FLAME *of* SEPARATION

Also by Des Kennedy:

Fiction
The Garden Club and the Kumquat Campaign

Essays
Living Things We Love to Hate: Facts, Fantasies and Fallacies
Crazy About Gardening: Reflections on the Sweet Seductions of a Garden
An Ecology of Enchantment: A Year in a Country Garden

FLAME *of* SEPARATION

Des Kennedy

INSOMNIAC PRESS

Edited by Adrienne Weiss
Copy edited by Emily Schultz
Interior design by Marijke Friesen

National Library of Canada Cataloguing in Publication Data

Kennedy, Des
Flame of separation / Des Kennedy.

ISBN 1-894663-64-0

I. Title.

PS8571.E6274F53 2004 C813'.54 C2003-907475-7

The publisher gratefully acknowledges the support of the Canada Council, the Ontario Arts Council and the Department of Canadian Heritage through the Book Publishing Industry Development Program. We acknowledge the support of the Government of Ontario through the Ontario Media Development Corporation's Ontario Book Initiative.

Printed and bound in Canada on 100% post-consumer recycled paper.

Insomniac Press
192 Spadina Avenue, Suite 403
Toronto, Ontario, Canada, M5T 2C2
www.insomniacpress.com

In memory of my parents
Tom Kennedy and
Eileen (Shevlin) Kennedy

Once upon a time Chuang Tsu dreamed that he was a butterfly, a butterfly fluttering about enjoying himself. It did not know that it was Chuang Tsu. Suddenly he awoke with a start, and he was Chuang Tsu again. But he did not know whether he was Chuang Tsu who had dreamed that he was a butterfly, or whether he was a butterfly dreaming he was Chuang Tsu.

—Wendy Doniger O'Flaherty
Dreams, Illusion and Other Realities

Part One:
Angel *of* Peace

Three faces in a dream
A trinity of children
Disembodied in the dark
Three faces only visible
Upturned, as to a light shining
Down on them
Darkness roils behind
Thick as mist shivered above sea cliffs
Impenetrable
But for gulls' cry
Dull rumble of surf
Some unknown depth
Beneath the surface
The faces make no sound
Nor gesture
Staring
Into what might be where you are
Eyes wide and bright
Famine orphans maybe
Waifs of some lost conflict
Asking nothing
Explicitly
Expecting no more
But mesmerizing still
Enticing you over and over
Some unseen edge
You tumble
screaming
Into the oblivion
Of waking.

One

"Good morning, everyone."

"Good morning, sir," the class chants back, singsong fashion, discordant, a reluctant choir practising a phrase it does not care for. Bright sunlight beams through classroom windows. Smell of chalk and young bodies in the room.

I check the attendance record—all present but for one. Susan Slater. Again. "Does anyone know what's up with Susan?" Mystified looks all round, some turning of heads, a couple of sniggers from the back-row boys. Nobody knows where Susan's gotten herself to. Or if they know they're not telling. I let it go.

"Alright, now where did we leave off yesterday? Yes, Francine?"

"We were to read the essay 'Dream-Children' by, er, Charles Lamb."

"Correct. Now who has actually read the essay? After getting through *Three's Company*, of course."

Titters. Hands rise in a wave, like seagulls off a landfill. A few hesitate, flutter uncertainly, providing time to grow comfortable with the fib, then rise straight as the others. "Excellent!" A judicious smattering of praise and ersatz enthusiasm, as a wise teacher once told me, can work wonders in what looks like hopeless circumstances. And, let's face it, Charles Lamb maundering over middle-aged grief and loss is not exactly a bona fide turn-on for your average eighteen-year-old whose glands are pumping weird chemicals into brain and body, everything bursting, breaking, accelerating like neutrinos down the freeway of I Love You, Say You Love, Me What Am I Going To Be? What's Any of This Mean?

I know what I'm talking about. I sat here myself not that long ago, at one of these same desks, in this same sarcophagus of a school, watching a parade of teachers do exactly what I'm doing now, a few of them brilliantly, most not. It never occurred to me that I'd be back here myself one day. I dreamt bigger dreams back then. I was bound for glory. I knew pretty much everything about everything back then—all except how a life can go rattling off on its own momentum, like a roller coaster after the first big climb, bouncing off other people, lurching around unseen corners and depositing you in a place you never imagined. Like here. Like now.

"What do you think the author's trying to say in this essay?" I glance around the room. The usual few hands rise confidently. Everyone else tries to be invisible. "Jim?" One of the bright ones. Jim Kubiak, already chosen as valedictorian for the graduation rituals that have, though still far on the horizon, begun to dominate the consciousness of every self-respecting senior.

"The part that was really neat," Jim riffles through his notes, "was the sentence where he says, let me see, yes: '…and how when he died, though he had not been dead an hour, it seemed that he had died a great while ago, such a distance there is betwixt life and death.'"

"Yes." Everyone in the room is aware that Jim's father died a couple of years ago, one of those dragged out death-by-cancer nightmares. I had to give Jim the news at school that day, hold him for a long while as he sobbed out a kid's incomprehension of death's arbitrary calculus. And the discussion stalls in a kind of strained embarrassment. Just then we're interrupted by a tapping on the classroom door. The door swings open and in steps the school principal, Mr. Stewart Danielson. The class stirs uneasily, sensing some excitement.

"Sorry to interrupt, Mr. Cooke," Danielson says, his dry English accent tainted, as usual, with just the faintest whisper of contempt. "But I have some extraordinary news." He swings to address the class directly. Everyone's attentive, not just because they're afraid of Danielson, but recognizing something big's in the works. Danielson's face—hawk nose, jade-pale eyes, the sallow skin a cross-hatch of sour lines, a mangy goatee—brightens into a rare smile. "As one of the two senior classes who'll be graduating this June," he pauses a moment for added effect, "you'll be delighted to know that Shallowford High, because this is the school's eighty-fifth consecutive graduation ceremony, has been selected for an official visit by the Governor General of Canada."

A bemused silence infuses the room. The Governor General. Coming here. For an instant no one knows if this is a good thing, a great thing, or not. Except Danielson, who proceeds to explain the importance of the event. I would guess most of the kids don't know who or what the Governor General is. A visit by Pierre Trudeau or Wayne Gretzky, yes, that would be something. Danielson is perfectly aware of their indifference but not at all fazed by it. Just what you'd expect from this bunch, you can sense him thinking. Danielson is not a native son, he's only been here a couple of years, though some days it seems far longer.

"So it will be incumbent upon us all," he instructs the class, "to have everything shipshape around here. I want this event to go off without a hitch, I want it to be the highlight of this academic year. Understood?"

A murmuring of assent from the class.

"Good." Danielson smiles again and begins to leave, then turns to me. "Oh, Mr. Cooke, may I see you in my office after class, please?"

"Of course." Now what?

After the bell I make my way down the kid-clotted corridor to the principal's office. As I tap on the door and enter, I catch Danielson sitting at his desk with his wife bending close to him. She straightens when I enter and looks at me with a silly smirk. Louise. A tall woman, younger than Danielson, a second wife, she works at the school as a volunteer, her primary task being to ensure that everyone acknowledges how important and clever her husband is. "Excuse me," she says, brushing past me with the same ridiculous smirk.

"You wanted to see me?" I ask Danielson.

"Yes," he puts his elbows on the desk, hands together, and peers at some documents lying in front of him. "Your mother phoned just now."

"My mother?"

"Yes."

Mother never calls me at school, but even this once, I can tell, is once too often for Danielson. He offers nothing more, playing some asinine waiting game.

"Is something wrong?" I ask.

"It's your father," he tells me, looking up. His pale eyes look completely passionless.

"What's happened?"

"An incident of some sort, I'm not sure." Did he say incident or accident? "He's at the hospital now. Your mother phoned from there."

"The hospital?" I feel a tightness in my chest.

"Yes." Still the cold jade eyes betray nothing.

"When did all this happen?"

"I'm not certain."

"When did you hear from my mother?"

"Oh," he glances at the wall clock, "about half an hour or so ago."

"And you didn't tell me right away?"

"I've told you as soon as it was practical to do so."

"Practical? You interrupt my class to talk about the Governor General coming to visit three months from now and you don't think it's 'practical' to tell me my father's been rushed to the hospital?"

"I didn't see any advantage to getting you upset—and I can see that you are upset, it's only natural—in the middle of a class. Nor did I think you'd want me to draw attention, in front of your students, to your father's, er…condition."

That's classic Danielson, the sniggering cheap shot. I breathe deeply. "Well, she wouldn't call if it wasn't an emergency. I'd better get to the hospital. Have you got someone who can sub for me?"

"Yes, I suppose we can cover for you," Danielson says dryly. "If need be I'll do it myself. Are your lesson plans on your desk?"

"Yes."

"Fine then."

"Fine." Two snipers on opposite hillsides, dug in.

I leave the office, cursing Danielson under my breath and almost bumping into his dreadful wife in the corridor. He could've offered his car, knowing I always walk to school, but didn't. And I'll be damned if I'd ask to borrow it. I sprint down the empty corridor and descend the stairs two at a time, then out through the little parking lot behind the school, wondering where my father's dementia has taken him today.

A quick sprint across the ball field, then down the path through the fringe of woodland along the river. Halfway across the old wooden footbridge, something catches my eye upriver. A girl running, it looks like, in panic. I lean on the guardrail, panting. The girl doesn't see me. Susan Slater, yes it's her, running as though some beast is at her heels. "Susan!" I yell against the slithering of the river over stones. "Susan!" And suddenly she's gone, disappeared into willow thickets along the bank. I wait a moment, my panting beginning to subside, now torn between getting to the hospital and finding out what's up with Susan, whether she's needing help.

I hesitate another moment, undecided, then sprint across the bridge and up the far side onto Walnut Street and along the two blocks to home.

Deirdre's in the kitchen as I burst in, again panting for breath. "Dexter, what is it? What's wrong?" She takes my arm. "Here, sit down." I rest at the breakfast nook for a moment, trying to catch my breath. Deirdre brings me a glass of cool water and I gulp it down.

"What on earth's going on?" she asks.

"Dad's in the hospital."

"Oh, no. How serious?"

"Don't know. Mother called the school. She didn't call here obviously?"

"No."

No surprise there. "Danielson was his typical cryptic self."

"I'll get the car keys; they're in my bag."

"You have anything on this afternoon?"

"Nothing special, why?"

"Well, if you don't need the car, how about I just take it? I may have to drive back to school afterwards, depending."

"Or I could come with you now and then just drop you off, if you like."

"I think it's simpler if I just go up by myself."

"Really?"

"No need to drag you into it."

"I don't mind. Really."

"I know. I guess I'd just rather go on my own. It's simpler—and it may not be any big deal anyway." I can see Deirdre's feeling excluded. Again. This is part of the dance we dance. But I don't have time for it now. "I'll call you from the hospital," I kiss her lightly on the forehead, taking the car keys from her hand. "Don't worry. I'm sure it's nothing to worry about."

"You look pretty worried."

"Do I? Well, he is my father."

"Yes." Deirdre's expression says a thousand other words.

"I'll call you when I know something."

"Sure."

Speeding through town, I'm wishing I hadn't hit that sour note with Deirdre. More sour notes than sweet ones these days. Can't be worrying about it now. Mother may really need me.

Along Main Street, there's hardly any traffic and only a smattering of shoppers gazing in the windows of the small shops I've known all my life. Twenty years ago, I would have turned left onto Laurel Street and the hospital would have been right there, a big brick building like the post office and high school, built a lifetime ago, with skill and an eye toward tomorrow. But not this tomorrow. It's where I was born, that old hospital, but it's gone now, knocked down in the name of progress. People cried the day they destroyed it; the demolition crew used explosives to blow the whole building right into itself while most of the town watched. All those births and deaths, broken bones and miraculous cures went down with a boom into dust. That was just last year. 1984. A group of citizens had wanted to turn the old building into a museum, to cash in on the new tourism economy, but it never happened. There's a second-hand car dealership on the site now and a couple of fast-food joints. Welcome to the 80s, George Orwell.

Now I have to drive to the other side of town and up onto the highway to get to the hospital. I click on the radio and Garth Brooks fills the car with heartache. The Health Board maintains it saved us taxpayers buckets of money putting the new facility out of town, but it's not convenient. The car glides up the side hill out of the valley. Cresting the hill, I see the jagged line of mountains off to the west, their peaks gleaming white with remnant winter snow. I speed past farms and ranches pretty enough for postcards. Their grasslands undulate softly toward the mountains, green waves breaking against black stone. Shallowford huddles in the valley to my right, a small town clustered along the banks of a serpentine river.

I wheel into the hospital's parking lot. A stark cinder-block building, the hospital sits in an otherwise vacant field like a big box dropped on an empty warehouse floor. The Board ran out of money before they could afford any landscaping, so the remnants of prairie and pasture lie in tatters all around. Winter-killed grasses shake arthritic fists at the building. I turn off the ignition and Crystal Gayle dies away. I get out of the car reluctantly, square my shoulders, take a deep breath and hurry across to General Admittance, thinking how it should be called General Denial.

Two

From a distance I spot Mother sitting alone in the waiting area. She's perched precise and upright, her straight back not touching the molded plastic chair, her hands resting on the small black purse in her lap. Staring straight ahead through a tinted plate-glass window, she looks vulnerable. I feel a quick pulse of protective love. The place is almost empty, the dead air smelling of antiseptic soap. Sounds echo down corridors like distant trains in a deserted subway station. They might be cries of dying, calls for help.

Mother sees me coming and rises to meet me. She's wearing a smart canary yellow silk blouse under a sage-coloured suit that shows her impeccably trim figure. Her hair, a flattering streaked silver, not grey, is recently permed. Mother's not the type to be caught in a crisis wearing a housecoat and slippers with rollers in her hair. We hug without saying a word. She smells of violets.

"I'm sorry to call you out, Dexter," she says, sitting back down, "but I'm afraid I wasn't sure that…" She looks away. I think perhaps she'll cry. Mother doesn't cry.

"What happened?" I ask, sitting beside her, putting my arm around her shoulders. I can feel her, brittle and light as a wounded bird in the hand. "How is he? What happened?"

"He's in some sort of trauma. I think he tried to drown himself."

"Drown himself? In the river?"

Mother hesitates. Looks away toward the window, as though into an unfamiliar dimension. "I happened to be passing the patio doors and I saw him at the far end of the lawn walking toward the river. He was wearing his old fishing gear—you know he hasn't touched it for years. He seemed to be moving very strangely, wobbling and weaving about."

"What did you do?"

"I put the groceries on the counter and went to the closet to get my rubber boots because it's still quite muddy down by the river. Then I hurried down there."

"And?"

"I found him sprawled on the bank, face down, his head in the water." Mother pauses, a catch in her throat. "I couldn't pull him out; I pulled as hard as I could, but he was just dead weight. And he's gurgling away underwater. It was dreadful." She tucks a wayward wisp of hair behind her ear and a tiny, delicate spasm flits across her face like the shadow of an insect flying above the still surface of a pond. This is hard for her, distasteful. She turns to me and I look directly into her pale blue-grey eyes. Thirty-three years of mother-and-son shimmer in the space between us. The ordeal of my father's slide into senility, my mother's stoic dignity through repeated humiliations, have left their mark on her still-lovely face, alright, but they haven't broken her spirit. Not until today, at least.

Suddenly we're startled by a scream that bounces off the cinder-block walls, crazy as a lacrosse ball, then flees, echoing down the solemn corridors. "I'm sure that was somebody else," I reassure Mother, though I'm not at all sure, nor is she.

Mother composes herself. "So there I was tugging helplessly. But finally his muscles relaxed; he went all slack and I pulled him out. I lay him face down on the gravel and tried pumping his lungs. You wouldn't believe the water that came out of him." Now the threat of tears again.

This awful image of my father sprawled on the riverbank is new, but his erratic behaviour isn't. At first, before we realized anything really serious was happening, his aberrations were sporadic; for months at a time he'd be fine, but then he'd have a spell of insomnia. He'd pace the house all night muttering to himself, forget things, seem to drift into a fog. After a few days he'd snap out of it and be himself again, as though nothing had happened. He'd be a bit disoriented because he couldn't remember the days when he'd been drifting away, but otherwise he'd be perfectly normal and cogent. Gradually the intervals between his disturbed bouts started to shrink. He became consistently irritable and then began suffering awful outbursts of anger. He'd never been an angry man, so we were shocked to see him enraged, to hear him violently curse. It wasn't until he began taking all his clothes off and walking naked down Main Street that finally we acknowledged the obvious: my father had tumbled into a profound dementia. I still cringe, thinking of his humiliation. His and Mother's. Understand, this is one of the community's most respected and eminent citizens strolling around town completely starkers, reduced to a public laughingstock. The cops would pick him up and throw a blanket over him—it got to be so regular for a while they'd keep a special blanket in the cruiser just for him—and bring him back home. He'd give them a lecture on constitutional law during the ride home, sounding lucid as Thucydides. Pressure built to put him in a home, of course, but Mother wouldn't have it. She wanted him at home with her and that was that. The last few years, he hasn't needed nursing so much as child care. Until today.

"You called the ambulance?" I ask her, the way one asks for specific details, as though by piling up enough insignificant bits one can climb high enough to peek through a window into the inexplicable.

"It seemed like the thing to do. I hated leaving him lying there gurgling water. I was afraid he might try it again. But I had to make a choice. So I dashed to the house and called for an ambulance."

"And you're sure it was deliberate on his part? Mightn't he just have stumbled and fallen into the water?"

Mother stares out the window again. "Oh, I don't know, Dexter," she sighs. "There was just something about his positioning, some deliberateness of posture that told me straight off that he was trying to..."

"Kill himself?"

She pauses, vacant, far away. "Yes," she whispers.

"Has anyone here told you anything?"

"The doctor's with him now."

"Charlie?"

"No, no, Charlie's away someplace. This is a new one. Dr. Prahamya or something like that."

Within a few minutes the doctor joins us.

"Oh, doctor," Mother introduces me, "this is my son, Dexter."

"How do you do?" the woman says rather solemnly, shaking my hand. I'd guess she's younger than I am, but I can't be sure. She's got a perfectly smooth coffee complexion and glistening eyes, like dark stones in clear water.

"Hello, doctor."

"How is he?" Mother asks matter-of-factly.

"I'm not quite sure," the doctor says. "He's resting now. I've given him a sedative to calm him." She speaks each word with soft precision. I know Mother wants to ask what sort of sedative, but doesn't.

"Do you mind my asking," the doctor seats herself across from us, "how long he has been afflicted like this?"

That's a considerate way of putting it, I think. An affliction from without implies a certain innocence, a victimhood, with none of the shameful complicity attached to inner debility. We are, after all, not enfeebled, but besieged. Mother doesn't buy into all the psychobabble about inherent pathologies and latent psychoses. Paradoxical as it might seem in someone impeccably dressed and with perfectly coiffed hair, Mother prefers a battlefield idiom: malignant forces emanating from the dark underbelly of civilization are to blame for the corruption of what's good and true. So Doctor Prahamya could not have framed her question more pleasingly.

Mother and I exchange a glance in which it's understood that I should do the talking. "It's hard to determine exactly when it started—" I tell the doctor "—at least when we started really noticing it. Maybe seven or eight years ago now. The last three years have been very difficult. Every so often there's an outbreak like today. But no one's quite sure if it indicates a gradual worsening or if it's just a random occurrence and doesn't indicate a trend in one direction or another."

The doctor nods, considering what I've said for a moment. "What's the diagnosis?"

"No one seems to know exactly," I reply. "He's been examined up, down and sideways. We've had him down to Vancouver several times, out at the university, they've got enough data on him to choke a supercomputer, but no one can figure out precisely why he's crazy. Some form of dementia is the best they can manage. Possibly premature aging of the brain." Mother is staring out the window again, as though she doesn't want to hear any more of this.

"Fascinating," the young doctor says, her dark eyes watching us. Under her placid scrutiny I'm wishing I hadn't sounded quite so strident about the specialists' diagnostic shortfalls. "With your permission," she says to Mother, deferentially, "I'd like to keep him in overnight, for observation, just to be sure."

Mother and I both know there's no being sure of anything when it comes to my father.

"Of course," I say. "We appreciate your help."

"Don't worry," she says to Mother, continuing to defer to her, "we'll take good care of him."

"I'm positive you will," Mother smiles. I can hear her adding "dear" in her mind, but she doesn't say it. Calmed by the soothing manner of the doctor, and with the shock of the crisis abating a bit, we're able to begin resuming our customary response to my father's madness. I don't mean to suggest that either Mother or I is indifferent to his condition, far from it. No, it's just that after several years of his escapades, we've grown accustomed to their chaos. Mind you, today was an aberration, perhaps an escalation, for he's never tried to harm himself before.

The doctor excuses herself, she has her rounds to do, and disappears.

"Quite an extraordinary young woman," Mother says, glancing at her watch. I can see she has her equilibrium somewhat restored. "Are you going to go in and see him?"

"Yes, I think I will, just for a moment."

"Good. I'm glad." She pauses, then continues, "You know, Dexter, nothing has pained me more over the years than to see you and your father at odds."

"I know that, Mother. I haven't been crazy about it either." My father and I have spent the last fifteen years or more in a state of elaborate estrangement. His worsening dementia eventually brought a closure of sorts to our mutual sourness, but an unsatisfactory one. It stranded us in different places, neutral but unreconciled.

Mother senses my tone and quickly changes tack. "Well, I think the worst of it is over, thank God. Shall we get together for a drink? Say in an hour?"

"No can do," I say. "Sorry. I've got another class this afternoon, and I have to pick my stuff up for the weekend. Why don't you come over for dinner?"

Again a slight flicker crosses Mother's face and is gone. I don't have to ask why she's vacillating. Dinner with Deirdre and Mother and me is not quite the same thing as a cozy drink together, just the two of us, where we can talk with an intimacy that's impossible when Deirdre's in the mix. "Alright," she says at last, "thank you, darling. I don't know that I could face the house alone tonight." We agree on six.

After I've walked Mother to her car, I reenter the hospital and get directions at the nursing station for my father's room. I pause at the open door and peer in, as though it were a cave awaiting exploration. There are four beds in the room, three of them occupied. For a moment I can't make out which of the three old men is my dad. They might be interchangeable, this ragged trinity, all of what made them who they were as individuals now dissolved into biographical mush and spooned like porridge into motionless lumps under hospital blankets.

My dad is in the bed closest to the window. He's asleep like the others, sprawled on his back, his head to one side of the pillow, as though he were looking out the window in his dreams. He's not an old man like the others, he's only sixty-three, but there is something ancient in his sagging, unshaven face, a grey pain that has spread itself across his handsome features like fine lines of ice crystals etched on a glass sheet. It hurts to see him like this, sprawled helpless in a hospital bed. My father. My hero for so many years. The man who stood like an oak tree in the centre of my dawning consciousness, all strong arms and deep roots. He would lift me to the sky and hold me there, so that I was not afraid, not in the grip of his firm hands. To me he'd been Gregory Peck in *To Kill a Mockingbird*, a man of principle and compassion. My dad.

I remember one day—I couldn't have been more than five or six—when my dad and I were walking along the river path. It was a cold afternoon with a grey sky and a keen wind whistling. Fallen leaves were skittering across the grass; I had been chasing them on our walk. We'd turned for home when suddenly two men appeared from out of the trees. They walked right up to us and I was instantly afraid. They were big fellows, rough and angry looking. I can't recall exactly what was said—I didn't understand most of it at the time—but I knew they were angry with my father about something. Much later I learned that he was representing a woman, the wife of one of these two, who'd been battered by him and wanted a divorce.

"Nice lookin' kid you got there, councillor," one of the men said, and even at my age I knew he wasn't being pleasant. Something sinister was in his tone. My father spoke sternly back, in a way I'd never heard him speak to anyone. I grew less afraid, sensing through a child's instinct that my father was not intimidated by these bullies, that whatever he was saying to them had stifled their aggression. Even I could see it, their slackening of resolve, their backing away from the force of whatever he was telling them. At one point my father stepped forward, right up against the big fellow who'd spoken about me, and the big man backed away. Eventually the two turned and left. They seemed to skulk back into the bushes like whipped dogs. My father stood looking after them for a few moments, then looked down at me, smiled and took my hand in his and said, as though nothing at all had happened, "Now let's get home for some of Mum's hot chocolate!"

A large bronze plaque hung outside the front of his office on Main Street, Philip Cooke: Barrister and Solicitor, it said, and underneath, the Latin motto: *Salus populi suprema lex esto*, The safety of the people is the supreme law. That was my dad.

He sometimes took me camping in the summertime. We'd stuff a big canvas tent, a cantankerous camp stove, axe, sleeping bags, fishing gear and all the rest into our old wood-panelled station wagon and drive to secret wild places far away. He had an amateur interest in paleontology and archaeology and was fascinated with how the world used to be, the forces that shaped it, the strange creatures that once roamed it. When the night sky was clear he'd identify planets and constellations and talk about the big bang and our expanding universe. "It's an astonishing thing—isn't it, Dexter—to look up into this immense tapestry of such breathtaking precision and realize it all began within the explosion of a spinning mass of energy no bigger than a turnip." I'd lie in the tent at night, listening to the sounds of the dark. My father would read aloud from Tennyson or Browning as I huddled in my sleeping bag, aware of wild creatures prowling outside, the imagined grunting and snuffling of grizzlies, but safe inside, safe so long as my father's voice held sway.

God, he taught me so much. Like fishing. He loved to fish. Normally he'd go alone. Not frequently, but every so often, he'd say to my mother, "I feel the river calling, do you mind?" Of course Mother didn't, and so on a Saturday morning he'd be gone before dawn, long before we were up, returning perhaps by lunch, occasionally not until suppertime, with several silvery trout in his creel. He'd cook them on the barbecue that night, and as we ate the delicate flesh, he'd recount the joyful mysteries of how he'd lured them out of their deep pools, tricked them into rising to his fly, and what great battles the trout had fought, leaping into the air to throw the hook, flashing silver in the sun, then diving deep to elude him. These were epic struggles, the way he described them, pure poetry, the fish such noble battlers we felt honoured to eat them.

One Friday night after dinner—I must have been ten or eleven by then—my dad looked at me long and hard. "Dexter," he finally said to me, "I think maybe it's time we went fishing together. Are you busy tomorrow?"

Busy? Are you kidding? I'd have cut off an arm and thrown it into the river for the thrill of going fishing with him. "No, sir, I don't believe I am," I said, bursting with joy. Several times before this, on a Saturday or Sunday, he'd taken me out to the backyard to learn the art of fly casting. I loved those times, him standing close behind me, gripping my hand on the rod, his index finger crooked across the filament, showing me how to work the rod back and forth, the line circling in the air like wisps of smoke.

"Good fellow," he'd say as I struggled to master it. "Well done!"

I worked and worked at casting. After school, before Dad got home, I'd carry the rod he'd given me out to the back lawn and set the line flying. I loved to see that rod and line come to life in my hand, feel it whip back and forth. This was magic, this casting of things beyond myself, a magic associated with my father. He taught me how to throw a football too, how to grip it with the laces at the tip of your fingers and fling it smoothly so that the ball spiralled tight and hard through the air. How to throw a sinking fastball so it dove wickedly, leaving the batter whiffing at air. The power of trajectory, of thrown things spinning through space and time, that's what he taught me. That and a thousand other things.

I hardly slept all night for excitement that first time my dad said "I think maybe it's time we went fishing together."

A series of magical expeditions with my dad began that morning. I began to learn about the river that would be such a big part of my youth and today, ironically, the place where he tried to kill himself. The Red Stone River gets its name from the canyons of red rock that it cuts through, up near its headwaters in the hills. Once it has tumbled down onto the grasslands it slows its pace to a graceful meandering through meadows and cottonwood groves, then right through the heart of Shallowford, where it flattens out into the great shallow arc that gave the town its name. Under my dad's patient tutelage I came to know the subtlety of its currents, the graceful langour of its back eddies, its insistent undercutting of banks. I'd work my way along the shallows while the flank of mountains off on the horizon glowed orange from the first morning sunlight and trout began rising from their pools to feed on caddis flies. I'd look up the river and see my dad working his rod like a maestro. I learned how to work the glides and runs and current seams along the riffles, casting my caddis so it would kiss the water's surface and drift naturally past a waiting trout. This was immensely difficult fishing and it took forever to get the hang of it.

"That's fine, son," my father would say as we lay on a grassy bank after the sun had put an end to the morning's fishing. "Anything in life worth doing is worth working hard for. The best things usually occur after you've fought your way through difficulties. The easy stuff is cheap and quickly fades." Coming from him these observations never sounded like platitudes or faded clichés. Lots of kids I knew disliked their fathers or were afraid of them or, at best, indifferent to them. But not me. I idolized the guy.

And look at us now. No, you can't step into the same river twice, old Heraclitus had that right. There's lots of water, literal and figurative that has flowed between my father and me since those inspired early days on the Red Stone. Gazing at him now, comatose in his hospital bed, I see how viciously unfair it is that he's been reduced to this, all his accomplishments lost in the slobber of an idiot. He must know it too, somewhere in the catacombs of his tortured brain, he must glimpse the pathos of his fall, the injustice of it. Small wonder he tried to drown himself.

Some years back I thought I'd finally let him go, detached myself. But I know I haven't. Because in a way he's dragged me into his darkness. I let him down. We each let the other down badly. As he lies crumpled in his bed, I can't help thinking the bitterness that triggered his unbalancing began to fester in the dark crevasse that opened up between the two of us.

Three

"Deirdre, darling," Mother says, as we sip our coffees, "that was a perfectly lovely meal. Thank you ever so much." Deirdre and Mother exchange icing-sugar smiles. "And thank you too, Dexter, for coming to the hospital this afternoon. You're both so very kind and thoughtful." Mother reaches out a hand in either direction, placing one on Deirdre's forearm, the other on mine. No doubt she's being sincere here, but something in the motion of her arms reminds me of how sidewinders leave tracks in desert sand like hieroglyphics that conceal their intended direction. Is she preparing to strike? Deirdre sees it too, I notice. But Deirdre doesn't flinch, just smiles in gracious acknowledgment, but I know she sees the serpent coiling.

To admit that there exists a certain dynamic tension between Mother and Deirdre is to understate the obvious. While all is discreetly polite on the surface, there's an ominous hum in the air when they meet, as though standing underneath high voltage transmission towers. Actual sparks might arc between the two women now and then, but this is rare. Voices are not raised and certainly tempers never flare. But there's a battle being waged here, a slow and patient prowling.

We're sitting at the dining-room table, the breakfast nook being too small for three, at least for this particular threesome, and somehow also insufficient for the day's solemnity, it's near tragedy of death by water. A neutral observer would likely have no idea of the tension coiled inside our seemingly innocent domestic dinner ritual. The setting itself betrays nothing, for Deirdre keeps an immaculate house. There's no telling disarray in the dining room, no incongruous detail to hint at hidden dysfunctions. The dining-room table and chairs are of dark cherry wood flecked with gold. The table can expand to seat sixteen easily, though we've never had that many in for dinner. And there's a matching sideboard and china cabinet. The china came from Mother as a wedding present. It was her own mother's set, Grandmother Peale, whom I remember from childhood as a tiny, fun-loving old lady who used to dote on me and who was always accompanied by an ancient and incredibly smelly basset hound whose stomach dragged along the floor. Mother's bestowing the china—Wedgwood with a delicate floral pattern—upon Deirdre and me was a symbolic act of the highest significance. The gift was a token that I'd been formally welcomed back into the family from which I'd strayed so disastrously. It also confirmed Deirdre's elevated position as repository of the family's future.

Fifty years ago, my grandparents on both sides, the Cookes and the Peales, were two of the most powerful families in Shallowford. Both my grandfathers, had in turn, served as mayor of the town. Back then I doubt anybody in Shallowford would have guessed that these twin dynasties were hurtling toward the brink of extinction. But Mother's two younger brothers were killed in a tragic car crash on their way home from university for Christmas holidays and Dad's twin sister, his only sibling, died of pneumonia before graduating from high school. My mother and father in turn had only one child, *c'est moi*, so now it's down to me—to Deirdre and me—whether the great lineages of the Peales and Cookes will continue as they have for generations or be snuffed out and lost in the dust of back country annals.

Right now the smart money would give odds on snuffing out, because Deirdre and I are childless. Not from want of trying, mind you. Oh, no, we tried so hard that blood was spilled in the effort. Nothing came of it but tears and the death of dreams.

Both Deirdre and I wanted kids right from the beginning. Deirdre passionately so. I think she wanted children more than anything else, certainly more than career or possessions. She was pregnant within a year of our wedding. We were living in Vancouver back in those days, on the lower floor of a great old house on the east side, just off

Commercial Drive. A wonderful old wooden place, with edge-grain-fir flooring and stained-glass windows, a home rich with the histories of families who'd occupied it over the years. It had a fenced backyard and remnants of old gardens, enormous hydrangeas and leggy rhododendrons. Deirdre was working at the public library downtown; I was finishing up getting my teaching degree. The day she came home from her doctor with the dream confirmed we whooped for joy. I called Mother right away and she preened with delight. "Oh, Dexter," she thrilled over the phone, "you have no idea how happy you and Deirdre have made me, me and your father too." I knew she'd longed for grandchildren almost as fervently as Deirdre wanted babies. And, yes, like Mother, I too hoped that a child, a grandchild, might help heal the ill feelings between my father and myself.

Deirdre swelled like a ripening fruit. Her skin shone almost translucent as her small body stretched to hold the new life growing inside. I loved to touch her swelling belly then, to lay my head on it at night, listening for movements. I think I loved Deirdre then with a purer love than any I'd known before. There was a chasteness, a sanctity about how she was, how she looked, how she moved as she ripened.

Deirdre and I were working in the yard one spring afternoon, putting a vegetable garden in so that we'd be able to puree fresh organic vegetables for the little one. Suddenly Deirdre cried out from the porch. I looked up to see her bent over with pain, clutching her belly. I dropped my spade and bounded up the steps. "What is it? What's happening?" But she could only gasp, wide-eyed. I saw a dark stain of blood expanding across her cotton dress. "I'm calling the ambulance," I said, and she nodded yes, her face squeezed by invisible pain. I dashed inside, dialled frantically, got the number wrong, dialled again, got the dispatcher, couldn't remember our address, remembered it and pleaded with her to hurry, for God's sake please hurry.

I ran back outside. Deirdre was gasping and making small noises like a dying animal. I could see a little rivulet of blood inching along one of the floorboards of the porch. I ran back inside and soaked a towel in cold water and brought it out. I mopped her sweating face with it. Her eyes were wild with fear and I couldn't look into them. I lifted her summer dress—she tried to prevent me but couldn't. She was clutching her stomach with one hand and reaching down to her crotch with the other, as though to prevent anything more from leaking out. Dark blood oozed over her clutching fingers. She was moaning horribly. I wiped the fresh blood from her legs with the towel. Her slender thighs smeared with blood. "Hold on, darling," I kept saying. "Hold on, it'll be alright."

Then the ambulance attendants were there, guiding me out of the way, lifting Deirdre onto a stretcher and quickly into the ambulance. I clambered in behind and huddled in a corner while they worked on her and the ambulance careened, shrieking through the crowded city streets.

It all was a blur after that. The big general hospital. Doctors, nurses, orderlies. Please fill in this form, sir. Please sign right there, sir. Do you have your medical card? No, I'm sorry, there's nothing to report yet. We'll let you know as soon as there's news. The doctor will be with you in a minute. Why don't you have a seat?

Meanwhile, phantasmagorical people, crazy and broken, on crutches and in wheelchairs, wandered around.

Finally a doctor, a young man, solemn and dark, needing a shave, approached me. "Your wife's going to be fine," he said. "She's lost a tremendous amount of blood, but we've managed to stop the hemorrhaging. It's going to take a little while, but she'll be fine." I knew he was trying his best to sound reassuring.

"The baby?" I asked.

"I'm sorry," he said, "the foetus was already dead by the time we got to your wife."

I don't want it to be a foetus, I want it to be a baby, a live baby. "What was it?" I asked, stupidly. Numb. Uncomprehending.

The doctor understood. And didn't understand at all. "I'm very sorry," he said. "I know it's a terrible loss to you. But your wife will be fine, and that's the important thing."

Was it? Was that the important thing? I couldn't think clearly at all, but clearly enough to know she wouldn't be fine. Not after this. Who would?

They let me in to see Deirdre sometime afterward. She was lying on a bed, hooked up to monitors and plastic packets of blood. At first I thought she was dead too, she was so ghostly white. She looked tiny in the bed, like a child herself. Her silky blonde hair was plastered to her head. I stooped to kiss her forehead. It was eerily cold. Her eyes were closed. I sat on the side of the bed and gently took her hand. There were needles in the back of it, attached to tubes.

"Darling," I whispered, "I'm so sorry."

She opened her eyes slowly, every bit of her wasted by sadness. Tears welled in her eyes and trickled down her cheeks. Her lips moved but no sound came out.

"I'm so sorry," I said again, and then I gave way and joined my wife in crying. I thought of the baby's tiny corpse and wondered what they did with it. No one asked if we wanted her buried or burned or anything. They must have just carted it away somewhere, like a little sack of garbage. You don't even get to say goodbye, to stand beside a grave surrounded by family and friends. There is no closure, just a sudden gaping hole where a day before there'd been a beautiful new life beginning. Hurt, lost and bewildered, Deirdre and I sobbed in one another's arms.

But then Deirdre gave me a pale imitation of her cheeky sidelong smile and the faintest squeeze of my hand in hers. At that moment my love and sorrow for her covered us both. We fused in our grief and loss, at least as profoundly as we'd ever done in happier times.

Twice more since then she's been with child and each time lost the baby, though never with the awful, shrieking, bloody madness of that first nightmare. We were as careful as could be during those pregnancies. Meticulous about our diets, faithful in doing the recommended exercises, avoiding anything risky. We walked on eggshells for months. But none of it mattered in the end. We couldn't hold the child for all our wanting and trying. After the third miscarriage, something vital was drained out of us. We'd lost so much blood, seen hope blossom and swell only to suddenly die. We lost something we both knew we'd never find again.

That last time, after I brought Deirdre home from the hospital, wan and pale, I cried in her arms again. But Deirdre didn't cry at all. She was finished with it, with the blood and the tears and the dashed hopes, all of it. "I can't do this again," she said. "I won't do this ever again." It was weeks before I dared touch her. But she pulled gently away. "I'm sorry," she said, "I can't."

"I understand," I said, and I did.

Thus a whole chapter of our lives came to a close. Eros packed her bags and left town. We simply stopped making love at all. A chaste kiss now and then, an occasional hug, sometimes a tender holding of hands—that's what our love life became. But that wasn't even close to the greater loss: knowing that we'd never have kids, that the core of our marriage was gone. We couldn't even talk about it. It just disappeared somewhere, like the dead foetus in the hospital.

Life goes on. Nowadays we walk a narrow precipice, Deirdre and I, with that blood-stained history on one side and the imperative to reproduce on the other, an imperative whose champion is my mother.

"Have you seen the doctors lately?" Mother asks. "You don't mind my asking, do you?"

"Not at all," Deirdre smiles, placing her cup on its saucer.

I'm mildly surprised that Mother has played the child card so flagrantly. Perhaps today's events have unsettled her more than I reckoned. She certainly knows better than to stick her scalpel into the tender tissue of our childlessness. Mother suffered with us through the hell of our trying to conceive and bring a child to term, and was a marvel of solicitude at the time. But as the years slipped past and Deirdre's biological clock began ticking down, Mother's desire for grandchildren became such an obsession it seemed to undermine her common sense. She couldn't leave it be. By hint and insinuation, by allegory and allusion, she sustained, and still sustains, a constant pulse of pressure that we should and must procreate. She means no harm by it; more than anything else she's misguided by love. But over the years her single-minded insistence on this one thing, ignoring the heartache the effort has already caused, has slowly blinded her to who Deirdre really is and how difficult this topic is for us. Though she certainly knows better, Mother blames Deirdre, not me, for our having no children. Without her even noticing, over time Mother's love and concern have curdled into something ugly.

Still, as irrational as Mother's behaviour is, I understand it; I can feel the force of her desire for grandchildren. It's not all that different from my own initial desire for children. The only difference now is I've given up on it and Mother hasn't. Even so, I don't judge her harshly, and this drives Deirdre nuts. "Why don't you stand up to her?" she demands after each of these skirmishes between the two of them. I urge Deirdre to take into account the added stress on Mother caused by Dad's condition. Each of the women seeks my support in alliance against the other, and I walk the finest of lines across their abutting minefields.

Deirdre's chin quivers. She blinks her eyelashes several times rapidly, and anyone who knows her well would know how hurtful this is for her. But for all her seeming brittleness, Deirdre doesn't break. "Not recently, no I haven't," she tells Mother primly. Fierce but unfailingly polite, Deirdre would never tell Mother to mind her own goddamn business. Instead, she's steeled her heart against Mother, bolted a door through which Mother will never be allowed entry. Knowing it, Mother stalks outside, thwarted, and plans new stratagems. All of this is unspoken, unacknowledged, but as real and tangible as the brick walls of this old house.

"Perhaps just as well," Mother says—and she actually reaches out again and pats Deirdre's hand consolingly. "It's good not to press things too much." This is the kicker, as we all know this issue has been pressed more enthusiastically than extra-virgin olive oil. Mother folds her napkin and dabs her lips with it. I look for blood.

I get up to begin clearing the table. I suppose it's my turn to talk now, to rescue the situation, because Deirdre's gone silent with resentment and Mother's retreated for the moment, perhaps satisfied, perhaps waiting for another chance to strike. I hate my role in this pantomime. Mother's interference is infuriating, and I suppose I should come down on her hard right now. I can if I choose to, oh yes. Mother has no armour against me. Nor weapons either. She feels no need for any, loving me as she does, unconditionally. Mother doesn't include my wife in her largesse, however, I think because she knows instinctively that Deirdre and I are not one person, that our conjugal love is not absolute. Not just because it hasn't borne fruit in children, no, something more than that: we are not what Mother and Father were—what Mother, Father and I were, once upon a time—we are not perfect. Deirdre and I are flawed. Incomplete.

The irony lies in how alike the two women are. They even look alike. Slim, fine-featured, poised, exuding an air of polished sophistication. People have mistaken Deirdre for Mother's daughter, some even for her younger sister, for Mother's younger than her years. Nor was it always awful between them. Quite the opposite. The first time I brought Deirdre home, you'd have thought she was the Rosa Mystica, the way Mother fawned over her. "Such a lovely girl," Mother confided to me afterward, "I sense a deep wisdom in her and a brave heart. You could do far worse in girls, Dexter darling, you could do far worse."

I knew exactly whom she meant, but said nothing.

Mother seized upon Deirdre, not with desperation, but with alacrity. Deirdre, she sensed—clever, sensitive, insightful Deirdre—would save me from stupid misadventures and a lifetime of regret. But that was long ago and Deirdre's no longer Mother's Rosa Mystica. Just my wife whose childlessness, to Mother, looks like selfishness.

So there the two of them sit, smiling sweetly while locked in constant combat, each angling for my allegiance. But I won't take Mother's side tonight, nor Deirdre's either.

"Would you like me to walk you home, Mother?" I ask after loading the dishwasher. I'll be damned if I'm going to sit around here for another hour watching these two spinning webs. "I'd love some fresh air myself." I don't invite Deirdre along, knowing she wouldn't come anyway.

"So soon?" Mother says, dripping disappointment. "I thought we might listen to *In Recital* together; they're playing Brahms tonight." Deirdre's eyes flash me an instant and unequivocal: don't you dare! Unlike Mother, Deirdre has both armour and weapons against me. Which is partly why I don't defend her against Mother's mischief. She needs no champion, at least on this particular battleground.

"Sorry, darling," I take Mother's arm, "I've got papers to mark and it's been a trying day for us all. Let's stroll home together and give Deirdre some peace and quiet." It feels inappropriate somehow to end the evening this way after the day's high drama. There ought to be something more, some coming-together in mutual affection from which we each draw strength. But there's nothing like that around here. There is no centre. Not surprising, when you sense the centripetal forces at play: the disjointed relationship Deirdre and I endure, our procreative failings, Mother's constant meddling and my father's retreat into his own demented darkness. Yes, something's missing in all this. Something's invariably missing as each day ends like today, flat and inconsequential.

"Oh, alright," Mother sighs, "I'll listen to Brahms alone at home. It won't feel the same without him there, of course, no it won't feel the same at all." She gathers up her things and prepares to go, but then does a wistful turn in the front hall. "Strange to be there in that big house all alone," she muses. "But Brahms I think will suit my mood." I'd wondered what she'd use for a parting montage, and this wasn't bad, this confection of herself sitting alone in her big house with violins sobbing in the dark. "Thank you, dear," she says to Deirdre, and the two of them exchange a ritual kiss, each posing a pinched face over the other's shoulder.

"I do hope Dad's alright," Deirdre says, "I'm sorry for what happened." She's sincere in this, I can tell, and Mother's touched, perhaps even momentarily contrite. Strangely, we didn't talk about Father's crisis at all, as though we'd tacitly agreed to ignore him just for tonight. Tomorrow he'll be home again and back on everyone's front page.

Mother and I walk to her house arm in arm. "Is there any place sweeter on Earth than Shallowford on a mild spring evening?" Mother asks and I'm happy to hear her speak of sweetness, no matter how qualified by the day's unsettling events. Only days ago the first warm winds flowed in from across the hills melting the last rags of snow piled in the town's shaded corners, and already I can feel a trembling of growth. We pause on the old bridge at the west end of town. The river runs hard and full underneath, swollen from snow melt. Thin willows and reeds along the banks are tugged by the lapping water, let go, then lash back only to be tugged again. I breathe in great gulps of green spring air, and listen to the chatter of river over stones.

"Your father loved this river, Dexter," Mother says with perhaps a shade more melodrama than necessary.

"I know."

Then neither of us speaks, as we separately dwell on the bathos of Dad attempting to drown himself in his beloved river. And on the tension between Deirdre and Mother, those two surgeons of the soul inflicting fine scalpel wounds on one another in the name of healing. Then we walk on and soon reach her place.

"Oh, Dexter," she says as we linger on the wide verandah, exchanging a long embrace, "darling, I wish none of this were happening."

"I know," I reply, hugging her tight, "I'm so sorry, Mother; I'm so sorry you have to go through all this." She clings to me and I'm happy to hold her, as I always am, remembering the times we'd spent together in this house. Remembering our walks around town. She'd stop to talk with neighbours and acquaintances while I stood watching, her smile glittering and her chestnut hair swirling around her shoulders in the sunlight. She'd include me in these conversations and her friends would cluck over me like broody hens, stroking my hair and telling me how handsome I was. And I was doubly blessed, because I had terrific parents and I never had to deal with what so many kids do, knowing instinctively that their parents don't really love them. Mine loved me and plainly loved one another. I remember them in a hundred happy cameos: Mother playing the baby grand piano in our parlour, with Dad standing alongside, one hand resting on the piano, singing in his rich baritone voice, the two of them exchanging laughing smiles. Another framed photo on Mother's mantle shows them walking barefoot together on a beach in Hawaii, young still and beautiful.

"Good night, Mother," I say at last, reluctantly leaving her embrace.

"Good night, darling," Mother says, "sweet dreams."

FOUR

I am stumbling alone through darkness, lost and afraid. Strange shapes loom and float past, silent and ominous. A light glimmers ahead. Old buildings shrouded in mist, the light liquid and refracted. I hear the shunting of trains, scream of steel on steel. Shouting voices and the tramping of heavy boots. Crowds of people shuffle past, their heads swathed in hoods and veils; I cannot see their faces. Each is silent, separate, a spectral drifting. I try to cry out, to warn them of danger, but the words clot in my throat. In an instant the crowds are gone, the shouts and screams recede until they are barely audible, a distant lamentation. I am perfectly alone again. Turning a dark corner, I come face to face with three children. The same three as always. Wanting something, I don't know what. Their eyes stare at me with a deep and patient grief. I want to reach out and touch them, but can't. I want to run from them, but can't. They have a power over me. I feel I am growing cold. I look down at my hands, see them slowly turn to stone. Grey lichens are growing on my fingers, tiny mosses creep down the lines of my palms. My whole body is hardening. The children are gone.

I'm jolted awake by birdsong, fragments of the dream still evaporating from the far reaches of my brain. Trying to separate what's real from what isn't. It must be just before dawn. Lying in the tangled sheets, I'm conscious of a gnawing sense of separateness and dream-spun loneliness.

I sit with coffee in the little sunroom we've added to the kitchen and watch light hatch in the eastern sky, pinks and rosy mauves and colours I doubt we have names for. Birds going mad with song, perched in impossibly perfect trees silhouetted against the sunrise.

I decide to mark the essays Danielson assigned the grade twelve class on Friday. Maybe get it over with before Deirdre is up and the day kicks into gear. After ploughing through several unremarkable essays, I'm surprised to find one from Susan Slater since she was absent on Friday. And I'd almost forgotten I'd seen her running in panic along the river. I should have called her home to be sure she's alright.

Typically, her piece is short, more a statement than an essay, written, as all her submissions are, on cheap lined notepaper in a graceful longhand.

An Essay About Dream Children

I really like this story, especially the ending, when the dream children disappear and they say, although they don't really say it, "we are nothing, less than nothing, and dreams. We are only what might have been, and must wait upon the tedious shores of Lethe millions of ages before we have existence and a name."

I think that this is probably true that there are millions of dream children out there somewhere who maybe died while they were still babies or maybe there was abortions or miscarriages or something but there's still part of them that's alive, like their spirit maybe and waiting to be born again to have another chance. I think maybe even old people do the same thing after they've died. That that's where ghosts come from and angels and evil spirits. And people try to make up religions to explain who these dream people are but they're just dream people. And I think maybe we can see them sometimes if were lucky and maybe they can tell us about how its like to be not alive but waiting to come alive. I would really like to meet one of these dream children and talk to them and find out. Because sometimes I wonder what its like if you don't exist. Do you feel anything or think anything? You must.

Interesting. Not certain I've read what I think I've just read, I go over it a second time. Yes, the kid has, uncannily, put her finger on several real sore spots in my life all at once. My father lying in his hospital bed floating in a sea of dreams. The children that Deirdre and I lost who haunt us still. And a couple of questions that I could be asking of myself if I had the stomach for it: what it's like to be not alive but waiting to come alive; what it's like if you don't exist.

I hear Deirdre rattling around in the bathroom, the shower's hiss. I reread the essay a third time, wondering.

"Good morning, darling," Deirdre says, coming out in her bathrobe and slippers, a towel curled around her head turban-style. "Sleep well?"

"I did, yes. You?" I don't tell her about my dreams.

"Perfectly," she smiles.

Perfect's the word for Deirdre, for she's an amalgam of minor perfections: fine-featured face, neck like a swan, silky blonde hair precisely clipped in a pixie cut, girlishly slim figure, gamine grace. No scars or blemishes show on Deirdre's cream-white skin. She is Audrey Hepburn in *Breakfast at Tiffany's*. Image-wise we fit together hand-in-glove, Deirdre and I, the perfect couple, comely and accomplished. Dexter and Deirdre, the Dream.

She kisses me softly on the top of my head and I smell the gleaming shower scent of her. Something in her posture, one hip stuck out, her turbaned head tilted, reminds me of the night when she first walked into my life. The first time I laid eyes on her all my vital organs shut down. The city was full of brilliant, vibrant women, a catwalk around every corner, but none had turned me on. I was in a rotten frame of mind in those days—away at university, I'd quarrelled with my father and had just been left by the woman I loved. I was drinking too much, smoking too much dope and wallowing in magnificent self-pity. One night, a gang of us were drinking beer at an old hotel near the waterfront. From its windows you could see the faint glimmer of lights from freighters moored in the bay. Our crowd was from the creative writing department, mostly clever young men fashionably unshaven, fashionably shabby, several with fashionably gorgeous girlfriends in tow. One of us, Georges, had gotten out ahead of the pack, at least temporarily, by having a short story published in a very little, very literary magazine.

Georges smoked a Gauloises, and spoke disparagingly of his accomplishment. The rest of us, itchy with envy, and aware of Georges' limitations as a writer—for hadn't we all been in workshops together, feverishly dissecting one another's work the way wasps will deconstruct a dead mouse?—were silently resolving to lay off booze and dope and buckle down to some serious writing. All except me. I didn't give a shit. I'd burnt the manuscript for my new play and doubted I'd ever write another. Besides, I'd had too many beers. At one point in the chanting around Georges' triumph I shouted over the crowd noise: "Kill the poets! Kill the playwrights!"

"Kill the critics!" shouted Marjorie, Georges' girlfriend of the moment, who was a much better critic, and writer, than anyone else at the table, though nowhere near as accomplished a drinker.

"I thought I might find you here, savaging the critics," someone said. I looked up through the blue haze of tobacco smoke and there stood an angel.

"Deirdre, you witch!" shrieked Marjorie "Come join us, we're starting a riot!"

"Yes, pull up a chair!" We all started shuffling to make room at the swilling table for her. But she just smiled, a kind of wise-guy smile that crept knowingly to one side of her face, and at that moment, without knowing her name or circumstances, after half-hearing only one sentence from her not addressed to me, soused beyond speaking and badly needing to piss, I fell entirely in love. Even through my drunken stupor, I recognized that the gods had sent me an angel.

"Do you still love me, Dexter?" Deirdre suddenly interrupts my reverie. She's still standing in the kitchen, towelling her hair.

The question catches me off-balance. Deirdre's not the sort of wife who typically asks if I love her. She's surprised me actually by posing the question, because it's broken one of our unspoken protocols. "Of course I do," I say, my tone implying that it's foolish of her to even ask. But the truth, as I'm sure she knows, is that I'm uneasy with the question.

"I know you don't feel as though your being's tied up with mine the way it once was," she says, looking away from me now, "that your happiness and mine are the same thing. Mind you, I'm not sure any men feel that way. I don't know if you're constitutionally capable of it." Deirdre's managing to sound both sentimental and menacing.

"You know I love you," I try putting a humorous spin on it, but even I hear how transparent I sound.

"I know you used to." And this is true. I fell for her like an avalanche. After that first meeting in the pub, Deirdre and I flowed together effortlessly. We didn't rush together panting. We didn't tear each other's shirts off and hump our way to the stars before we knew each other's names. No, Deirdre and I drifted languidly into orbit together, into a tender and extended pas de deux. We talked then alright, oh, yes, we talked for hours, and walked for miles through the city, looking at buildings and sculptures and poking into gardens down back alleys to see what bizarre fruits and vegetables the Portugese and Chinese and Italian gardeners were growing. We ate at offbeat bistros and went to little theatres and gallery openings and afterward laughed together at the pretentious clones in *de rigueur* black all standing around exchanging witticisms while eyeing each other's accessories. Later we'd make love by moonlight, candlelight or the bright lights of the city.

I remember the day I proposed to her. We were already living together by then and I was back at university, at Deirdre's urging, getting a degree in education. We'd been to see a matinee showing of *Love Story* at the old Hollywood Theatre on Broadway and I guess we were in a sentimental frame of mind. Maybe I confused Deirdre with Ali McGraw. Whatever. It was pouring rain when we came out of the movie house and we dashed together down the sidewalk to a little café where we often hung out. Shaking the rain from our hair, laughing giddily, goofy in gooey love from the film, I reached across the table and took Deirdre's hand in mine and asked her to be my wife. I hadn't planned to, and I certainly didn't have a ring to slip on her finger, we hadn't ever really talked about it, except in a joking way, but there it was: a bona fide proposal. And Deirdre, who normally kept her wits about her, accepted on the spot. So here we are.

"You haven't really answered me," Deirdre prods, examining her African violets on the windowsill. Well, no, I haven't and I don't want to either. What would I say without hurting her? Of course I love her, quite profoundly in some ways.

And as wobbly as we are, paradoxically, there's something solid about Deirdre and me, something that holds us together beyond habit. But it isn't romance. It hasn't been romance for quite a while. So when Deirdre asks if I love her, I interpret her to mean: am I romantically passionate about her? Which I'm not. And I won't say that I am. But I can't say "No, I don't love you" either, because there are all sorts of ways in which I love her and trust her more than anyone. I want to be with her and can't imagine living without her. This is love dammit, in its own elliptical fashion. I reassure myself that it's pointless and unfair to compare a well-worn affection like ours to the mindless trajectory of initial sex.

And it's hard to talk coherently about this half-life love. We don't have the words; at least I don't. The feelings are there, but not the words. Other items in love's catalogue haven't deserted me, but romantic passion and the words to speak it have. I don't say any of this to Deirdre, not today, not ever. I tell myself for the hundredth time that you can't compare the forms of love. The love I felt for Deirdre the day she first told me she was pregnant, the love I felt for her when we lay in one another's arms after losing our first baby—these were as strong and real and true as any other form of love known to man or woman.

Five

"Thank you for coming along with me this morning, Dexter." Mother squeezes my arm affectionately as we stroll down Elm Street beneath the skeletal limbs of overarching trees. We're returning to her house from Sunday service, as my parents did for years together and we as a family used to do long ago. Our familial piety always drew us to Saint James Anglican, an imposing stone and stained-glass structure with a Gothic spire that pierces the leafy canopy of town like the sword of a crusader flashing in the sunlight of Palestine. The spire is by far the tallest structure in town, our sole stab at a skyline.

I was glad as a boy that our family attended communion and vespers at Saint James, though I couldn't have said why. I just knew I liked being inside that cool stone sanctuary. I could tremble at the might of the great pipe organ when it thundered a recessional, then skip outdoors to play a game of catch with the gang or go ramble the fields with my dog, unencumbered by scruples or crippling religious guilt. This was the glory of Anglicanism in those halcyon days: transcendence without tragedy, membership in a community of belief that steered clear of excesses and fanaticisms. We had no statues that would weep real blood on Good Friday afternoons, no Wailing Wall to bang our heads against. The whole affair was eminently civilized, like high tea at a proper British hotel.

I've long since abandoned belief in any of the church's flabby orthodoxy. I think Mother has too; sometimes I suspect everyone in the congregation has. But the ritual of attendance and the solemn liturgy itself, rich with ancient canticles, are aesthetically satisfying. When the weather's fine, as it is this morning, we walk the few blocks from Mother's house to church, just Mother and I, no Deirdre. Strolling the tree-lined streets, passing the stately old homes in this part of town, with their neatly mowed lawns and clipped shrubs, their elaborate finials and bargeboards, newels and balusters, is at least as soul-soothing as the service itself. Today's sermon proved particularly dull—the new vicar is hopelessly muddled among beatitudes and platitudes—and nothing in the service could compete with the thrilling, palpable surge of awakening earth.

"It's very sweet of you to still do this with me, Dexter," Mother says, as though she's read my mind yet another time. "I know it's not quite your thing anymore, but it means so much to me for us to be together like this, especially with your father the way he is."

"Yes." What we don't say aloud is that my father's condition has worsened. The little squall in which Deirdre and I were caught yesterday morning was interrupted by a call from Mother saying the doctors didn't think it a good idea to release Father after all: new talk about disturbing symptoms, a turn for the worse. They would like to keep him in until Monday at least, for further observation. Could I drop over to the hospital and see what was going on?

"Sure," I said, "can I pick up anything for you?"

"Not a thing, darling, thank you," Mother said, "if you'll just deal with the hospital I'll feel ever so much better."

"What's wrong?" Deirdre asked as I hung up. "Has something happened to him?"

"Dad's worse," I told her, "I have to go over there."

"Oh, Dex, I'm sorry," she said, dripping goodness, forgiveness. Too good and forgiving really, which can be irritating when, as now, she has nothing to forgive.

"I'll be back in a bit," I said. Personally I'm not all that good at forgiving, though I work at it intermittently. I enjoy the juiciness of a grudge, something you can sink your teeth into, like rare steak.

Driving through town, I suffered a mild attack of remorse. I don't like the way I treat Deirdre, or she me. After a skirmish like the one we'd just had I end up feeling brutish, wishing I were more generous, more open with my love. I wish she were someone who excited love as something more than a duty.

I left my ruminations in the hospital parking lot, which is easy to do because a hospital, any hospital, has a way of absorbing you into its rhythms and perils and smells. After a few visits, it seems you've been coming here forever, and will do so until the day they carry you out in a body bag. The station nurse was flushed with overwork, her shoulders slumped forward and saddlebags hung under her eyes. She explained hurriedly that they'd moved my father to a semi-private room and directed me to it, adding that Dr. Prahamya would see me during her rounds.

Again I paused at the door of my father's room. Nearby in the corridor, a near-corpse lay on a stretcher, bags of blood and bloodless liquids hanging from above the body and dripping down through tubes. I entered the room and found my father lying on his bed staring out the window. We could see the mountains from here, though they looked unreal, more like a landscape painter's notion of mountains in the distance, with stylized clouds clinging to the highest peaks. There was another empty bed in the room.

"Dad?" I ventured, drawing close, as I sometimes used to, finding him asleep in his lawn chair on a Sunday afternoon, a case book lying open against his chest. His gaze came back from the mountains and searched for me in the room. I smiled and sat on the edge of the bed.

"How are you?" I asked, reaching with my right hand to touch the little mound of bedclothes where his feet lay. His gaze lingered on me for a moment then wandered off to the window again. I wondered if he knew me. His lips moved as though he were trying to speak, but the thought was too far away. Looking into his eyes was like staring through holes in hoodoos where round bits of sky are framed in sandstone. Nothing there, just blue vastness.

I was not aware of her entering, but suddenly became conscious of the doctor being in the room. "Good morning, Mr. Cooke," she said.

"Hello, doctor." I rose from the bed, aligning myself with her. "What's going on with him?"

She shook her head slightly as she went over to the bedside. "The human mind," she said, "is a most peculiar instrument. It is capable of so much we simply don't comprehend." She bent over my father, touching his forehead with her hand while her words fell gentle as cherry blossoms shaken down by breeze onto his bed. "The nurses thought perhaps he'd had a stroke overnight," she continued, "but there's no indication of that, no sign of trauma at all. That's the mystery of it. As though his brain went down another step into the darkness for some reason of its own. I'm sorry not to be more helpful." She glanced at the chart hanging at the foot of the bed and shook her head again. "A mystery," she repeated, smiling slightly at me. Her voice was quiet, but perfectly distinct. "I know it's distressing for you and your mother, but try not to worry, will you? I don't believe he's in any immediate danger, but it would certainly be best if we were to keep him here for observation. Perhaps on Tuesday I can confer with Dr. Samuels and see where we go from there."

"Whatever you think best," I said. "I'll let Mother know." I couldn't think of anything else to add. She's right about the human mind, of course, the mystery at the bottom of it. But when your own flesh and blood is lying on a hospital bed with less awareness than a lizard, you'd like a more mechanistic analysis. I wanted her to say, We've discovered a blood clot in the left temporal lobe and we'll operate this afternoon to remove it and the prognosis looks excellent. With the taxes you pay, you don't want a medical establishment baffled by mysteries.

After the doctor had gone I pulled a chair to the bedside and sat down. I didn't know what to do. My father shifted again and looked toward me, his lips moving like an old sinner mumbling prayers of repentance, but I couldn't make out what he was saying. They might not even have been words. I reached out and took his hand. It was not emaciated or feeble, but neither was it warm and vital. The hand that gripped the football over mine, the fly rod. More urgently than ever, I thought of his death, of never again talking to him, father to son, man to man. Of maybe never having a chance to reconcile with him what's lain like a grudge between us.

"I like the ritual too," I tell Mother as we near her house, "but only because we do it together." She squeezes my hand in gratitude. It's strange to see her even the tiniest bit shaken or dependent. She's normally always in control and keeps nothing under stricter control than herself. Quite brilliant in her own right, she could have had a professional career had she chosen to, but instead she dedicated her life to her husband and child. I can't imagine it really fulfilled her, but you'd never hear her complain about the limitations she's lived under; she simply did what was expected of her, the *Ladies' Home Journal* vision made real. Nowadays she reads her feminist authors voraciously, but never does she think herself hard done by. "I'm privileged, Dexter, and so are you," she'd often say to me. "Self-pity is particularly distasteful among the privileged." She taught me to be like her, to maintain self-discipline. "You can do anything you want, be anything you want, Dexter, darling," she'd tell me over and over again. "You're smart, you're strong, you're gifted, you can reach for whatever star you choose. You need never be afraid of being second best; you're the best there is and I'm so awfully, awfully proud of you." Then she'd hug and kiss me and damn near smother me with loving. I basked in this attention as a kid and at the time never considered what a burden her expectations might become.

I give Mother a hug at her front gate, decline her offer to come in for coffee and sweet rolls, and turn down the street for home. Deirdre will have brunch ready.

A few blocks along, an old beater rumbles up the street and idles to a stop alongside me. A woman at the wheel gestures to me. As I go over to the car, wondering who this could be, she reaches across and swings the passenger door open. "Hello, Dexter," she greets me like a friend, "hop in." It takes me a second to click: Ann Slater, Susan's mother. "I thought I might find you around here," she says, as I slide into the front seat. The car's sour with the smell of cigarettes and beer. Now why would she, of all people, be looking for me?

"Hello, Ann," I say," how's tricks?" Her eyes scan me quickly, trying to read if I'm being funny at her expense or not, so I throw in, "Haven't seen you in a donkey's age."

"Ah well," she sighs, like an afternoon soap-opera queen, "we've all got our own lives to live, haven't we? Not like the old days."

"True enough," I admit. Time has not been especially kind to Ann. She's wearing a cheap green cotton dress with a shabby mustard cardigan thrown over her shoulders. It appears she's just recently hennaed her hair to a rather unfortunate orange. Coral lipstick accentuates the corona of fine smoker's lines etched around her mouth. Her fingernails are painted the same colour as her lips. I don't dare look at her toenails.

"Wanna go for a ride?" she asks me. "I need to talk to you and I've got something I think you'll be very interested in."

Christ! I think to myself, but smile. "Fine," I say, "but I have to be home by one."

"No sweat," she says, shifting to drive and pulling out. The car backfires loudly, like a shotgun blast, and Ann giggles. "I guess I need a new muffler," she says.

What you need is a one-way trip to the auto wrecker's, I think, but say only, "I guess." I notice Ann's legs are purpled with bruises and varicose veins, and this strikes me as even sadder than her awful hair and lipstick. As a kid I knew Ann only from a distance. We all did because, in her prime, Ann Slater was a dish. Several years older than me, she was the hottest thing at Shallowford High my first year there. Blessed, or cursed, early with a woman's body, she wore her skirts high and her sweaters tight. A scent of scandal clung to her, whispers of who she did it with, at a time when most of us only did it in imagination. While we dated princesses by day, many of us Shallowford studs-in-training stained our sheets by night with dreams of Ann Slater's body. She paid us little twerps no attention at all; she ran with older guys, wild guys. I don't know what happened to her after graduation—I think she dropped out before graduating—but I'd guess a lot of booze and drugs and a few too many cowboys with larger cocks than brains. She married at least once, I know, and I seem to remember she lost a child in some horrible accident, a fire it might have been. I'm not sure who Susan's father is, or was, and maybe Ann isn't either.

She pulls the old clunker into a parking spot near the river: Shallowford's version of Lover's Lane. "Hope this is okay," she says, and you can see the flirt hasn't quite died inside her, no matter how much grief it's brought her.

"Fine," I say, "what's on your mind?"

"Smoke?" she asks, tipping an open pack toward me.

"No thanks."

"Mind?" she asks, again flashing me her lipstick-smudged smile.

"Go ahead. I'll just roll down the window." Fresh air washes in through the open car window. I can smell the river, muskrats rutting in the mud. She snaps a silver lighter open, lights her cigarette, winces from the sting of smoke in her eyes, then exhales a long flume of smoke out her window.

"There was something you wanted to tell me?" I perhaps sound impatient but I really don't want to sit here for the rest of the morning in the company of pathos-made-flesh.

"It's about Susan," she tells me in a confidential tone, implying that it might be any number of issues other than the single thing we actually have in common.

"Yes?" I prompt.

"She's not been herself lately," Ann says, drawing on her cigarette and trying mightily to look deep.

"What do you mean exactly?" I'm feeling impatience rise against her, this ridiculous coyness.

"She's been acting very peculiar, very peculiar indeed." Again the soap-opera stare away toward the river.

"What do you mean? What's she been doing?" I'm conscious of pressing too assertively, of not letting her tell the story in her own way. Maybe this is hard for her. Maybe I don't care what she has to say. Why, I wonder, do I feel so little empathy for her?

"She's off in Never-Never Land," Ann says, running her hand back and forth across the top of the steering wheel. "She makes things up."

"What sort of things?"

Ann gives me an appraising look, as though not entirely convinced she should tell me what she's going to. "She's seeing apparitions."

"Apparitions?" I sense a door swinging open that I'd just as soon keep shut. "What do you mean by apparitions? Did she tell you this?"

"Nope, I read about them in her diary," Ann stubs her butt in the ashtray, giving me a sly sidelong glance. "Keeps a diary hidden in her room. Thinks I don't know where it is, silly little fool. She puts a long strand of hair in it in a certain way and I'm always careful to put it back exactly the same. This way I can keep an eye on her, see, know exactly what she's been getting into. You can't be too careful with young girls these days, can you, with so many filthy buggers running loose?"

I almost have to bite my tongue at the irony of Ann Slater presenting herself as a born-again commentator on public morals—not that she isn't right about the surplus of filthy buggers. But sneaking around reading her daughter's diary is repulsive and I'm tempted to tell her so.

"No, you can't," I agree instead. My best bet's to end this exchange by the shortest route possible.

"Here it is," she says, reaching in front of me to the glove compartment. I notice a large brown mole growing at the base of her neck, several dark hairs sprouting from the mole. She takes out a paper bag and from it a diary bound in fake leather.

"You mean you've brought it with you?" This really is repulsive. I don't want to look in Susan's diary.

"Don't worry," she says, "Susan's away for the day. I'll have it safely back before she's home and she'll be none the wiser." For Ann Slater, it's obvious, ethics is only a question of whether you get caught. Here again the sly smile. "Just take a look at this." She begins leafing through the book, carefully so as not to leave smudges. I feel a creepy sensation of being complicit in ugly dealings, as though I were sneaking into the girl's bedroom to steal furtive looks at her diary. A violation I want nothing to do with.

"I really don't want to look at Susan's diary," I tell her, just as she finds the page she's been looking for.

"Oh, I think you do," she says, cunningly, almost a sneer.

"No, I don't, Ann. And I really need to be getting home; my wife's expecting me." Her plucked and repainted eyebrows rise archly. I wonder why the hell I'm feeling defensive, so not the master of the situation my parents trained me to be.

"You care for Susan, don't you?" she asks with a hint of belligerence.

"I care about her." I correct what I'm not sure was an insinuation or not. "Yes, I care about all my students."

"Then read this," she says, shoving the opened diary at me, "and help me out for God's sake, I'm at my wit's end."

I take the diary from her. It's opened to Friday, April 18, 1985. I read the entry:

Dear Diary:

Today was so weird. I felt the pull again, only stronger than ever, and it was really scary. It happened before class, when I was sitting on the bleachers by the playing field. It was sunny and warm, really beautiful, and I was reading the essay for English class. It wasn't making any sense to me at all, I couldn't figure out who the people in it were and I didn't much care. It just seemed like one of those stupid school things they do because they can't think of anything better. Not Dexter, I mean Mr. Cooke, of course, you know Diary, that I still have a thing for him. Anyway, I was kind of only half paying attention to it. You know, Diary, how you can read words sometimes and you know what the words are, but they're kind of outside your head, they don't come in and make real sense the way other words do at other times, when you really know what they mean. Then all of a sudden, WHAM!!! I read a line near the end about the so-called dream children where they say "we are nothing, less than nothing, and dreams. We are only what might have been…" That was so incredible. It's just what I feel sometimes too, that I'm nothing, only a dream, less than a dream, only what might have been. So I was sitting there thinking this and I started hearing music, like from faraway, like how they do it in the movies sometimes, music that seems to start from a long way away and gradually draws closer. I looked around, but there was nothing. Nobody with a ghetto blaster or anything. And the music was different somehow, I can't explain it. I felt like something was tugging at me, like all of me was being pulled in one direction. Like maybe how it feels when an undertow pulls you down in the ocean.

Pretty soon I was walking along the riverbank away from school. I don't even know how I got there. The sun was glinting on the river like diamonds and you could see all the buds on the trees starting to open, like tiny green babies being born. There were birds singing in the bushes, I guess they're starting to build their nests already. It was so beautiful I wanted to cry. But still I felt the force drawing me on. So I came to the fence where the sanctuary starts. I've never been in there before. The signs say No Trespassing and the kids say there's big dogs in there running loose. I've never seen one. But I was scared to go in, even though whatever was pulling me wanted me to. I sat down on a log to think, but I kept hearing the music, sometimes it seemed to come from the river or the trees, or sometimes from the hills higher up. I had to go in even though I was so scared. I found a gap in the fence where I could just slip through the barbed wire without getting tangled. The second I was through a strange feeling came over me, as if I was in a magic place or something. I felt so light I could float away like a dandelion seed. I did a little dance right there in the grass under the cottonwood trees. If anyone had seen me they would have thought I was crazy. But you see, Diary, I didn't care. I was lighter than air, and my feet danced across the grass like I was a famous ballerina. I didn't care about playing hooky or trespassing or anything. I was FREE!!! Wild and free!!!

I wandered further along the river that way, only now I wasn't being pulled anymore, I was just drifting like a cloud in a clear blue sky. I don't know how long I walked for, it could have been an hour or more. There was no one around, no sound at all except the river splashing and birds singing. Then all of a sudden, my heart stopped. I saw a man through the trees. He was really tall, and had long hair and a beard. He was dressed all in white and was mega-weird looking. I froze right there. I don't think he saw me. He was just standing there, staring up into the trees like he was praying to them. I was so scared I almost pissed my pants. I tiptoed backward, and kept him in sight for as long as I could, trying not to step on anything that would make noise. I was sure he'd come after me, do something horrible to me, but he never moved. When I couldn't see him anymore, I turned and ran. I ran and ran. My lungs were bursting, my heart pounded like a drum. Twigs and branches kept lashing me as I ran. I didn't care. I was so scared. After a while I had to stop because I couldn't breathe, I couldn't get any air in. I thought I was having a heart attack my heart was pounding so loud. I tried to listen to hear if he was following me, but a flock of ravens up in the trees were screaming to each other. I didn't hear him coming over their noise. I got up again and ran and ran. I promise you one thing, Diary, I will never, ever, go back into that weird place again.

I close the book. I don't know what to say.

"D'you think she's doing drugs?" Ann Slater asks me.

"I have no idea." And it's true, I have no idea at all. But for the second time this weekend Susan's writing has provoked a visceral response in me, because I know the mysterious man in white she's describing. Or should I say knew him. Knew him and loved him. Brother Gabriel he called himself. He was something special: tall and beautiful with charisma to burn and a troop of loyal followers that included my first true love, my long-lost Angela. For a brief, brilliant time Gabriel became one of the most important people in my universe. He and Angela together turned my life upside down. That was when I discarded the discreet piety of Saint James and ran ridiculously wild, in the highlands of spiritual ecstasy, and of sexual ecstasy too, with Angela. Brother Gabriel was her spiritual guide and mine, and between them they set a whirlwind loose that ripped apart everything I'd ever known and believed in. And then they disappeared, and nothing's been seen or heard of them since. I don't think much about that old episode any more, but if you rub deep enough, as Susan's just done, the rawness is still there. I can feel it now. I don't want to read any more of Susan's diary, and I'm already late for brunch, so I escape, promising Ann I'll do whatever I can to help with her daughter.

Six

Hurrying toward the gym for theatre rehearsal, I hear Danielson call out, "Oh, Mr. Cooke!"

"Yes?"

"I hope you don't mind my asking." The principal sidles up to me. "How's your father? Nothing too serious, I hope?"

"He's still in the hospital. They're running some tests on him."

"Hmm. I'm sorry to hear it. I do hope he comes through it alright."

Though his tone is one of genuine concern, I've learned through experience not to trust a word out of Danielson's mouth. With him, nothing is what it seems. Always there's some other game being played that you don't know the rules of. It's no coincidence that his favourite pastime is playing chess; he's quite an accomplished player, sometimes travelling to Calgary or Vancouver to compete in tournaments. Danielson is someone who invariably makes a move not for its own sake, but as a prelude to subsequent moves and eventual entrapment. Sometimes I believe it's his way of maintaining control in the school; other times I'm convinced that he takes delight in setting up his little ambushes, outflanking and outwitting you on a playing surface of his own devising.

Whatever it is, I try to avoid him as much as I can. Most of the staff dislike him as thoroughly as I do; his maneuvers are a favourite topic in the staff room, so long as none of his intimates are within earshot.

Just this morning I had a chat with Miss Phillips, the biology teacher. She's a timid soul and perfectly harmless, but too fragile for the rough-and-tumble of explaining the subtleties of paramecia to hulking grade-eleven boys. "Oh, he just gets under my skin!" she hissed at me this morning.

No need to ask who. "What was he on about this time?"

"The prehistoric recurrence of mass extinctions," she looked at me guilelessly through her oversized tortoiseshell glasses.

"What's that got to do with anything?"

"I think it has to do with him knowing more about biology than I do."

"What did he say?"

"The usual rubbish…"

But at that point our conversation was interrupted by the sudden appearance of Louise Danielson and I left Miss Phillips to whatever further torments awaited her.

"By the way," Danielson asks, "Did you get the essays from the grade twelves on Friday?"

"Yes, I did. Thank you."

"Excellent." A pause. "How's that group coming along? I mean in terms of the provincials? Everything in hand?"

"Yes, I think so," I wonder what he's trolling for now. "They're a pretty bright bunch."

"I'm sure they are, but bright alone won't suffice, will it?"

"No, I suppose not." I'm determined not to get into it with him.

"I'm sure you realize that the Governor General's visit makes it doubly important that we have all hands on deck graduating with flying colours."

"Of course."

Danielson pauses a moment. You can almost see his hand hovering above the board. I'm wanting to get down to the gym, see if I can maybe have a word with Susan Slater before rehearsal begins. I start inching in that direction, but Danielson's not to be denied. "How's that play of yours progressing?" he asks. "Rehearsals going well?"

"I'd say so. I think the production's quite promising." This is an outright lie, but no more than Danielson deserves.

"You're on your way to rehearsal now?"

"Yes, I should get down there." A few more steps away.

"How would you feel," Danielson sidles up to me again, drawing too close, "if I were to sit in?" This is something he's never before asked to do. He knows full well I can't say no.

"Sure," I try to sound as nonchalant as possible.

"I'm just thinking," he says, "You know, if the production's really up to snuff..." he pauses here, so that I get the message unmistakably, "we might consider having a gala performance for the Governor General's visit."

Shit. This I don't need. It means Danielson with his hands all over the production. Doing it his way. In short, a nightmare. "Hmm, that's interesting," I stall for time, "very interesting. Let's see how the production unfolds in the meantime. Whether it's, as you say, up to snuff. We don't want to embarrass ourselves."

"Exactly. Well, why don't you get on with it. I'll be down shortly. I'll just slip quietly in. I don't want to intrude on your work."

Like hell you don't. "Fine," I tell him and head toward the gym.

We're labouring on a play I wrote myself. At first we'd rummaged around the standard school play fare—*Pygmalion*, *Our Town*, *The Crucible*—but couldn't find anything that clicked for the kids involved. That's when Patsy Reynolds—one of those annoyingly bright kids who thinks of clever things before you do—suggested we develop our own production. Maybe I could whip up a rough script and we would workshop the thing from there. Against my better judgment, I allowed myself to be flattered into it. Naturally I'd wanted to be hip and relevant; otherwise why bother? We could have just remounted *Oklahoma!* and ridden off into a corny sunset of irrelevance. But I had to try my hand at gritty realism. Recently I'd reread Margaret Atwood's *Surfacing* and borrowed the notion of a group of young people off on a camping trip. The classic journey of discovery. I developed seven main characters: two sets of boyfriend/girlfriend, two other girls who may or may not be incipient lesbians, and one lonesome cowboy guy. This took care of most of the kids who really wanted to act, while the rest would do lights and props, makeup, be assistant director and so on.

Fine. The story's alleged tension relies upon a mounting friction among the players, a stripping away of layers so their souls are bared for all to see. It's been pretty tough, sitting at rehearsal in the school gymnasium-cum-theatre, occasionally cringing as the kids on stage fumble through lines, looking embarrassed as they try to dredge up an existential angst that's as foreign to them as Aristotle.

"Okay, Sharon," I call from my chair. "Can you try that line again, walking from stage left, and stop just this side of the tent." Sharon, playing Beth, nods, repositions herself and walks stiffly forward:

BETH: (exasperated) Oh, Peter, aren't you ever going to grow up?

"Good!" I call. "Go on, Gordon." This to Gordon Corsault, kneeling by the tent, playing Peter.

PETER:(looks up at Beth with an exaggerated sneer) You didn't seem to have any complaints about how grown up I was last night.
(Beth blushes and looks embarrassed)
(Diana enters from stage right, panting as though she's been running)

Susan Slater's in this role and I'm instantly reminded of that scene by the river and her strange diary entry.

PETER & BETH: (Looking up in surprise) Diana? What is it? What's happened?
DIANA: (strides forward) It's Alix. She's gone.
BETH: Gone?
PETER: Gone where?
DIANA: I don't know. I think she's lost and confused. She must be somewhere out there, trying to find...something.
BETH: What could she be trying to find?
DIANA: (pause) Maybe...herself.

Susan looks much taller on stage than in real life and her voice is surprisingly strong. Suddenly, the gym doors swing open and Danielson steps into the gym, with Louise trailing dutifully behind. They take up a position against the far wall, watching the action on stage.

"Focus!" I call to the players, who've been thrown off by Danielson's arrival.

PETER: Should we go look for her?
DIANA: (staring straight ahead) You'd never find her out there in that wilderness, not unless she wanted to be found.

Susan's Diana is taking control of the scene and the strength of her presence is carrying it forward but, my God, it's going to take some doing to make this vapid writing breathe.

A few minutes later, I notice Danielson and his wife leaving the gym, whispering to one another.

None too soon the final bell rings. "Thanks everybody!" I call out, "It's coming along very nicely." The kids shuffle off the stage, picking up jackets and books. I'm gathering up my script and notes when Susan Slater approaches me. "Can I talk to you for a minute, Mr. Cooke?" she asks. "In private?"

"Of course," I say. There's no need to go anywhere for privacy as the other students are already banging out through the swinging gym doors. Susan sits down one chair away from me and sets her books and sweater on the chair between us. She looks uncomfortable.

"Well, what do you think?" I ask her.

"About?"

"About the play. Be honest."

She brushes a tumble of raven-dark hair back from her face with one hand. Something in the gesture is acutely familiar, mirroring lost moments from my past. This girl has an enigmatic quality all her own. She lacks poise and self-assurance, but her allusiveness is appealing.

"Really?" she asks.

"Yes, really."

"It's pretty weird," she says, laughing nervously, swallowing the laughter, then bowing her head so that the long hair spills forward again. She glances at me sideways. Is she flirting? I can't tell if it's just shyness or not.

"Weird how?" I ask her. "Do you mean offbeat or ridiculous?"

She rolls her eyes the way TV's taught kids to do. She is flirting, I think, remembering the line from her diary that she "had a thing" for me. "I guess both," she says, smiling.

"It's not the play you want to talk about, is it?"

Her face changes again, darkening. "No," she replies, then pauses. "Can I ask you something?"

"Of course."

"Have you been talking to my mother?"

Christ, here we go. I don't want to deny anything Susan already knows about, but neither do I want to give away things she doesn't. "Yes," I reply, ever so casual, "I ran into her on Sunday morning and we had a bit of a chat."

"About me?"

"Among a lot of other things."

"What did she say about me?" With each question Susan becomes a little more focused and intense, her shyness retreating.

"The same things you'll maybe say yourself about your own kids a few years from now: how you want them to do well, to succeed, to have a good life." I realize as the words spill glibly out that I'm taking liberties with Ann Slater's questionable motives, but what option do I have? I'm hardly going to tell this kid what I think of her mother.

"Did she tell you about my…my apparitions?"

"Your what?"

Susan looks over her shoulder, as though she's afraid someone may be listening in, and lowers her voice. "My apparitions," she repeats, embarrassed.

"She did say something about your seeming very distracted these days," I say, carefully.

"But nothing about apparitions?"

"I'm sure I would have remembered that," I say. "Do you mean you've been seeing things?"

"Yes," she says, almost to herself. Her manner's distracted, she's someplace else, withdrawing inside herself.

"Do you want to tell me about it?"

She doesn't answer for a bit. Her hands fidget together in her lap. I notice her fingernails are brutally chewed down. Still she doesn't want to tell me whatever it is she wants to tell me. She does and she doesn't. Just like I do, and do not, want to hear what she has to say. I like Susan a lot; she's a bit of an oddball, but she's nobody's fool. I don't like to see her struggling and pathetic. I wait, in the cool dimness of the gym, a faintly acrid smell of years-old sweat staining the atmosphere.

"Susan? What is it?"

She raises her head slowly and again brushes back her hair. Tears are streaked across her cheeks. Her face is distorted, swamped by bloated coarseness like her mother's. She fumbles for a Kleenex in her bag and blows her nose. "I'm sorry," she blubbers, "I can't help it. I'm so scared."

"Why don't you tell me about it? Just take your time and tell me what's happening. No need to be embarrassed or afraid."

She blows her nose again and dabs at her eyes. The sobs subside. She turns away from me, still sniffling, to compose herself, then swings back. Her eyes are rimmed with red and her cheeks glisten from the tears, but the ghost of her dreadful mother is gone from her face. "Something's going on with me and I don't know what it is," she says. "Sometimes I think I'm going crazy."

"What's happening?"

"I'm seeing someone. Up at the Conservancy."

"You mean you have a boyfriend?"

"No, no, nothing like that."

"What then?"

"I go to the Conservancy. I can't seem to help myself, I just have to. And then I see him."

"Who do you see?"

"It's a man. Always the same man."

"Can you describe him?"

"Easy. He's, like, very tall and he's got long blonde hair, beautiful hair."

"How old would you say he is?"

"Not as old as you," she says, then I can see she wished she hadn't. "I dunno, maybe he's like twenty-eight or thirty or something."

So it's not Gabriel; he'd be pushing forty-five by now, an old man to her. Am I relieved or disappointed it's not him? Would I really want to see him again? "What clothes does he wear?" I ask Susan.

"White cotton pants and shirt. And sandals. And a green necklace."

I'm wondering who the hell this could be. I don't doubt Susan's telling me the truth; she's far too agitated to be spinning all this out of nothing. But who the hell could it be? "Do you talk to him?"

"Sort of," she shrugs.

"What do you mean, sort of?"

"Well, it's not like we're really talking, like you and me are right now."

"You and I," I correct her, prissily.

"Right," she says, "you and I." She stops then and again stares down at her fidgeting hands. The Kleenex is shredded between them.

"But?" I prod.

"Well, even though he's not really talking, he does sort of say things to me." Her sentence ends on a rising note, as though it were a question.

"So you're up quite close to him?"

"Oh, sure. At first I wasn't. The first time I was scared shitle...I was really scared."

"But you went back, even though you'd been frightened?"

"I couldn't help myself, that's the weird part, it's like I have no control over it. After that first time I swore I'd never go back in there again. But I lay awake all that night, and I thought I could hear that same music from a long way off. I knew I had to go back the next day. There was some reason I needed to go back. I can't explain it."

"So you went back and weren't afraid?"

"Not so much, no."

"And you gradually drew closer to the man?"

"Uh huh. At first it didn't seem like he knew I was there, or maybe didn't care. Then he'd, like, maybe smile at me for a second and turn away again."

"But he wouldn't say anything?"

"Not that day. But I knew he was harmless, and I felt kind of...kind of..."

"What?"

"Oh, I dunno...I felt kinda...it seems dumb even saying it..."

"No, go on."

"Well, it was like I was sort of lifted up, like I was stoned, only I wasn't."

"And what happened?"

"Nothing else. I just kind of drifted home, sort of in a daze. But I couldn't sleep again that night. I thought about him all night. I knew I had to go back again on Sunday."

"And you did?"

"Yes. And by then I'm, like, right up to him and I'm not scared at all."

"Then he'd speak?"

"It's like I was saying, he doesn't really talk, his lips don't really move or anything, but you kinda hear his voice anyway. Like it was coming from someplace else or something. It's truly weird."

"Can you remember anything he said?"

"Yes, he talks about the trees a lot and the birds. The grasses. It's kinda like poetry how he talks."

"Do you have any idea who he is or where he came from?"

"He told me his name."

"He did?"

"Yeah. He says his name is Gabriel."

"Gabriel? You're sure that's what he said?"

"That's right. And he says he comes from the Divine Oneness."

"What?"

"Mr. Cooke! Mr. Cooke!" I snap to and see Danielson's calling me from the door, his disapproval bouncing off the gym walls. "I'm locking up now, Mr. Cooke, do you mind?"

I quickly gather my stuff up, and Susan hers, and we hurry out of the gym. Danielson's rattling his big knot of keys like an impatient prison guard, holding the door open with his other hand.

"Everything alright?" he asks me as I pass him, insinuating that it doesn't look that way.

"Yes, yes, everything's fine," I tell him impatiently, as the gym door bangs shut behind us. Susan's already disappeared down the corridor.

Seven

I pull the Subaru off the gravel roadway, stopping in front of the Conservancy gate. It's the original old ranch gate, with two tall pine log posts and a big log crossbar from which a wooden sign hangs down by two chains. The chains complain with a rusty squeal as the sign pitches in the wind: Dancing Grasses Conservation Area. Unauthorized Access Prohibited. I climb out of my car and lock it. Off to one side there's an information board with a map of the property and a description of its ecosystem. Only you can't read it because its face is covered in plexiglass, which has been shattered by a buckshot.

Nobody's around, nor is there apt to be anybody around, because the gate's at the end of a gravel road on which nobody lives. Barbed wire fences stretch in both directions, taut lines etched against billowing land and sky. A red-tailed hawk perched on a fence post stares disapprovingly as I climb the aluminum gate and drop down onto the roadway inside. As though bored, the hawk launches itself into the air and glides away on the wind. Perfectly alone, I set off down the road.

No plough has broken this ground, and the meadows have been only lightly grazed by horses, so the native grasses remain. My father taught me their names years ago: Sandberg bluegrass and bluebunch wheatgrass mostly, with prairie sagewort, junegrass and rabbit-brush scattered here and there, their new growth shimmering green. Vivid patches of colour—the pink flowers of long-leaved phlox and bitterroot, the brilliant yellows of arrow-leaved balsamroot—bring a stunning contrast to the landscape. The meadows fall away gently, undulating down toward the river which is lost in a green veil of poplars and cottonwoods.

This ranch is over a thousand acres, two full sections, running up almost against the town on its eastern side. The place was homesteaded back in the 1870s by two brothers named Clagg, each of them getting a section. Just how they survived isn't clear, because they never broke the land or ran cattle the way their neighbours did. They fenced the whole spread, more to keep other people's livestock out than theirs in. The brothers built one big house together and a small barn for their horses and after that they pretty much left well enough alone. Neither married, and after they died the property went to unknown relatives who lived in Boston.

It was never clear whether Gabriel had inherited the place or not. He carried on as though he owned it. But he'd have carried on that way if he didn't. Gabriel seemed to own whatever or whomever he touched. After he and the rest of them disappeared the place sat empty again. Eventually a couple of suits from the city showed up, representing something they called the Dancing Grasses Foundation which would be managing the property as a native grasslands reserve. They put up their signs, ran an announcement in the local paper to the effect that trespassing on the property would result in criminal prosecution, and other than a once-yearly site inspection, left the place to sit undisturbed.

And so it has. Until now. Disturbed now by Susan's unlikely tale of seeing Gabriel and hearing from him about his trademark "Divine Oneness." Someone who'd disappeared from here before she'd entered kindergarten.

Though it was fourteen years ago at least, I remember like yesterday the afternoon when Gabriel first stepped into my life. Gabriel and Angela both. A bunch of us were hanging out at Mellinson's Café on Main. They had a jukebox in there and big old high-backed booths—they still do—and it was the place to go. A coke 'n' smoke kind of place. We played Roy Orbison and Van Morrison records on the jukebox and this was considered extremely wild.

One summer afternoon I had my Buick convertible parked on the street outside the café, I could see it through the window, gleaming in the sun. My dad had given me the car for my sixteenth birthday: a 1966 Wildcat convertible, 425-cubic-inch nailhead, buckets, console, power antenna, tilt steering wheel. A total dream machine. "You deserve it, Dexter," my dad had said to me, handing me the keys on the morning of my birthday. "Your mother and I are proud of you. You deserve to drive in style." No lectures about driving carefully or not drinking and driving, none of that. Always positive. Always aimed at excellence. And I wasn't disappointing. I was pulling down straight A's and starring at football and hoops. My hair was right, my clothes were right, girls clustered like grapes around me. They said I looked like Troy Donahue. I mean, how good can you stand it?

So me and Eddie Fanning, Diana Burroughs and a couple of other kids were sitting at a booth in Mellinson's drinking milkshakes. Patsy Cline was crying on the jukebox. Mellinson's has a bell that tinkles whenever the door's opened, and we'd look up to see if it's maybe one of the gang coming in. Only this time we looked up and if we hadn't been so determinedly cool our jaws might have dropped like we were a bunch of hayseeds. A bizarre trio was standing there. Two women and a guy. One of the women looked like what I imagined gypsy girls did, with long, straight hair hanging halfway down her back. She wore a flimsy flowing cotton dress, brightly patterned and beaded, and was barefoot. The other woman was older and much more conservatively dressed, but her hair was cut close to her scalp in a way I'd never seen on a woman before. The man with them was the most dramatic-looking character I'd ever seen. Well over six feet tall, he had long blonde hair and a small goatee. He was dressed entirely in white cotton, with thick leather sandals and a necklace of polished green stones. By then we'd seen plenty of photos and news clips of hippies in San Francisco and Woodstock and all that, but these three looked different. There was nothing scruffy or juvenile-looking about them at all. And—though I couldn't have described it at the time—I was aware of a kind of serenity that seemed to envelop them and set them apart from their surroundings. Against the familiar backdrop of old Shallowford, where the unpredictable seldom occurred, these three stood out as if they'd just landed from Mars. In our neck of the woods men didn't wear necklaces, or dress all in white, or wear their hair like a woman's. "Jesus Christ!" I said, under my breath, and that's who he looked like, Jesus.

"Can I help you?" Joanie Aiello asked them nervously from behind the counter. Joanie was one of our gang, working at the café for the summer. All the rest of us were staring, though coolly.

"Do you serve herb tea?" the man asked her, his voice surprisingly gentle.

"Herb tea?" Joanie stammered, obviously not sure if the regular old tea bags Mellinson would throw into a pot of hot water were herb or not. "No, I don't think so," she said at last. The two girls at our table started giggling which caused the man in white to turn and look at us. For a moment his eyes locked onto mine and I felt strangely transparent under his gaze, as though he could see something in me I'd rather he didn't. He smiled slightly, maybe even nodded as though in recognition, then turned back again to Joanie.

"Thank you," he said to her. The three of them huddled for a moment in conversation, smiled at Joanie, then sidled out of the café, the little doorbell tinkling behind them. The moment the door closed, our group was shrieking hysterically and Joanie was staring across her cash register out the front window as though Roy Rogers himself was riding Trigger down Main Street. That was Gabriel's Shallowford debut.

On that lazy summer afternoon, my life's course was already laid out as precisely as the gardens at Versailles. I would complete grade twelve the following spring at the top of the honour roll and be class valedictorian at graduation. I would win a scholarship to a prestigious university where, combining excellence in academics and athletics, I would become in due course a Big Man on Campus. I would graduate with honours and proceed to law school at an even more prestigious university and then article with and join a prestigious law firm in a city of my choosing. Eventually I might—and here was the only potential variable in the script—perhaps return to Shallowford to raise a family and take over my father's practice. My grand march into manhood and profession stretched before me like an already-familiar highway. I had enjoyed long conversations with my parents about it, debating the virtues of this university compared to that one, the particular merits of various fields of law. But never once questioning the fundamental premise. "You'll make your mark, son, I'm certain of that," my dad told me, while Mother beamed approvingly. I was certain of it too.

I was working part-time at my dad's office that summer, helping out with filing and filling in for the receptionist while she took her holidays, simple stuff. I'd done the same the summer before—Dad thought it'd be useful to get a bit of "hands-on lawyering" before going off to university. Evenings and weekends I'd get together with the gang; we'd swim in the river and sit around a bonfire at night, paired off like pigeons, falling in what we thought was love, and finishing up with ferocious necking. I was hooked up with Diana Burroughs, a sweet little prom queen, who treated me as though I were a semi-deity and let me fondle her breasts.

I was sitting at my dad's receptionist's desk one languid afternoon, probably daydreaming about being with Diana that night, how we'd kiss, how she'd resist, but eventually give way, how our tongues would explore each other's mouth, how my hand might wander into caressing her thigh or cupping a breast, when the office door opened and there stood the younger of the two women I'd seen in the café. Startled out of my reverie, I damn near lost my cool, but when you have as much of that commodity as I thought I had, you can lose a lot without losing it all and I quickly recovered.

"Good afternoon," I said. "May I help you?"

A wry smile lit up her face for a moment. It was a face that could use some lighting up. For one thing, it was far too large for the rest of her. Had it been any larger, it would have bordered on grotesque. The face itself was neither ugly nor handsome, but primitive: full, coarse lips, no lipstick, deep-set eyes under dark and heavy eyebrows, and high cheekbones. Her hair looked native, long and lustrous black. Shallowford girls wore their hair in ponytails and pixie cuts and Sandra-Dee curls, not in a long tumble like hers. She wore a light cotton blouse and a short, free-flowing skirt. The blouse was cinched under her breasts so that it exposed a tawny midriff, which was so perfectly flat and beautiful I wanted to touch it. She stood with her legs slightly apart, like an athlete balanced for action, her muscular thighs outlined beneath the thin cotton. There was something provocatively physical about her. Though her outfit was far less revealing than the skimpy bikinis Diana and the other girls were wearing to our swimming parties, it was far more erotic. She smelled of a fragrance I didn't recognize, something like incense. I guessed she was a couple of years older than me.

"I'd like to make an appointment with Mr. Cooke," she said in a husky voice, like Dinah Washington singing "What a Difference a Day

Makes." I must've wigged out or something for a second, because she said, in a slightly louder voice, "Hello?" and smiled at me.

"Yes, yes, of course," I said, scrambling for a pen and the appointment book. We found a time that suited her. "Could I have your name please?" I asked her, resuming the proper professional voice my dad had instructed me to use with clients.

"No, you can't," she said, smirking, "I need it for myself; but if ever I decide to give it away, you'll be first on my list."

It took me a split second to click on her joke. "Very funny," I said. I was accustomed to adulation from girls, but this odd sock was plainly not the adulation type. She was different from what I might have expected. I guess all the gossip around town about the outlandish newcomers had set me up to expect someone who'd be slovenly and a bit slow on the uptake. Drug-addled or inbred or something. But this girl—more a woman than a girl—was anything but slow. I realized that I was a bit intimidated by her.

She told me her name—Angela Lang—and after I'd written it in the appointment book, she asked me mine. "Dexter?" she said, delighted. "What a wonderful name! And are you, in fact, dextrous?" I put down my pen and looked at her. Again that enigmatic smile, almost taunting, lighting up her oversized face.

"I suppose I am, yes," I replied and smiled myself, determined not to be unnerved by this oddball. But I couldn't come up with something clever to toss back to her, like afterward when I realized I should have said, "And are you in fact an angel?"

Instead I said nothing, just grinned at her knowingly, the way I knew girls liked. "Are you the lawyer's son?" she asked me.

I told her I was and she asked if she could sit down. "Sure," I said. As she slipped into a chair across the desk from me, I became aware she was not wearing a brassiere. This too was not done in Shallowford; I'd tussled with enough treacherous bra fastenings to know that. But what was strange for me was that, after just a few minutes alone with this woman, without her saying or doing anything to make me feel this way, I was embarrassed of my hometown and its townsfolk. Even the bleeding madras shirt and white chinos I was wearing seemed pathetically preppy compared to her exotic appearance. Under this peculiar woman's scrutiny I felt the country bumpkin. Naive and klutzy. All the things I never am, have never been. Stupidly, prodded by an unfamiliar sensation something like panic, I wanted to tell her about my Buick.

"Do you dance?" she asked me out of nowhere. Her eyes were large and dark and watched me intently, as though for some purpose she wasn't revealing. Her voice and smile were faintly mocking, but her eyes weren't at all. Maybe that's why I was unnerved by her—I got several different messages from her at the same time and I couldn't tell which one, if any of them, was real.

"A bit," I told her, dripping false modesty. In fact, I love to dance. Mother taught me when I was still a kid. And there were few things I loved more than sweeping around the living room in her arms, Rhett Butler to her Scarlet O'Hara! We'd tango and we'd swing too, all kinds of crazy dances, Mother knew them all. And though I loved to dance for its own sake, especially with Mother, I appreciated dancing's tactical advantages too—that there was no surer way of enticing a desirable girl than to take her in my arms and twirl her masterfully across the dance floor. By grade six or seven every girl in the class could more or less dance and hardly any boy could. Most of the boys nailed themselves to the gymnasium walls whenever we'd have an after-school sock hop, but not me. I danced as I had with Mother, smooth and confident, loving the thrill of the dance itself and the adulation of the dance-mad girls.

"Wonderful," she said, "perhaps we'll dance together sometime." Which was a weird thing for a stranger to say, and the way she said it struck me as provocative, as though she were daring me. With that, and a final smile, she rose suddenly and left my father's office.

Several days later she came back for her appointment, but my father was there and she said little to me. Still I was conscious again of her strange allure. Afterward, I tried to wheedle out of my father what she'd wanted, but he wouldn't say. To him confidentiality was sacred. "A fascinating young woman," was as far as he'd go.

Damned if she wasn't fascinating! I had to admit I was turned on to her. I sometimes caught myself daydreaming about her instead of Diana, thinking about that slim, delicious abdomen. What the hell was it about her that I found so irresistible? It made no sense: she wasn't beautiful at all, I knew nothing about her, had had only one brief conversation with her which had left me feeling inadequate. But I was fascinated by her. Not the hot ejaculatory fixation I'd had for Ann Slater when I'd come roaring out of puberty. Angela was no Ann

Slater any more than she was Diana Burroughs. She was something else entirely, something we Shallowford studs didn't have a category for. I needed to know about her and that, in part, was why I was determined to visit Dancing Grasses that first time.

Driving out of town this morning I'd smiled to myself thinking how much I'd changed from the young buck I was when I first took this same route to visit Gabriel and Angela. I'd driven up in my Wildcat back then, convinced, I'm sure, that I'd make an impression in it. But though I had a cocky swagger to my step in those days, I doubt it went with me on that particular expedition. I was feeling totally jacked up as I turned the Wildcat's nose into the ranch. I hadn't told my parents where I was going or when I'd be back. There was something uncharacteristically furtive about what I was doing.

Strange that today I registered a faint facsimile of that same furtiveness, not nearly so strong, but unmistakable. I didn't tell Deirdre what I was planning to do, nor have I told her about Susan's diary. Deirdre wouldn't approve—of my reading the girl's diary to begin with, of Ann Slater or my renewed imaginary dealings with Gabriel and Angela. There are blocks of black-and-white in Deirdre's world view, though not many halftones. But the history of this place, and its former occupants, is for me one long trail of greys.

Though there were no greys at all the afternoon of my first, tentative visit. It was a brilliant summer day, much like today, vibrant with blues and greens. I parked my Wildcat right here, on a hill above the river in what's left of the old Clagg homestead. The original house still stands, fashioned from pine logs with dovetail notches at the corners. The logs have weathered to a silver patina and much of the chinking has fallen out from between them, so bars of sunlight gleam between the skeletal logs. The shingles on the roof have curled like dried leaves from too many summers in the sun and the whole building sags as though it has lost heart. The small barn nearby, also of logs, leans at a tipsy angle, pushed out of shape by the wind. Bits of old farm machinery lie rusting in tall grass, like the skeletal remains of dead animals.

I'd expected the newcomers to be making use of the buildings. Instead I found them in an encampment of three big tipis down near the river. As I approached, I saw five of them—the three I'd seen in the café and two others—sitting in a circle in the grass, eyes closed, meditating. I lingered at the edge of the clearing, not wanting to intrude, and was just on the point of quietly withdrawing when the one who looked like Jesus raised his arm and beckoned me to come forward, though how he knew I was there I don't know, because he had his back to me. As I approached the group, he and the man beside him separated slightly, wordlessly, creating enough room for me to join the circle. All of them still had their eyes closed and continued with their rapt meditation. I felt a complete fool, not knowing what to do, awkward in the unfamiliar lotus position. But I closed my eyes and let my mind drift, felt the warmth of the sun, the touch of soft breezes, heard a miniature symphony of rustling and twittering. Where my mind drifted was mostly across the circle to Angela sitting opposite me. Pretending to keep my eyes closed, I squinted through tiny bars of light, seeing a blurry image of her. My thoughts were blurry too. What was I doing here? Why was I letting myself be pulled along by an irrational fascination with this woman? Sitting self-consciously in that earnest little circle, my meditations primarily upon Angela, I had an unwarranted but unmistakable sense of danger.

Afterward, Angela introduced me to the group: Cheyenne, the butch-cut woman I'd seen in the café; Brewster Luckacs, a thin young guy with rimless glasses and wispy beard, wiry and intense, wound tight; and James York, a bulky and affable black man smiling from inside a tremendous head of Afro hair. They had come from San Francisco and were determined, they told me, to establish a community on the land. They would do away with private property and all the cursed trappings of capitalist consumerism (at which point I'd wished my Wildcat, parked on the hill above us, was a little less obvious). They would seek the greater good, a collective well-being that would nurture both body and spirit. They would dance and write poetry and meditate. "Each of us needs to establish our place in the world," Gabriel said, "and to answer the fundamental question: how am I to live my life? For us, that place is here and we plan to live together, simply and spiritually." I was, they told me, always welcome to join them.

I smiled and thanked them and didn't mention I was no more likely to join them than I was to join the French Foreign Legion. There was a far larger world awaiting me beyond the narrow confines of this buttoned-down little town I'd known all my life. As much as I loved this place, I wondered who'd want to live here after living in San Francisco. I wondered if they knew what they were getting themselves into.

Still I found myself, in those carefree summer days, returning to the ranch not just for the chance to see more of Angela, but from a desire to converse with Gabriel. I was as captivated by him as by her. He was a man of extraordinary force, compelling charisma. Talking with him it seemed as though the normal course of events was suspended while I entered a consecrated place. He took me into unknown spaces, enfolded me in an embrace that had nothing sordid or contrived or manipulative in it. I simply felt lifted up, borne along by a gentle current.

We were looking at these old log buildings in the homestead one day, he and I. "Black Elk speaks of the damage done to native consciousness," Gabriel said, "when the people were compelled to abandon their tipis and live inside straight-walled cabins. The energy is not the same; how could it be? Moving from circles to squares. No wonder the nations waned for a while. No wonder the spirit withered." Gabriel would muse like that and smile in a way that implied we were soulmates voyaging together through a universe that was in turns tragic, absurd and brilliant. I never felt as though I was being instructed by him, not in a school-teacherish way, and certainly never patronized. He included and honoured me, and had no need to prove himself superior. I loved him from the start. Him and Angela both.

"We make love to the universe," he told me another time. "We copulate with the galaxies, feeling our fingertips dance along the flesh of the Pleiades." A poet as well as a mystic, his words to my young ears were touched with scintillating brilliance. Listening to him, I felt implicitly and absolutely that I was somehow part of a tremendous spiritual mystery. The allure of Dancing Grasses, to me was that I left behind the stupid minutiae of everyday life and entered a place of enlightening tranquility and bliss.

"Consider the grasses of the fields," Gabriel said to me one day. "Empty your mind of clutter, continue emptying it, until the clutter is no more and complete calm prevails. Sit among the grasses. They will teach you all you need to know of birth and death and the great wheel of life on which we turn." Intent upon enlightenment, I sat and watched grasses for hours at a time. "Don't watch them," Gabriel told me gently, "be in them and of them. Be among them as you are among all living things, one of them, linked inextricably to all the rest, enmeshed in the web of life. Don't struggle. Just be." I spent whole afternoons sitting in the lotus position on a hill above the river, striving mightily to obtain a glimpse of what he was talking about. Sometimes Gabriel would sit there too, unmoving, his eyes closed, his face lit with a rapturous glow. That's what I wanted for myself, the power of his peacefulness.

But how could I be anywhere in that place where Angela lived and not be consumed by her? I might struggle all afternoon to clear my mind of sensory shadows, struggle not to struggle, but I couldn't clear it of her. She was always there, smiling her enigmatic smile, not frequently speaking to me, but there.

I visited the ranch maybe half a dozen times, slipping away on evenings or weekends or whenever I could. One Sunday morning I'd begged off going to church with my parents and went up to Dancing Grasses instead. "Dexter," Gabriel said to me shortly after I'd arrived, "I do believe it's time you looked at the face of God. Do you think you're ready?"

"I think so," I said, not really knowing what he meant, but unwilling to appear afraid of whatever it was he was proposing. A blasphemous streak in me thought I'd already seen God's shining face couched in Angela's dark eyes, but I didn't say so. "Eat this," he said to me, handing me a small piece of cake made from fruit and coarse grains.

"What is it?"

"Manna," Gabriel smiled, "bread from heaven. Have no fear of it; it will take you to the Godhead." It was obviously a hallucinogen of some sort, I don't know what. I'd never taken drugs before. They were still basically non-existent in Shallowford in those days; booze was what we kids went for. Gabriel continued smiling benignly as I chewed the grainy cake and he chewed a small piece himself. "Let's walk for a bit," he said, and we went off together, arm in arm, just the two of us, gradually working our way up one of the side hills. Already I was feeling a bit peculiar, slightly off-focus, the way you do as a little kid when you whirl to make yourself dizzy.

"There is a spiritual world," Gabriel was telling me, "locked inside the physical one. The goal of the pilgrim is to break the locks, break through the membrane that seals us from the spiritual world. Once we've broken through we begin the long ascent toward discovering that which lies beyond the illusions of time and place." Though my mind was spinning like a prayer wheel by this point, his words were perfectly lucid.

We came to the crest of a hill and looked back across the valley below us. Far off to the east, I could just make out the spire of Saint James piercing the canopy of trees, and I felt an unbidden pulse of love for my parents kneeling at prayer in their church.

After what seemed a long time, Gabriel said, "Sit here," and I was glad to sit down, for my head was spinning and the world around me was tilting crazily. "Don't be alarmed," Gabriel sat down beside me. "Don't cling to control; let it go. The Truth lies not in logic but in life. What we seek is beyond our control. We seek union and immediate communion with the Divine Essence. That which flows through everything."

I don't remember him saying anything more after that. I was only dimly conscious of him sitting just slightly behind me chanting. I was viscerally aware of the sun on my back and of the wind riffling through the grasses nearby. I focused on the golden stems of grass bending and waving ceaselessly, their ripe seed heads shaking. The wind in the grass played an insistent, rhythmic rustling. Following Gabriel's instruction, I tried to withdraw my consciousness from circumference to centre, to place my attention upon just one thing.

Gradually I began to lose sense of time and place as I drifted off in what I took to be ecstatic rapture. All I remember from it now is the grasshopper. As I stared at the spears of grass, suddenly there seemed to emerge from the earth an enormous grasshopper. Its body was a vivid yellow and green, its big hind legs muscular and spiny. But there was something wrong. It lay on its side and struggled to move but had no strength. It stared at me through one of its bulging eyes. Plainly it was dying, and as I peered closer I became convinced that it was trying to impart to me some tremendous and terrible secret. I focused on it for what seemed like hours. At some point a red-headed ant approached and touched the grasshopper's outstretched leg with its antennae. The grasshopper flinched but couldn't kick the ant away. Soon another ant appeared, then several more. Growing bold, they swarmed the grasshopper's body, moving with a dreadful jerky purposefulness. The grasshopper's beady eye was still fixed upon me, intent even in its death throes to tell me the secrets of a grasshopper cosmos. Was this the face of God that Gabriel had promised: the tortured face of a dying insect?

I saw the precise moment at which life left the grasshopper's eye. An instant of transition after which the insect was just a corpse being disassembled by the engineering ants. And I felt at that moment that I'd been shown the secret of life and death, being and non-being.

Eventually, I returned to myself, still awash with what I felt was transcendent love, but also touched with wistfulness as I withdrew from that exalted state. I was sitting in darkness. The wind had dropped away to a whisper and an enormous sky vaulted above, brilliant with stars. I saw and felt and heard and smelled everything around me with perfect clarity. Gabriel was still behind me chanting his mantra, which sounded now like a song the earth might sing to itself.

I felt as though the paradox of life had been resolved for me that afternoon—a paradox I hadn't even realized existed a month before. I had escaped for a brief interlude from the mists of unknowing and had beheld That Which Is. I knew two things with absolute conviction: that my life's course had unalterably shifted and that this afternoon's vision was one I would carry with me always and would recall at the moment of my own death.

As I linger here now, looking at where the three tipis stood around the fire pit, hearing the wind gossiping in aspen leaves, I'd give anything to be seventeen and meeting Gabriel and Angela for the first time. But it's obvious I'm not going to meet either of them today. There's no sign of anyone having been about. No campfire or litter or trampled grasses, nothing at all. The place is deserted. I wander slowly down along the river which is running high and fast, charged with mountain snow melt, and meander along in the direction Susan described, inhaling the heady scent of cottonwood. Still there's nothing to indicate that anyone's been here, no matter what Susan says. But ghosts? Oh, yes, there are plenty of ghosts in this place, some of them of my own making, and I have the sense that if I lingered here long enough, I'd surely begin to see them too.

EIGHT

"You seem unsettled, Dexter," Mother says, cutting a precise, tiny piece of her quiche. "Is something bothering you?" We're sitting at her kitchen table, just she and I. Deirdre's got an author's reading at the library, some noisy sound poet from Calgary.

"I'm sorry, Mother. No, it's just one of my students is having some trouble and I don't know quite what to do about it." That's the minimalist version. Truth is, I'm starting to obsess about this whole Susan-and-Gabriel thing. I can find no rational explanation for what Susan says is happening to her. It's possible she's making the whole thing up, maybe even believing it. A delusion.

"Perhaps I can help," Mother offers.

"Thanks, Mother, but I think you've already got more than enough on your plate." I smile at her lovingly in a way that I know she can't resist. "I'm sure that it'll work itself out."

"I hope so, darling." While I'm being less than candid with her—same as with Deirdre—it's true that Mother's got as much as she can handle right now, because Dad's back at home. The doctors concluded there was no point in keeping him in hospital any longer. He'd gotten neither better nor worse and multiple tests told them nothing.

Eventually Doctor Prahamya melted back into whatever post she'd held before and we were left to the expertise of our old family doctor, Charlie Samuels. Charlie's more a medicine man than a doctor: he specializes in gentle reassurance cut with the occasional quack cure. He's a devout believer in the medicinal properties of Napoleon Brandy, and he and my father spent many a winter evening in the early years philosophizing over their snifters by our fireplace. It was strange to see Charlie fussing over my dad when we brought him home. Twenty years ago I'd have sworn that it'd be the other way around, that my father's Spartan discipline would have outlasted Charlie's puffy self-indulgence.

Mother and I converted Dad's old study into a bedroom for him, situating the guest-room bed so that from it he can look through the French doors out across the yard and down to the river he loved and almost died in. After much discussion, we installed a television set too. It's sitting on the stand where Dad's giant *Oxford English Dictionary* used to rest in authoritative dignity. The TV's Charlie's idea. Dad had little use for television and rarely watched it. For unmistakable moments in history—John F. Kennedy's funeral, Neil Armstrong stepping onto the moon—he'd join us in the family room and watch absorbedly, but for little else. He never ranted about television's asininity the way some people do, nor did he resent having it in the house; he simply ignored it. Doctor Charlie was quite insistent on his having it in the sick room. "His brain requires stimulation," Charlie argued, "so unless you or your mother want to sit here all day reading or talking to him, he's better off with the idiot box than nothing."

The implication that my father's been reduced to the level of an idiot was lost on Charlie, but not on Mother. "Oh, Dexter," she said to me later, "it seems so much worse here than when he was in the hospital." I knew what she meant. His vacant stare, the perpetual dribble from the corner of his mouth, his incoherent mumbling; in the hospital these seemed the symptoms of an illness for which a cure was being devised amid the hum of instrumentation and squeak of nurses' shoes along the corridors. But here at home, surrounded by the familiar objects and rituals of family life, those same symptoms loom far larger as manifestations of irreversible breakdown.

"Mother," I say, "I don't feel comfortable about your trying to cope with him alone here. I think we're going to have to get somebody in." The kitchen in which we're sitting is, as always, immaculate. There's a dishwasher now which there didn't used to be—in the old days my dad and I always washed and dried as our contribution to Mother's meals. But the rest of the room's the same: the marble countertops are clean;

the oak cabinets still hold dinnerware and glasses; pots and pans and implements are in their precise places. On the table where we're sitting there's a beautiful bouquet of violets and miniature narcissus that Mother has forced in her glass house. Grandfather Peale's old clock strikes the quarter-hour out in the corridor as though only minutes, not years, have elapsed.

"Funny, isn't it," she muses, "how suddenly everything changes. Your father and I had such great plans for this part of our lives. There was so much we wanted to see and do, a whole world to be explored. Now to have him lying in there like that. He's barely sixty years old, Dexter, and look at him!"

She's obviously not able to talk practicalities yet. But we'll have to get somebody in to help her; she can't possibly deal with him by herself. I'll help, of course, but there's a limit to what we both can do. I know they've socked a fair whack of cash away—it was supposed to carry them to London and Paris, the pyramids and the Taj Mahal. Now's the time to spend some of it before Mother's flat on her back too from stress and exhaustion. She'll wear herself out looking after him, worrying over him. Helping to death.

After dinner I go into the study to sit with Dad while Mother has her lie-down. He's the same as always, propped up in his bed, staring at the television set. The curtains are drawn across the French doors so we can't look out across the lawn down to the river. A burst of canned laughter explodes in the gloomy room. Two young women with perfect teeth and hair and fabulous bodies are exchanging insults in staged competition over a brooding hunk. Shrieks of laughter greet every volley, although the scripting is vapid. The expression on my father's face doesn't change. No single facial muscle moves, no matter how hysterically the laugh track demands a response. Having been the perfect lawyer, perfect husband, perfect father, my dad's become the perfect television viewer: staring with rapt attention at the flickering screen, dutifully absorbing whatever rubbish it hurls at him.

He barely acknowledges my arrival. When I sit on the bed, touch his arm and say hello in a forced-cheerful voice, he turns his blank face my way and stares for a moment. He might as well be staring at Mount Rushmore. There's not a flicker of recognition. I could be the latest sitcom or an item on the evening news. Even when I look right into his eyes, there's nothing there. I wonder what goes on in his brain. Is it all just a distant numbness, an elongated version of that dizzying second before the anaesthetic puts you out? Is he drifting, free of memories and dreams, of ideas and anxieties? Maybe he's slipped off the wheel of suffering altogether, found the peace that surpasses understanding. The laugh track shrieks again.

We blew apart, my father and I, over Gabriel and Angela. Even with huge deposits of mutual goodwill from those Norman Rockwell early years, we came, as though from opposite directions, to a hazardous corner where we collided.

I hadn't told my parents where I was going nor where I'd been, those first few times I went to Dancing Grasses. Normally I didn't keep things from my folks and I had no reason to believe they'd disapprove of my visiting there. The few times the topic of Dancing Grasses had come up in conversation, they'd both maintained an open attitude about what most townsfolk saw as the weird newcomers. I didn't stop to wonder why I was being so secretive, I just was. I guess I wanted to be sure about Gabriel and the others before I told my parents that I'd been spending time with them. Once I'd become convinced that Gabriel was a holy man, a saint, I was anxious that my parents meet him and confident that they would see him that way too.

It was a warm afternoon, I remember, and we were sitting outside, my parents and I, on big Cape Cod chairs in the shade of apple trees. Bluebirds were swing dancing among the branches, their plumage brilliant blue against green leaves. I had an exhilarating sensation those days of seeing everything more distinctly, the colours and shapes and textures of everything seemed to glow intensely. I smelled and touched and listened with enhanced awareness, as a person would who'd emerged into the light after years spent in a dim cell. I frequently felt close to tears. That particular afternoon I was also incredibly nervous about introducing Gabriel to my folks. I wanted desperately for each to like the other, to approve.

Then he was there, standing in the grass, dressed in his customary white cotton. We hadn't heard him come up, and there was an instant of shocked surprise to see him standing there, as if he'd materialized out of nothing. I introduced him to my parents. Gabriel joined his hands in front of his breast, as though in prayer, and bowed in turn to my mother and father, then shook hands with them.

"Sit down, please," my father motioned Gabriel to an empty chair. Mother bustled away to fetch refreshments. We sat there for a moment in the shade, nobody speaking. Three men sitting in lawn chairs in the dappled shade.

"And how are you finding life in Shallowford?" my father asked Gabriel, in his professional breaking-the-ice voice. My father was wearing a shirt and tie and dress pants held up by suspenders. Next to Gabriel's loose cottons, his clothes looked stuffy and old-fashioned in a way they never had to me before.

"Deep," Gabriel replied, smiling. "Deep and rich." It seemed as though he was about to add something more but stopped. Then he said to my father, "You've lived here all your life I believe?" Gabriel's manner was smooth.

"That's right," my father replied, "all but my university years and articling. And, of course, my time overseas during the war. This has been my home and I suppose it always will be. My grandfather built this house and I can't imagine living anyplace else."

"I envy you your sense of place," said Gabriel. "Something I haven't been blessed with myself. Not until now anyway." I thought Gabriel's phrase, "a sense of place," was lovely; I'd never heard it before.

"Where's your family from?" my father asked. It occurred to me I'd never asked Gabriel that question. I knew nothing about his past. I thought my father was just making polite conversation and I was interested in knowing more of Gabriel's background.

"I have no family," he replied, again with that gentle smile.

"None at all?" my father asked, and I could hear in his tone a faint echo of his courtroom voice, the one he employed to pry information from reluctant or thick-headed witnesses.

"Correct," Gabriel said. "How did the Nazarene put it? 'Verily I say unto you, there is no man that hath left house, or parents, or brethren, or wife, or children, for the kingdom of God's sake, who shall not receive manifold more in this present time, and in the world to come life everlasting.'"

"I see," my father said, and it was obvious that he saw far more than these two words acknowledged. Even I found something not quite right in Gabriel's response. Something inappropriately patronizing in the stagey quotation. As though he was deliberately slighting my father for his attachment to home and family. Or was this my imagination?

"I would have thought," my father said, after an uncomfortable silence, "that you might have taken for your text those lines from Jalal ad-Din Rumi—let me see if this old memory serves—'O you who are milk and sugar, O you who are sun and moon, O you who are mother and father, I have known no kin but you.'"

"Just so," Gabriel smiled at my father, plainly impressed and I think a little surprised. I was surprised myself. My father was more apt to quote Wordsworth than a Sufi poet. "But let's not forget the following line from our good poet," Gabriel continued, "'I have no business save carouse and revery.'"

My father smiled but said nothing. I didn't quite understand this exchange, but I knew enough to realize that the meeting was not going as I'd hoped. I don't know what I'd expected, foolishly—that these complete strangers would at once commingle in graceful symmetry of spirit, for no reason other than that I admired them both. I ransacked my brain for something to say, something that would steer the conversation in a more amicable direction. But what?

"Do you enjoy reading the law?" Gabriel asked, and now I had a definite sense of a charge in the air, the way it feels moments before a thunderstorm breaks across the prairie.

My father pondered a moment before answering, surveying our guest with a discriminating look. "Yes, very much," he said at last, also smiling. "I feel it's been a great privilege for me to practise law all these years." My father's arms lay along the armrests of his chair, his open hands palm-down, so that he looked like the classic image of Abraham Lincoln. "Do you know much of the law?"

"Hardly," Gabriel said with a soft laugh. "I'm afraid I think of it as one of those things that are Caesar's and are best left unto Caesar."

"I see," my father said a second time. I could tell from his expression that he was unimpressed with Gabriel's reply. Bluebirds chittered in the ensuing silence.

"We had a dog called Caesar once," I put in, stupidly, but anxious for something, even this idiotic non-sequitur, to distract us from the nervous tension.

"What sort of dog was he?" Gabriel asked, and I could see that he too wished to avoid any further unpleasantness.

"Irish setter," I said.

"Aha!" Gabriel enthused, "and was he high-spirited, this Caesar of yours?"

"I'll say. You couldn't get him to sit or heel or come or anything, could you, Dad?" Why was I feeling and acting like I was eight years old? Caesar had been my first dog and I'd worked hard to train him, but he'd had a wild streak and was uncontrollable. Even my dad, who was good with animals, couldn't bring that dog to heel. He'd slip the leash and be gone and no amount of calling or searching could bring him back. One day he disappeared and never returned. "I'm sorry, old man," my dad had said to me at the time, "mostly for whatever happened to that poor silly creature, but you're better off without him. A dog that won't be trained is no damn good to itself or anyone else." That had seemed to me to be a harsh judgment because I'd loved poor Caesar, even though he was stupid.

Again I realized that our conversation had run around a little loop and brought us back full circle. I was mystified, because here were the two greatest talkers I'd ever encountered—my father who could ramble on brilliantly for hours about dinosaurs or stars or God knows what, and Gabriel whose mystic discourse flowed fluid as water—and their conversation together was as stilted and trivial as the most inane exchanges at the supermarket. Worse than that, it seemed underlain by a fundamental mistrust, a sense of inhabiting separate solitudes, some Balkan outpost in which ancestral antipathies had festered for generations. A place where all the good will in the world was no guarantee against sectarian bitterness breaking out over the slightest insult. I don't know how I intuited all this at seventeen, but I did.

Things lightened up considerably when Mother reappeared with her tray of little cakes and iced tea. I saw her genius then, how she flattered and cajoled the men, found scraps of common ground for them, small hillocks upon which we could stand comfortably and laugh, even as the waters rose all round us. Under the force of her charm, we became players again in an ideal scene, a merry group sitting in the shade on a lazy summer afternoon. But I was not fooled for a moment, nor I suspect was anyone else. There was a line drawn in the dirt that day, a line that I must or must not cross and, unmistakably, whether by crossing or not, I'd be led into a landscape more complicated and perilous than any I'd known before.

I questioned my father about what had happened when we went for a walk together after Gabriel had left. But he wasn't himself that day; he was withdrawn in a way I seldom saw. He seemed absorbed by far horizons and barely conscious of my walking alongside him.

"Dad," I said to him at last, "can I ask you something?"

"Of course," he said, reeling his attention back, smoothly, the way he'd taught me to reel in a dry fly. "Shoot."

"You didn't care for Gabriel, did you?"

"Oh, I wouldn't go that far, old man. I trust your judgment a lot, as you know. I'm sure you see some qualities in him that I haven't been exposed to yet."

This, I knew, was Dad being diplomatic, confirming my worst fears. I waited for him to say more but he didn't.

"What is it about him you don't like?" I picked at it as you would a scab, to see how much could be pulled away before bleeding.

"I never like to judge a man prematurely," my father said, stopping in his walk and looking directly at me. "I prefer to give anyone the benefit of the doubt. Far too many of the world's woes come from people drawing wrong conclusions and making rash decisions based on how others look or talk or dress, without any real understanding of who they are." This was Dad's standard anti-racist etcetera prologue. Even I could hear the "but" coming, like a semi-trailer roaring down the freeway.

"But I'm afraid there's something about your friend Gabriel that sets my teeth on edge."

"How so?"

"Alright, son, I'll be as honest and forthright with you as I can. I've heard some things about your friend, some very disturbing things, but I suspended judgment until I'd seen him up close for myself."

"What sort of things?"

"I'm afraid I'm not at liberty to disclose what I've heard. I'm sorry, but I'm not." I hadn't thought to ask if this had anything to do with Angela coming to see him that time. "But I will tell you this," he went on, and his tone was now as grave as he could make it, "the little bit I saw of your friend just now unhappily confirms some of the worst I've heard."

"I didn't think he was that bad!" I blurted out, a hot flush of defensiveness washing over me. I almost said "No worse than you," but didn't. "What did he say that was so awful?"

"Perhaps it's more what he doesn't say, what remains unsaid between the lines."

"Such as?"

"Such as his preference that you disregard what your mother and I have to say to you and instead follow his advice."

"He never said any such thing!" I was getting angry now. This was not fair. It was doing what my father had from day one taught me never to do.

"I don't blame you for being angry," he went on, "it's what happens at your stage of life and it's perfectly natural. Your anger at me will allow you to begin finding your own self, your own way in the world. And that's fine. That's how it works. The problem is if you don't find your own way but instead are seduced by unscrupulous characters like your friend. To be blunt about it, the fellow's a clever fraud and no more. It's an old, old shill, the one he's playing at. The self-appointed mystic who stands outside and above the world of ordinary human affairs and passes judgment on all he sees beneath him. There's nothing of genuine spiritual love or commitment in the attitude, no going out of your way for the benefit of others. It's all me, me, me. All attitude. Posturing. It's a particular sickness of the young, this playing the religion game, though it's not only the young who suffer from it. Frankly I find his brand of arrogance and self-indulgence insufferable. There, now, you've asked and I've answered. You don't like it, I know, and I'm sorry."

"How can you even say that, Dad?" I was choked at what he'd told me. "You've never even heard him, how he talks. What he's got to say is so much more intelligent and profound and...spiritual than anything in those stupid, boring sermons we've been listening to in church every Sunday." This outburst sounded hopelessly sophomoric, even to me, but now I was flashing with passion. However, my father remained immovable, my frustration and anger beating against him as ineffectually as rain against a rock face.

"It isn't the saying that's at issue," he replied calmly, "it's the doing. There's no denying that your friend's got a golden tongue. But I'm not interested in tongues. I'm interested in minds and hearts and that's where your friend stumbles badly." I wanted to yell at my dad: Stop calling him 'your friend,' his name's Gabriel! My father continued in the same calm voice, "I'm not saying he's corrupt, not yet anyway, but he's no business setting himself up as a guru. He'd do far better to go find a teacher for himself rather than pretending to be one. Perhaps then he'd learn a bit of humility, a bit of respect for others. But he's a long, long way short of being a teacher or spiritual guide and I dread to think what will become of you if you continue under his spell."

I couldn't have been more devastated than I was by my father's words. I trusted my father implicitly, admired him immensely, and now here he was telling me that the new pathway that had opened up for me, about which I was so excited, led in fact to something he despised. We spoke no more about it, but over the ensuing days his disapproval hung in the air like smoke. I sensed my father, in tiny but unmistakable ways, withdrawing himself from me, which is something he'd never done before. I resented him for it. I was hurt by what I saw as his arbitrary withdrawal of respect and affection. Though her disapproval was every bit as strong as Dad's, Mother didn't confront me directly about it, nor did she distance herself from me as I felt he was beginning to do.

I wrestled for weeks with my father's opinion of Gabriel, unable to reconcile it with what I knew to be true. I was painfully aware that this was the first time ever that I'd not accepted my father's judgment as necessarily correct. At last, when I couldn't stand the tension another day, I slipped away to Dancing Grasses to speak to Gabriel directly. I would observe everything with infinite care and see for myself how much truth there was in what my father said.

"Is Gabriel around?" I asked Cheyenne who was kneeling on the ground, making tortillas over a small cooking fire.

"Went into town," she replied, not looking up.

"Which way?"

"River path."

I considered following that way. "Do you know when he'll be back?"

"Nope," she slapped down another tortilla.

I turned to go back to the car, and there was Angela emerging from one of the tipis. "Hi, Dexter!" she called to me, waving an arm. "Gorgeous day." She was wearing an oversized Grateful Dead T-shirt and cut-off blue jeans, her hair pulled back and tied at the nape of her neck. I walked over to her, hearing a grunt from Cheyenne behind me.

"What's up?" Angela asked.

"I was looking for Gabriel; wanted to talk to him."

"Want to talk to me instead?" she cocked her head mock-coquettishly.

We'd seldom talked at any length on my previous visits. But I watched her every move, and I'd seen her observing me sometimes with that same half-mocking air she'd used in my father's office.

"Sure," I said.

"Let's hike along the river."

"Great. Maybe we'll meet Gabriel."

"No, not toward town," she said, "let's go upriver."

"Okay," I said, the urgency of my talk with Gabriel suspended. We wandered off along the riverbank. Sunlight flashed across the water that afternoon too—it seems in my imagination that there was always sunshine lighting up those days. "Such a beautiful place," she mused dreamily, her fingertips caressing the tops of tall grass as she walked beside me. "I don't know that I've ever felt such peace." Which was ironic because I was being twisted about by more chaos and confusion than I'd ever known. Unfocused yearnings churned inside me, sensations I had no experience in handling.

At one point in our walk, Angela took my hand in hers. She didn't look at me, she had her head bowed, nor did she speak, but our hands spoke poems back and forth. Her hand in mine smouldered with tension. We had come to a copse of aspen trees growing close by the riverbank in such a way that they surrounded a small grassy glade at their centre. As we wandered into the glade, I spotted something in the grass just in front of us. At first I thought it was a dead animal. We peered down at it and I realized it was a tiny fawn lying perfectly still, its dappled white spots against its cinnamon hide making it strangely difficult to focus on. The creature seemed to have some magical property of camouflage.

"Is it wounded, do you think?" I whispered to Angela.

"No more than you and I," she replied, and at that instant, in a single fluid leap, the fawn exploded from its resting place, bounded away and vanished into the aspen grove. The movement was so perfectly instantaneous it seemed, after a moment, that the animal had never been there. Angela released my hand and knelt where the fawn had lain. She reached out and ran her palm across the flattened grasses. "It's still warm," she said, lifting her fingers to her nose to inhale the scent of deer. "Things disappear and reappear, but they leave a scent to tell of their passing."

I knelt beside her and touched the deer's bed too. I could smell the musky warm scent of animal, mingled with the scent of Angela. Our heads were almost touching as we knelt together in the grass. I guess I knew what was about to happen. I entered a kind of mist, much like a dream, in which perceptions dissolved and intermingled. Aspen leaves fluttered, birds chattered, and sunlight glinted on the river. It was as though the earth had suddenly tilted and I was tumbling downward, powerless to stop. I reached out and touched the warm tawny skin of her forearm. She raised her head slowly and gazed at me. Her fingers closed upon my hand and guided it up along her arm then across to her breast. She pressed my hand against her breast and an impish smile lit up her face. We knelt that way, suspended in sunlit space and time. When she reached behind her head to release her hair, her breast swelled against my hand and her hair fell in a black cascade around her shoulders. Then our mouths were together, tongues exploring hungrily. My swelling cock pressed against her. Then I undressed her, the loose T-shirt sliding up over her head in one fluid motion, the black hair again cascading, the cut-offs, then her panties, slipping down her long legs. I tore my own clothes off in a fever of caressing. When I mounted her, entered her, my whole self dissolved into pure organism, stilled within, like the fawn, though panting and thrashing in the sunshine grass. She shrieked wildly, and when her body arced up out of the warm grass, breaching on a sea of green, I came inside of her, pouring everything I was into her. For the first time in my life I tasted the salty flesh of ecstasy. When I collapsed against her, sated and insatiable, I could hear her heart pounding like a buried stone. We lay there in the scented grass for what seemed like hours. I wanted never to leave that place, that woman.

It was all intoxication after that. Everything else—friends, family, sports, studies, even Gabriel's precious meditations—dwindled into background noise to which I was oblivious. I was on fire for Angela. I dreamt of her, longed to be with her, delighted in her when we came together. We made love with the carefree abandon of young animals.

Lovestruck and giddy, I wrote love poems for Angela. I'd never written a poem in my life and certainly not a love poem, but suddenly they gushed out of me in a torrent of lovestruck lyricism. I'm sure they were dreadful, throbbing with "sunsets and thighs as smooth as silk," but at the time, writing them was thrilling, inseparable from the intoxication of love. I remember the day I presented her with what I thought at the time was my masterpiece, a lyric titled "Love in Quarter Time" or something like that. All I can remember now is how it described my dancing away from Artemis into the arms of "golden-breasted Aphrodite." Angela took the sheet from me, read the poem through, beamed at me cunningly and unbuttoned her shirt. In hindsight I see this was a clever way of her avoiding having to give an opinion on the lyric.

That astounding summer unwound and slipped into autumn and I was back at Shallowford High for my senior year. But all I could think of was Angela. I'd be sitting in class, dimly aware of the teacher droning on about Heisenberg's Principle of Uncertainty while my imagination chased Angela through shining aspen groves and tumbled with her in a sweaty tangle. My grades began to slump. I quarterbacked the football team again and we had a not-bad season, but even there my focus was blown. I no longer roared onto the field with the single consuming desire to win this game at all costs. I was far more concerned to see if maybe Angela was somewhere on the sidelines admiring my play. She never was. "Neanderthal head-banging" she called football, and after she'd said it, winning a game never again seemed the peak of excellence it had been.

No matter what I was doing, or with whom, always my inner self was taken up with Angela, looking for her, wanting her.

Mother noticed almost straight off, of course. "Dexter darling," she said to me when we were alone one evening that autumn, "you don't seem at all yourself these days."

"What do you mean?" I replied casually, smiling my polished smile for her sake, though I was instantly on guard.

"I mean you seem terribly distracted, darling. Your father has noticed it too."

"Distracted? No, I wouldn't say I was distracted exactly," I replied. "I'm just really busy. I've got a lot on my mind."

"I'm sure you do," Mother said archly. "But nothing you wish to share with your poor old mother?" She pouted at me in her mock-flirtatious manner. Though I'd always been charmed by it before, now her pouting seemed ridiculous to me, almost embarrassing. I had no further use for games, other than the ones I played with Angela. In the ensuing silence I realized that for the first time in my life I was doing something, being something, that I absolutely didn't wish to share with her in any way. She obviously knew it too.

"I'm doing just fine, Mother, really. Please don't worry about me."

"Oh, I'm not worried about you, darling, I'm just curious. You know me, always butting in where I'm not wanted."

"Mother!" I cried. Now she was playing the half-mocking martyr game.

"Now why haven't we seen anything of sweet little Diana lately?" Mother's not one to give up easily. She has a perfect nose for where something might be festering. "Have you two had a lover's quarrel?"

"No, we haven't." I was beginning to resent Mother's persistence. "We've just sort of drifted apart." Which was total bullshit, as I suspect Mother knew. For the past year or two, Diana Burroughs had been stuck to me like crazy glue. We were no more likely to drift apart than apartment buildings are. The truth was I'd just begun avoiding Diana, making feeble excuses why we couldn't get together. I hadn't even had the decency to tell her directly that I was no longer interested in her. But I wasn't. Her superficial schoolgirl chatter rankled me now that I was immersed in Angela's fierce sexuality. Fiddling with Diana's hopeless bra strap while she giggled and twittered seemed repulsively childish. I knew she'd invested all her social capital in being with me, and being seen with me, riding around town sitting tight up against me in the front seat of my Wildcat. She was Dexter Cooke's girl; she was at the top of the heap. Then suddenly she wasn't and she knew it; but her pride, cruelly inflated by her time as my first lady, would not admit that I'd lost interest. Instead she feigned disinterest of her own. She flounced around school laughing excessively at her own flimsy wit, parading her scanty accomplishments like trinkets for all to admire. But inside I knew she was humiliated; who wouldn't have been? But what was awful—such was the state of my bewitchment—

was I didn't really care if she was hurt. I was oblivious to the pain of love's withdrawal.

"I see," Mother said. "Well, that's unfortunate. Such a lovely girl."

Horseshit, I wanted to reply. I knew Mother had always considered Diana a twit.

"Is it something about your friend Gabriel?" Mother ventured. We were by now all fully aware that Gabriel was persona non grata at our house.

"Is what something?" I almost snapped. "Mother, I'm fine." I softened my tone, "I'm busy, I'm preoccupied and I'm fine."

"Alright, darling," she backed away. "But you know I'm always here to help if I can."

"Yes, I know that, thank you, Mother," I said, rising abruptly and kissing her goodnight.

The real sticking point came in late September with my decision to abandon the long trek toward a law degree. I'd decided to become a playwright, to take courses in creative writing and theatre after graduation. In hindsight I see that both Gabriel and Angela played a part in this choice, though at the time I considered it my own decision. I wasn't born with a passion for writing or the stage as some kids are, but a door had swung open when I started writing poetry, a door I knew I must step through. "You're a born storyteller," I remember Gabriel saying to me. "There's no greater gift," he continued, "than to tell and re-tell people their stories. It's an ancient art, a venerable profession, older than priesthood, older than prophecy. The telling of stories, the singing of songs, the painting of pictures—these are the ancient high orders at the heart of being human. Generations of storytellers lived and died before the first shaman was born, before the first king was crowned." He talked about the actual magical power that was communicated to the poet by a divine patron. He told me how Hesiod had received such a call and been given a rod as symbol of this magical capacity; how the Muses...

A branch of laurel gave, which they had plucked,
To be my scepter; and they breathed a song

In music on my soul, and bade me set
Things past and things to be to that high strain.
Also they bade me sing the race of gods,
Themselves, at first and last, ever remembering.

Yes, that's what I wanted more than anything. Part of me still knew that the superhighway I'd always planned to cruise—university, law school, maybe someday joining Dad in his practice—was right and admirable and would lay solid foundations for a rewarding and distinguished career. I'd never wanted anything else. But now I did. Now I wanted to be an artist, a bohemian, a free spirit. I wanted to roam the world, explore the outer limits of consciousness. I wanted to run with the coyotes and howl at the moon. Sure, Gabriel and Angela had kindled this new fire in me. I wanted to be like them. I wanted to be what looked like free.

Thus it was on one late September afternoon, I sat for hours on a log down by the river, wrestling with the question of my future. I felt something close to despair. At one point I looked up into the tree canopy and was shocked out of my preoccupations by the beauty of the big cottonwood gone to gold. The great tree's arms arched outward, darkened to indigo by a recent rain, through a blizzard of yellow and green-yellow leaves that fluttered as though still alive. A multitude of golden birds turned constantly against the sun, their voices amplified. Astonished by its beauty and impermanence, I felt duty and desire fuse within me and I knew with sudden clarity that I should become an artist. I should tell my stories to the world. Yes! My mind was made up. I heard my muse beckon me through the beauty of the green-gold tree.

Composed, determined, I rose and strode toward the house. My parents were sitting on the patio, enjoying a glass of wine before dinner. By a trick of the sunlight pouring across the yard they looked young and beautiful and the red wine in their glasses glowed like molten rubies. I told them my decision. I'd never spoken harder words to them than these. I loved them both and I wanted them to love me and approve of what I did. No part of me wanted to be doing things they'd scorn. "Theatre school?" my father said, masterfully concealing disbelief, but that was all. Mother said nothing, which was truly ominous. I suppose at that moment the sun should have sunk behind a bank of dark clouds on the western horizon, but it didn't. The light held, catching us in an incandescent tableau, a final glowing brilliance.

We scarcely spoke at dinner that evening; even Mother's ameliorative skills seemed blunted by the severity of this break. Afterward my father invited me into his study—the same room I'm sitting in now. He seated himself behind the big oak desk and asked me to close the door, a sure sign that important, manly words were to be exchanged. He'd done the same thing when I'd hit puberty, invited me into his study, that solemn sanctuary lined with law books, and given me a long and detailed description of what were called the facts of life: ejaculation, copulation, conception; he marched through all of it in a manner calculated to strip the subject of any fear or mystery. He didn't trade in fear or mystery.

"Son," he said, "I believe I understand what you're going through. It's not so different from what I felt myself at your age. And I know you think you're fully aware of what you're doing and what the consequences will be. But you're not. The world's a far rougher, unforgiving place than anything you've seen yet. Your mother and I are concerned that you're making an unwise choice that's going to wreck your chances."

"I know that's what you think, Dad, and I appreciate your concern." I'm sure I sounded like a patronizing ass to him, but that's how he sounded to me too. "But I know what I'm doing, believe me."

"I wish I could, son, but I don't believe you. It's plain as rain you have no idea what you're doing. Your cock's doing all your thinking for you right now, and it's not a trustworthy decision-making organ." Somehow he must have found out that I was balling Angela, but how I don't know.

"My cock's not doing all my thinking for me!" I replied hotly. There was a tone of nastiness in the term, a taste of acid in both our voices.

We let it go at that for the moment, but I think we both realized that the rift between us widened dramatically that day, a rift that would get even wider with time and eventually leave us standing far apart, virtual strangers.

Just as I'm about to leave the sick room, my father turns unexpectedly from the television screen and looks directly at me. "Dexter," he says in a voice dry and raspy as an old floor board creaking in an attic. It's the first coherent word he's said in weeks, disturbing and wonderful to hear. He's coming back, I think instantly, thank Christ he's coming back!

"Hello, Dad, how're you feeling?" My own voice sounds almost as shaky as his.

He seems to waver for a moment, wobbling between worlds, then focuses on me again. "Dexter, old man," he smiles, "I think it's time you and I went fishing together."

I feel a hot flush of tears behind my eyes and start to answer, elated, as I was long ago when he'd spoken the same words to me. But before I can say anything in reply his eyes glaze over again, then close, and he's back in the dream world.

Nine

"Is this okay for you?" I ask Deirdre as we get out of the car. We're parked at Trout Lake up in the hills west of town for our Sunday afternoon walk. It's church with Mother on Sunday morning, a walk with Deirdre Sunday afternoon. Across the bunchgrass steppes, last year's crumpled old stems are shot through with a shimmer of green fire. The lake lies in a small basin where grasslands and aspen forest clash in their ancient game of territorial domination.

"Fine," she says, zipping up her red windbreaker. A cool breeze off the hills, skipping across the lake, kicks up shoals of small ripples and lashes the lakeside willows. Deirdre's fine hair flirts wildly around her face. Small trees surrounding the parking lot bend eastward like supplicants to Mecca, bowed against the pressure of incessant wind. I lock the car—we didn't use to around here, but now we do—and we set off along the footpath. Over to our right, sheer and stony mountains bulk up, their highest reaches and peaks marbled with snow. Ragged white clouds tear themselves apart crossing the hills. The grasslands drop away to our left. We walk for a while without talking. I can feel the little chambers in my brain creaking open to take in the sweep of this vista.

"Oh, look!" Deirdre exclaims, pointing off to the side of the path. "Shooting stars and yellow bells." I hadn't noticed them—clusters of tiny flowers blooming in masses all through the tattered brown grass.

Trust Deirdre to pick out the perfect small detail amid the Wagnerian grandeur. "Oh, they're so lovely," she says, wading into the meadow and stooping over a cluster of shooting stars, her fingers caressing the tiny white petals. Drawing near, looking down at her thin shoulders etched by the wind against the fabric of her windbreaker and at her slender neck, white and fine as eggshell, I feel a pang of love.

I decide to take the plunge. "Do you believe in apparitions?"

She looks at me queerly. "Apparitions?"

"Yes."

"Why? Have you had one?" Deirdre can be impertinent when she's in the mood.

"No, I haven't." Smiling. Should I confide in her? Why not? "One of my students has. Or says she has."

"A girl?"

"Yes. It usually is, isn't it? And a Catholic. It always seems to happen to Catholics."

"Is she?"

"I don't think so. Unless she's maybe one of those Catholics nobody knows is a Catholic."

"Like me?"

"Yes."

"And she's told you she's had an apparition?"

"Recurring apparitions. Yes, she has." I'll skip the whole bit about her mother and the diary.

"What has she seen?"

"A man dressed all in white, she says. She describes him as a sort of spectral presence. And he communicates with her, though he doesn't appear to be speaking."

"Um. What does he communicate?" Deirdre's taking this whole thing seriously. But then she takes most things quite seriously.

"Oh, pseudo-mystical stuff. The Divine Oneness, that sort of stuff."

"Sounds familiar." In our early times together, before the grey days began, I'd told Deirdre a lot about Gabriel, less about Angela, and she's quick to make the connection now. I steer her away from what became a sore spot between us.

"So do you believe in them? In apparitions? Do you think they're real?"

"I used to. Good little Catholic schoolgirl that I was. You know Lourdes, Fátima, the Virgin of Guadalupe."

"And now?" Deirdre and I seldom ever discuss spiritual notions.

"Now I don't know," her fingertips still dance lightly across the wild flowers. "I remember the question came up a lot in one of my psychology courses. We had an old Jungian professor—what was her name? Professor Arquette. One of those mad genius types."

"What was her take on visions?"

"Oh, the typical Jungian thing: they're part of a whole body of transcendent reality that we've learned to suppress in our craven submission to rationality."

"But that they're real, not just psychic projections?"

"I'm trying to remember. That they originate in a place that isn't quite human. She used a phrase, 'the breath of nature' I think it was. Most of the talk was about primitive peoples. About the dream world, dreaming the world into existence, that sort of thing. That dreams, visions, prophetic occurrences were all things our ancestors knew about and accepted as completely real. That it's only recently in human history that we've learned to ignore that parallel universe, disregard it in the name of reason and progress."

"But not that it doesn't exist?"

"Oh no. That's why the Jungians are so into their dreams. Our unconscious selves are still very much in touch with the dream world. Even to the point that we can dream things that are going to happen to us long before they actually do. I remember we were all totally turned on by this stuff at the time. It was one of those revolutionary insights we were always having in those days, remember?"

"Yep." Deirdre and I gaze at one another and neither of us says anything for a moment. Remembering.

"In the Catholic tradition, the stuff you were taught as a child, was it always a woman who appeared?"

"I think so. The ones I remember anyway. It was always the Blessed Virgin Mary. They had a special name for them, what was it? Oh, of course—the Marian Apparitions!" Deirdre looks up at me from the wildflower bed, an apparition herself.

"Hmm."

"If you're really interested, you should go talk to the priest at the Catholic church."

"I don't want to hear a lot of Catholic drivel, present company excepted."

"Remember the church's name?"

I must have passed it hundreds of times over the years, but damned if I can remember what it's called.

"Our Lady of Fátima." Deirdre makes a little nose-wrinkling face. "Ring any bells?"

"Hmm. Named after one of the apparitions."

"Not only that. They have a little library in there on the subject—I've referred a couple of people there from our library—and apparently the priest is something of a home-grown expert on the topic. You should talk to him."

"Why are your suggestions always so clever, do you think?"

"Miraculous, isn't it?" She smiles at me again among the shooting stars.

The big front door of the rectory swings open revealing a small old lady peering at me suspiciously through thick bifocals. "Yes?" she asks in a voice that's surprisingly strong coming from such a frail-looking body.

"My name is Cooke. I have a three o'clock appointment with Father Luscombe."

"Oh, yes," a welcoming smile erases any trace of suspicion. "Do please come in." She closes the heavy door behind me then totters across a dark wood-panelled foyer and ushers me into a small parlour. "Do please have a seat. Father Luscombe will be with you shortly."

The room is lined with bookcases containing leather-bound religious texts. A pungent scent of furniture polish and candle wax permeates. A crucifix hangs on one wall above a small gas fireplace that isn't burning. A large, framed print on the opposite wall depicts the Madonna as a beautiful young woman dressed in long white robes with her hands joined in prayer. She is suspended in the air, her sandalled feet resting on a small cloud through which the branches of a shrub protrude. Beneath the cloud three children—two girls and a boy—kneel on the earth, hands also joined in prayer, staring in rapt devotion at the Lady above them. Two sheep lie on the ground beside the children.

The whole thing is unbelievably hokey. Definitely a mistake coming here.

I hear footsteps approaching and rise from the stiff-backed chair to meet the priest. "Good afternoon, Mr. Cooke," he greets me formally in a quiet voice. His hand in mine feels bloodless. He gestures for me to sit again and seats himself in a chair a few feet away. Probably in his late fifties, small and pale, bespectacled and dressed in full clerical black suit and collar, he gives the impression of someone who's dwelt for many years in a dark, secluded place.

"How can I be of assistance?" he asks in the same gentle voice, like the turning of pages in a sacred text.

"I'm interested in knowing a little bit about apparitions." My own voice sounds coarsely loud.

"I see." He pauses for a moment. "And what precisely is the nature of your interest?"

"I'm sorry?"

"Why do you wish to know about these things?"

"Oh, I see!" I'm trying to maintain an informal tone, but the little priest's quiet solemnity possesses a remarkable strength. The tormented Christ on the cross eyes me with a disconcerting combination of accusation and forgiveness.

"You're not from the newspapers or anything like that?" He asks the question in a completely neutral tone.

"No, not all," I assure him. "A purely personal interest."

"Good."

"I'm a teacher at the local high school."

"Ah, yes. Cooke. Are you by chance Mr. Philip Cooke's son?"

"That's correct."

"Ah, yes. A very fine man indeed. A good citizen." The priest allows himself a pale smile. I wonder if he knows what's become of my father, but he gives no hint. "So: apparitions." He seems slightly more at ease than he did.

"I understand you're quite an expert in the field."

"Oh, I wouldn't say that, oh, no!" Another pale smile. "I've done a little bit of reading on the subject. We have quite a little library on it here." He gestures to the books surrounding us. "I've been here at Our Lady of Fátima parish for a good many years and naturally developed an interest in our blessed namesake." He inclines his head slightly toward the print of the Madonna. "But I claim no expertise in the field. I'm certainly not about to be called by the Vatican and asked my opinion on the subject." A gurgling chuckle bubbles up from his plump stomach.

"What's the Vatican's position?"

"On apparitions?"

"Yes."

"Well, naturally, the Church doesn't accept any of them as authentic until they're studied extensively and confirmed by the local bishops."

"But they do happen? More than just the famous ones we hear about?"

"Oh, yes, all the time."

"Even now?"

"Perhaps more now than ever."

"Fascinating."

"We're fortunate to have a quite recent statement from the Vatican on the subject. Let me see if I can find it now." He goes over to a writing desk recessed into the bookshelves, rummages about and returns with a document. "This is a statement made last year by Joseph Cardinal Ratzinger who is head of the Church's Congregation for the Doctrine of Faith. He writes: 'One of the signs of our times is that the announcements of Marian Apparitions are multiplying all over the world.' And he goes on to say that, in addition to the Marian Apparitions, there are many other signs including Eucharistic Miracles and the manifestation of the charisms of the Holy Spirit. Numerous souls are receiving the gifts of prophecy, healing, knowledge and other signs of the presence of Christ in our midst." He lifts his eyes from the document.

"Why do you think these things are happening?" I'm far from believing that they are, which I suspect the priest fully realizes.

"It's most important," he tells me, "to study the Gospels in order to understand why these mystical occurrences take place. We must pray to the Holy Spirit for discernment in these matters."

"Might they just be dreams? Or hallucinations?"

"Of course they might. And some undoubtedly are. Just as surely some undoubtedly are not. We have in the Church, you know, the 'Somnia a Deo missa' the dream sent by God. A person can choose to believe in such things and have his or her life informed by them, or they can choose to think it's all hocus-pocus and ignore it completely. That's the beauty of free will." Father Luscombe smiles, comfortable in the unassailability of his position.

"What about Fátima? Can you tell me a bit about that?"

"Certainly." It's odd how this priest never looks directly at me; his pale grey eyes are always focused slightly off to the side and away, as though the intimacy of direct visual contact would be improper. "During the Great War in Europe, His Holiness Pope Benedict XV worked tirelessly for the cause of peace, but to no avail. Finally, in May of 1917, he made a direct appeal to the Blessed Virgin Mary, asking for her intercession to bring an end to that dreadful war. A mere week later, the Lady appeared miraculously to three young children at Fátima." Again the slight inclination of his head toward the print on the wall.

"I remember reading a magazine piece about it, about the pilgrims who travel there seeking cures, like at Lourdes. But I've forgotten where it is. Italy?"

"No, it's in Portugal, a tiny village about seventy miles north of Lisbon." The priest's small white hands flutter like trapped moths against the black serge of his suit. " It was actually about a year earlier, in 1916, that these same three children had their first supernatural experience."

"Also an apparition?"

"Correct. As they were out in the countryside taking care of the family's sheep, there appeared before them a dazzlingly beautiful young man who shone as though he were composed of pure light."

Now I'm getting interested. "Who was he?"

"He said to the children: 'Do not be afraid. I am the Angel of Peace. Pray with me.' Then he knelt down, bending forward until his forehead touched the ground and repeated three times the words: 'My God, I believe, I adore, and I love You! I beg pardon of You for those who do not believe, do not adore, do not hope and do not love You.' Then he vanished. He subsequently appeared to the children several times throughout the summer. The final time he appeared, in autumn, he brought a chalice, which hung suspended in the air. A Host hovered above it and from the Host drops of blood dripped into the chalice."

Going to the bookcases again, the priest finds and opens a book, searches through it, finds what he's looking for and brings the book over to me. "There are the three children." He indicates a faded photograph that shows three little peasant kids standing in front of a stone wall and staring quizzically at the camera. For an irrational split second I half expect them to be the three childish faces that haunt my dreams, but they're not. "That's Lucia dos Santos, age ten," the priest's index finger points to the eldest child, a girl on the left, clasping her hands at her waist and wearing a traditional shawl, blouse and a long, loose skirt. "And those are her cousins, Francisco and Jacinta Marto, aged eight," he points to the boy in the centre, "and seven," indicating the little girl on the right who is dressed like her cousin.

The priest returns to his chair, still holding the book open. "The angel prostrated himself before the chalice, then he gave the host to Lucia to eat and let Francisco and Jacinta drink from the chalice, saying—" and here he looks at the book and reads "—'Take and drink the Body and Blood of Jesus Christ, horribly outraged by ungrateful men. Repair their crimes and console your God.' Then he prostrated himself again and disappeared forever."

"Did the kids tell anyone about this?"

"Not until after the events of the following year. It's thought that the angel was sent to prepare them for the coming of the Lady. And indeed on the following thirteenth of May, the Blessed Virgin herself appeared to them."

"In the same kind of way?"

"They had taken their sheep to pasture in a little place known as Cova da Iria. They'd eaten their lunch and prayed the rosary when suddenly there was a bright flash of light, like lightning, then a second flash, though it was a clear sunny day. They looked up and saw the Lady. Here's how Lucia described her—" again he referred to the book on his lap "—as 'a lady, clothed in white, brighter than the sun, radiating a light more clear and intense than a crystal cup filled with sparkling water, lit by burning sunlight.' The children stood there astonished, enveloped in the light emanating from the apparition. The Lady smiled at them and said: 'Do not be afraid, I will not harm you.' Asked where she came from, the Lady pointed to the sky and said: 'I come from heaven.' She told them she wanted them to return to the same spot on the thirteenth day of each month for the next six months. After the children had pledged to offer themselves to God and to bear great sufferings as an act of reparation for the conversion of sinners, the Lady opened her hands from which a light streamed down onto the children which allowed them to see themselves in God." The little priest looked solemnly at the floor between us.

"What does that mean?"

He paused for a moment, raising his head but still looking slightly askance. "I confess I'm not exactly sure. I suppose it is what we would call the Beatific Vision."

"That's looking on the face of God?"

"More than just looking, I believe. Being subsumed completely within it. Then the Lady finished with an instruction to say the rosary every day in order to bring peace to the world and put an end to war. Then she rose into the air and moved off toward the east until she finally disappeared."

We're interrupted by the entrance of the ancient housekeeper carrying a large tray.

"Ah, here's our tea," Father Luscombe says. "Thank you so much, Mrs. Sketchley."

The old lady totters to the desk and places the tea tray on it. "Can you look after yourselves then, Father?" she asks.

"Perfectly well, thank you, Mrs. Sketchley."

The housekeeper clatters out and Father Luscombe pours me a cup of tea and brings with it a plate of dainty pastries.

Sipping tea and nibbling in the silent parlour beneath the baleful stare of the crucified Christ, mulling over the miraculous experiences of Portugese peasant children, I feel I'm in a different world from the one I know. We might be in some late medieval shire discussing the mystical insights of Mechthild of Magdeburg.

"And as the Lady foretold," Father Luscombe picks a few crumbs from his breast, then dabs his lips with a linen napkin, "the following month she reappeared and informed them that Jacinta and Francisco would be joining her in heaven soon and, indeed, the two children died in the great influenza pandemic of 1918. Interestingly, there were about fifty witnesses to this apparition. One of the witnesses, a woman named Maria Carreira, testified that at the point of the Lady's departure, she herself heard a sound like a rocket, a long way off, and saw a small cloud a few inches over the tree rise and move slowly toward the east until it vanished.

"Well, naturally all this caused an absolute sensation throughout the country. Politicians and the press got involved, trying to get the children to disclose certain secrets the Lady had told them. By October 13th there was a huge crowd assembled, come to witness the miracle the Lady had promised to perform that day. Here's what the Lisbon newspaper, *O Dia*, reported." He puts his teacup and plate aside, takes up the book, turns a couple of pages, then reads:

> "At one o'clock in the afternoon, midday by the sun, the rain stopped. The sky, pearly grey in colour, illuminated the vast arid landscape with a strange light. The sun had a transparent gauzy veil so that eyes could easily be fixed upon it. The grey mother-of-pearl tone turned into a sheet of silver which broke up as the clouds were torn apart and the silver sun, enveloped in the same gauzy grey light, was seen to whirl and turn in the circle of broken clouds. A cry went up from every mouth and people fell on their knees on the muddy ground. The light turned a beautiful blue as if it had come through the stained glass windows of a cathedral and spread itself over the people who knelt with out-stretched hands. The blue faded slowly and then the light seemed to pass through yellow glass. Yellow stains fell against white handkerchiefs, against the dark skirts of women. They were reported on the trees, on the stones and on the sierra. People wept and prayed with uncovered heads in the presence of the miracle they had awaited."

Father Luscombe gazes at the page for a little while without looking up. I have the sense he's struggling to contain his emotions. "There was another account," he continues, "written by a newspaperman named Avelino de Almeida, who had previously written a bitterly sarcastic piece about the apparitions in his newspaper, *O Século*. Here's what he wrote on that dramatic day:

> From the road, where the vehicles were parked and where hundreds of people who had not dared to brave the mud were congregated, one could see the immense multitude turn toward the sun, which appeared free from clouds and at its zenith. It looked like a plaque of dull silver and it was possible to look at

> it without the least discomfort. It might have been an eclipse, which was taking place. But at that moment a great shout went up and one could hear the spectators nearest at hand shouting: 'A miracle! A miracle!' Before the astonished eyes of the crowd, whose aspect was Biblical as they stood bareheaded, eagerly searching the sky, the sun trembled, made sudden incredible movements outside all laws—the sun 'danced' according to the typical expression of the people."

"And the Church believes that miracle to be authentic?" To me the whole thing sounds like mass hysteria.

"Absolutely." The priest retrieves the teacups and returns them to the tray. "A rigorous examination of the facts was undertaken and thirteen years later the Church pronounced the Fátima apparitions to be authentic."

"And you believe that they were?"

"Oh, yes, without a shadow of doubt." He stands beneath the picture of the Lady, hands together, slightly stooped, but unshakable in his conviction. "I have every confidence that those apparitions did in fact occur. Absolutely. Even skeptics and non-believers were witness to the miracle. There's no doubt in my mind whatsoever."

And that's what's remarkable about this little cleric: he has no doubt. His conviction's as absolute as granite. I see him carrying his faith around like a very small locked box in which untold precious treasures are stored. An ecclesiastical golem living contentedly here in the dimly lit rectory, as removed from the brutal machinations of the secular world as a medieval monk.

I envy him his faith, his steadfast assurance of what is real and what is not, what is truly miraculous and what not; a man comfortable with an Angel of Peace appearing as a dazzlingly beautiful young man shining as though composed of light; at ease with a Lady in white appearing to little peasant kids, confiding secrets in them, showing them visions of hell and beaming rays of light onto them in which they can see themselves in God.

As the big rectory door closes behind me and I step back out into the real world, I'm even less sure of what I know and what I don't than I was when I went in.

Part Two: Angel *of* Death

Speak to me, Angel,
Of how it is
That you can look into the eyes
Of a child and decide
This one shall live
This one shall die
What conferred this spectacular conceit
Upon you, Lucifer,
Sweet bringer of light
You who shone brightly
Once
Now cloaked in black
Dispensing death
And never looking back
To see perhaps if this one
Or that
Were worthy of reprieve
Might glitter as you yourself once did
Given opportunity
Spared the gagging gas
Toxic fumes
Of what is bound to be
Or not
Contingent on your whim
Speak to me, Angel,
For I am disconsolate
And would hear your explanation
For these corpses in my arms.

Ten

Beth: I don't think what's happened here should concern anyone else but us.

Diana: How can you possibly say that, Beth? Look at her! (Pointing to Alix who sits upstage staring vacantly and quietly humming.) She's totally freaked out!

Beth: Well, who wouldn't be freaked out spending a night alone out there, lost. Wolves howling all night. I was freaked out even being here with the rest of you.

George: I think Beth's right. Let's keep this to ourselves.

Peter: I agree.

Diana: (exasperated) So we'll just pretend nothing happened? We'll ignore the fact that Alix has gone catatonic. And if anyone should mention it, we'll just say, 'Oh, no, Alix is fine; if you knew her as well as we do, you'd recognize that.' Great plan, guys.

Beth: I'm sure she'll snap out of it by the time we leave.

Diana: (incredulous) By the time we leave? What are you talking about, 'by the time we leave.' We've got to leave today, right away. You can't expect her to keep camping up here in that condition!

Peter: Well…

Diana: (insistent) You guys don't seem to realize, this isn't fun and games. She's been traumatized. Badly. And we need to get her help, like right now.

"Okay, folks, that's great," I call up to the stage. "Good work. We'll pick it up again on Tuesday, alright? We'll be moving to the next scene, so try to have your lines completely memorized, okay?"

The players desert the stage. Their shuffling despondency confirms my fear that the production's as flat and vapid as an overexposed Christmas carol. Except for one thing: Susan Slater's performance is riveting. She's devoured her role, whole and bleeding. At each rehearsal she brings an increasingly intense ferocity to Diana. But never before like today. Today it was almost scary watching her, because it's not clear how much of her performance is acting and how much is coming out of what's happening in her life. The other players are lost, whispering and tiptoeing through their roles, as though afraid that Susan's mania will wash over them and sweep them away. Decidedly out of my depth, I'm not sure what direction to give Susan. I could try to tone her down, but I don't really want to because what she's doing on stage is the most interesting thing about the whole sad sack production. After rehearsal, she reverts to her usual quiet shyness and quickly slips out.

As I'm packing up my stuff, Danielson approaches me. He's been hanging around at rehearsal more, sometimes with his wife, the two of them standing against the far wall of the gym, whispering to one another. I've been tempted to ask them to please be quiet or leave.

"Well, what are your thoughts about the production, Mr. Cooke?" Obviously a prelude to the principal giving me his thoughts about it.

"I'm pleased with how hard the kids are working on their parts."

"Yes, indeed," Danielson agrees. "The Slater girl seems especially keen."

"She's very good in her role."

"Yes, most impressive. Now, about the story line itself..." Danielson makes his move.

"What about it?"

"Well, from the little bits I've seen, it does appear to be becoming increasingly...how shall I put it?...gloomy."

"Does it?" Deadpan.

"Yes."

Danielson and I stand as armed combatants on the field of battle.

"Does it have a happy ending?" Danielson's maybe the least happy person I know, but he's serious about this.

"Happy? No. I wouldn't say happy."

"What would you say?"

"Oh. Provocative. Ambivalent. Something along those lines."

"Not upbeat then?"

"Well, more upbeat than beat up I would say."

He ignores my cleverness. "Is the crisis with this traumatized girl resolved satisfactorily?"

I give a little snort. I'm not sure anything in my script is dealt with satisfactorily, but I'll be damned if I'll give Danielson the satisfaction of my admitting it. "I'd say so, yes."

"Mr. Cooke, let me be perfectly frank." Again he draws too close to me, staring with his rheumy eyes. I can smell a sourness on his breath. "In discussions with the Governor General's office, it has been agreed that a public performance of some sort, with His Honour in attendance, would be a highly desirable feature during his visit. The only likely candidate we have to fill that role is this drama."

"I'm not sure…" I begin, but Danielson raises an index finger between us, decapitating my sentence.

"I would very much like this play to be performed, and for the production to be exceptional in all respects. Something the school can be proud of presenting to an audience containing a number of very distinguished persons. But to be perfectly blunt about it I have some very real concerns that the theme of this play, the message it conveys, is not sufficiently…uplifting."

"Mr. Danielson, I don't…"

Again he cuts me off. "I have no objection to realism, or to stretching the boundaries a bit. But I want a play that speaks to the best in human nature, not the worst. I want a play that's appropriate for students who are leaving us to begin making their own way in the world. There should be some optimism, some excitement, some sense of wonder. What there shouldn't be is a lot of doom and gloom, a lot of crawling around psychiatric back alleys. It's not appropriate for children of that age and it's certainly not appropriate to force the Governor General to have to sit through it."

Danielson has succeeded in getting under my skin and I'm working really hard at not reacting to him. Before I can say anything, he asks, "Do you have a complete copy of the play that I might borrow?"

So here it comes. Already I can see Danielson and Louise sitting up all evening, tearing my script to pieces. "No, I don't have an extra copy."

"Have one made for me, Mr. Cooke, if you would, please. I'm sure my wife would happily photocopy it for you."

"I'm certain she would."

Danielson registers my sarcasm. "Have it on my desk by tomorrow afternoon, if you'd be so kind." He smiles his feral smile and bids me good afternoon.

Shit.

An hour later, walking over to Mother's place after school, I'm still steaming about Danielson. It's not just his meddling, his bullshit controlling, but his criticism of my writing. Doom and gloom for Christ's sake! What's really pissed me off is the jerk's provoked me into remembering my great belly-flop attempt at becoming a playwright.

What a farce. Or maybe a tragedy. I was down in Vancouver alone, having graduated from Shallowford High with not quite the anticipated honours, intent upon learning the playwright's craft. Though it was my first real time away from home, I wasn't homesick at all, not nearly so much as I was missing Gabriel and Angela. Over the course of the previous year, my senior year, without fully realizing it was happening, I'd gradually and completely switched my allegiances from my parents, friends and school, everything really, to them. I'd let my hair grow long and would have grown a beard if I could. I took to wearing Indian cotton shirts like Gabriel's, reading Sufi poets, eating vegetarian.

Angela came down to the city in early October. I met her at the bus depot on a dripping wet afternoon. "Hey, you," she said, slinging a backpack over her shoulder, smiling, mischievous as ever.

"Hey, yourself," I beamed back at her, barely containing my elation at having her with me. I'd missed her dreadfully. One of my early poems described myself as being drawn toward her as Earth's waters are pulled by the moon. No matter what I thought, believed or told myself, no matter what common sense said, the waters of my cells surged toward this woman and I could no more check the surge than King Canute could turn the tides.

We took the Fourth Avenue bus to the Naam Café, which was my main hangout at the time. "So what are you doing in town?" I asked her. The windows of the café were steamed up and she was drawing mandala shapes on the dripping glass.

"Could be I'm looking for a place to stay," she said offhandedly. "Know of anything?"

Was she proposing moving in with me or not? "No, I don't. Beginning of school year's really tough. I guess people start dropping out in a couple of months, then some places open up."

"What's a girl to do?" she asked in her half-mocking way.

"You could bunk in with me for a bit." I wanted to say "forever" but didn't.

"Really?"

"Sure."

"What would your parents say?"

"Nothing if they didn't know."

"Not ashamed of me, are you?" A teasing challenge.

"Of course not. It's just my parents don't like any of the choices I'm making right now. So the less they know about what I'm doing, the better."

And that was that. We set up house together in my musty little basement suite in Kitsilano. A few days stretched into weeks, then more weeks. I was thrilled to have Angela with me. The world was already turned completely on its ear in those days, old forms had collapsed in the turmoil of the sixties and everything was up for grabs. I whirled through those crazy, sexy, mismatched days with Angela, she and I dancing together like flames. I was totally wired on the writing life, writing rapaciously as Angela puttered around the apartment. Words poured out onto the page almost by themselves. Sitting up late at night, I'd review what I'd written and be thrilled by its cleverness, incisiveness. Rich with mythic allusion. One of my pieces was being workshopped by a little theatre collective. I was convinced people were beginning to take notice.

One morning, early in November, my landlady, Mrs. Selz, called down the stairs saying there was a phone call for me. I took the call at the wall phone in her dark corridor. "Hello?"

"Hello, Dexter." My father. "I hope I haven't caught you at a bad time."

"No, not at all." A confusion of questions stampeded through my brain. Mostly why was he calling, what did he want. "Are you at home? Is something wrong?"

"No, no, nothing like that," he said. "I'm in Vancouver. At the airport."

"What's going on?" I felt instantly threatened by his proximity. We'd had less and less to do with one another over the past year. We didn't argue but neither did we connect in any real way. We'd just drifted away from each other. I'd long ago ceased to be his shining prodigy just as he'd ceased to be my Atticus Finch.

"One of these legal workshops we have to take. You know, keep the old duffers from wandering too far off-track." His stab at humour sounded contrived.

"Is Mom here too?"

"No, she isn't." This was ominous, as I knew Mother would have loved to see what I was up to, where I was living, was I looking after myself? It occurred to me that I hadn't answered her several letters, hadn't written home since I'd gotten here. So much writing, but none for her, none for them. I was terrified that my father was going to ask to come over to my place; or, worse still, if he could stay with me. "I'd like to get together with you," he said, "Do you have a bit of spare time in the next day or two?"

"Sure."

"I could take a cab over to your place, if you like."

I didn't like. Not with Angela there, her panties drying on the radiator, the stench of hemp and sex permeating the place. "Where are you staying?"

"Hotel Vancouver. The workshop is there."

"I can catch a bus down there easily."

"You sure?"

"Yep. My apartment's…difficult." I wondered if he suspected. We agreed to meet the following afternoon.

The overwrought lobby of the old hotel—potted palms, grand chandeliers, Muzak Mozart—was almost deserted. My father and I greeted one another with an awkward, tilting gesture, like armless mannequins trying to hug. We sat together in opposing high-backed wing chairs near a fireplace. My undergrad cottons and sandals felt out of place in the stuffy lobby. Everything about the place—stout pillars, deep rugs on marble floors, enormous bronze doors and cast moldings—was large, solid and heavy. Like my father.

"How're you getting on then?" he asked me.

"Fine. How's Mom?"

"She's fine. Bit of an empty nest. She misses you."

"I'm sorry."

"Has to be, sooner or later. Mothers and sons, you know." He was speaking in clipped little bullets, like a sergeant major in a bad British film. None of his old easygoing eloquence shone through. It never occurred to me that he might have been as nervous as I was. Except I did notice, just above his right eye, a small tic flickered under his skin. Funny, in hindsight, how such a small detail created a sense of vulnerability in him, though I paid no attention to it at the time.

We skirted carefully around a number of innocuous topics: the weather back home, the dreary workshop he was attending, the lamentable state of Shallowford High's football team this year. All the time I could see he was circling toward the reason for this meeting.

"You must be very, very busy these days, are you?" he asked.

"I seem to be writing morning, noon and night." Though it would have been more accurate if I'd said "writing and fucking."

"But not to your mother and me."

"No, look, I'm sorry about that. I had no idea how long it's been."

He waited a few moments, observing me. The flickering of his tic seemed to intensify. "Is there something you'd like to tell me, Dexter?"

"Not particularly, no." Only a million things there are no words for.

"Something you're hiding from your mother and me? Something you're perhaps ashamed of?"

"Not at all. What would I be ashamed of?"

"I would hope nothing. But cutting your mother off that way, when you know full well how devoted she is to you…"

"I'm sorry. I'll write this week. I promise."

"Not exactly the same thing, is it?"

"What isn't?"

"Writing from guilt rather than affection."

"I'm only feeling guilt because you're making me feel it." I miscalculated in escalating the tension like this, but he was already provoking me.

"I'm not making you do anything. Or feel anything."

"Yes, you are. You're making me feel like there's something wrong with what I'm doing and there isn't. I'm doing exactly what I want to be doing. I'm sorry it's not what you want me to be doing, but it's my life." I was digging in and, I'm sure, sounding defensive.

"I'm only suggesting that you might spare a couple of minutes now and then to drop your mother a line or give her a call."

"Yes, and I've said I'll do that."

"You missed her birthday entirely."

"Oh, for Christ's sake!" I knew then that it wasn't Mother he was concerned about—he was using that as code for a far deeper criticism. I realized he must know that Angela was here, but didn't want to bring her up. He glanced at his watch, as though he had something else more important to get to.

"Well, Dexter," he said, ignoring my outburst and bearing down on me as I'd sometimes seen him bear down on a hostile witness, "there's no sense beating around the bush. You know your mother and I are extremely disappointed with the choices you've made and the company you're keeping."

"Yes, I know that." I wanted to tell him to lighten up. I was living with the woman I loved and studying the writer's craft, which I also loved. The old blueprint was burned long ago, but somehow he didn't get it. Or wouldn't accept it. Most of the time I felt like I was rocketing toward the stars: being with Angela wasn't always easy but it was brilliant; my writing was going well; I loved learning about theatre. What was there to get so uptight about? What was there not to be proud of?

"You had it all," he said, shaking his head. "You had it all right there on a silver platter and you walked away from it. Unbelievable!"

His words betrayed a dishonesty and a cheap sentiment unworthy of him. "You walked away from me," is what he meant, and that was true. He was no longer the dependable mass that held my planet in orbit. I'd broken from the pull of his gravity, as one must, as he'd known all along I would. What didn't make sense to me was how stubbornly he clung to the old constellation long after it had vanished. His dabblings in astronomy, archaeology and paleontology had given him a marvellous perception of celestial movements and the fluxes of time and space. But when it came to my getting on with my own life in the way I chose, he seemed as stubborn as a beaten mule.

We shook hands before parting, but I walked out of the hotel with an acrid taste of stalemate in my mouth.

After that everything came down in a crash. It was a desperate night in late November, wind and rain pummelling the city, when I came home dripping wet, and found Angela stuffing her backpack. She told me she was leaving.

"What do you mean, leaving?"

"I have to go back to Shallowford."

"Why would you want to go back there?" I couldn't grasp what was going on.

"Gabriel needs me."

"Gabriel needs you? Gabriel doesn't need anybody."

"Weird things are happening at Dancing Grasses. I have to get back there."

"Now? In the middle of the night?"

"Yes."

"When will you be back?"

She stopped her restless packing and looked at me. Her eyes glistened moist and miserable.

I understood in a flash. "You're not coming back, are you?"

"No. I don't think so."

A huge boulder crashed to the bottom of nothing. "Why not?"

"Dex, it's really hard to explain."

"Try." I was fighting back panicky tears.

"I don't think our being here together the way we've been is right."

"Right? What d'you mean, right? What kind of shit is that?" I was almost sobbing.

"Ever since your father's visit..."

"My father! Did you talk to him?" Always there was this smouldering subtext that she and my father were having conversations about which I knew nothing.

"No, just what you told me."

"And?"

"I think he's right. You've cut yourself off from your family and your friends. And you'll stay cut off so long as you're with me."

"That's how I want it."

"Dex, you're losing perspective. You're getting to be really obsessive about this writing thing and, to tell you the truth…" She hesitated, resumed stuffing clothes into her backpack.

"What? Tell me what truth?"

"I don't want to say anything to hurt you."

"Like you're leaving, for example. No, that doesn't hurt at all! So tell me: what's the great truth?"

She looked straight at me again and now her eyes were brimming with tears. "I think maybe you're making a mistake with this writing thing."

"What?"

"Maybe you should think again about what you really want to do. Maybe about law."

"Law? I can't believe you're saying this. You think my writing's no good."

"I didn't say that, I…"

"Well, that's bullshit! You know it's good."

"Dexter, I have to go."

"You're leaving me?"

"For now. Yes. I'm sorry."

"You're sorry." A well of hot tears. Blubbering like a baby.

"Don't cry, Dexter," Angela said, laying her hand like a cool salve along the side of my face. "We're both better off if I go, you know that as well as I do."

"No, I don't!" I cried, while the wind panicked through the creaking timbers of the house, "I don't know that at all!"

She kissed me gently and sweetly, my salty tears on both our lips, and then smiled. "Farewell," she said. "It's just farewell, not goodbye forever." Then she was gone. Just like that. As I closed the door behind the now empty space, the power went out and I tumbled headlong into pathetic fallacy. I couldn't get my head around her leaving. I hardly ate or slept for weeks. I smoked dope constantly and drank toxic plonk from gallon jugs. I prowled the city streets at night, a loner, a loser, new recruit to the underclass. The basement suite we'd shared became a squalid toad hole I couldn't bear to be inside. I could smell fungi and bacteria in there, eating the walls. I walked for miles along the city beaches, in wind and rain, letting the elements strip me down to heartwood.

My writing collapsed like a bad soufflé. I became tentative, where only weeks before I'd roared with passion. I was no longer willing to send my words outdoors into dangerous neighbourhoods where they'd be cut to pieces. I began to see how banal my writing was. Glib and derivative. Cowardly, and in the end, embarrassing. Angela was right: I was deluding myself thinking this shit was worth trying to build a career on.

The pressure boiled inside of me and finally erupted during an evaluation session I had with Milton Gorman, the resident literary lion on campus. I was still desperately depressed the morning I tapped on Gorman's office door and entered to his shouted "Come!" I'd submitted a one-act play for his review, and I knew before he said a word that it was poorly written. "Your work shows definite promise," Gorman told me offhandedly as we sat on opposite sides of his desk. He was wearing a magenta silk scarf draped artily across his denim shirt. Throughout the interview his manner gave the impression that his brain was doing something else entirely while he was talking to me. "But you really must," he said after trotting out a few rote compliments, "drop this small-town Pollyanna bullshit. You're not Eleanor Hodgman Porter and you never will be. Unless, of course, you want to fashion a career writing Hallmark cards. Which, come to think of it, is undoubtedly more lucrative than writing for the theatre." He tossed all this off as though he were Oscar Wilde cavorting at a party and appeared delighted by his own wit.

"Could you be more specific?" I asked him, feeling myself getting prickly at his dismissiveness. I wondered if he'd even read my play.

"If you like," he replied, rising from his chair and sauntering over to his bookshelf where he scanned the volumes as though searching for something relevant to our conversation. His hair was tied in a ponytail, which was a radical statement on campus in those days. He plucked a book from its shelf, glanced at its fly leaf and laid it on his desk. "I have no wish to pry into your personal life," he said to me, "but if you insist on the bitter truth, I have to tell you that your writing is incredibly naive. It's as though you've never been anywhere or done anything real. If you're serious about becoming a writer, the best thing you could do is go live on the downtown east side for a year and watch how real people live. Don't write a word, just observe. Get the sense of it, the smell of it, the blue-green iridescent sheen of pigeon feathers amid the squalor. Observe the hookers and addicts and broken-down old loggers. Listen to their lingo, smell the stale beer and cigarette butts. Maybe after that you'll have some characters we'd be interested in viewing for an evening." He carried on in the same patronizing vein for another five minutes.

Listening to him I saw Gorman clearly for what he was: a third-tier poet who'd written beautifully as a young man but nothing memorable since, still riding high on a long-exhausted reputation. All the anger I'd been feeling since Angela left came boiling out in one hot jet aimed straight at this poor faded poet. "And here's the bitter truth from my perspective," I raged. "You're the most miserable fucking excuse for a teacher I've ever encountered." I could see fear in his eyes as I got right into his face. "You're supposed to be helping and encouraging people, not crapping all over them for your own sadistic entertainment. I may be a failure at writing, but you're a way greater failure at teaching, and as far as I'm concerned, you can take your blue-green pigeon feathers and go fuck yourself!" I snatched my play from his desk, stalked out of the office and slammed his door hard enough to crack plaster.

I see now where my rage came from: what Gorman said out loud was what my own fears had been whispering to me since Angela went. I'd gambled everything on being with her and being a playwright. The twin obsessions of my life: to be caught in her smouldering sexuality, and to take from our fiery lovemaking the elements I could weld into the framework of bold theatre. Now, with her gone, I could no more write than fly. For the first time in my life, I was conscious of being second-rate. One night I threw the manuscript for my new three-act play into a box, and all my notes and revisions, my character sketches, everything I could find in the shitbox my apartment had become. I carried the boxful of papers down to Kits Beach, out onto a rocky point. I took the pages one by one from the box, lit the bottom of each one with a lighter and once the flames licked up the sides of a sheet, cast it into the wind, so it flew out over the water, a flaming piece of failure.

Time proved Angela, my father and even Milton Gorman correct, the most recent evidence being this lacklustre school play I've produced. But I'll be damned if I'll give Danielson the satisfaction of my admitting it. Sad now as much as angry, I'm startled out of my ruminations by the rumble of a rusted muffler, and there's Ann Slater's old beater pulling up alongside me again. Christ.

"Hello, Ann," I say, leaning a forearm on the roof of the car and peering in at her from the passenger-side window.

"You better get in, Dexter," she says. "We got trouble."

I don't like the smell of that "we." "Trouble how?" I force myself to sound jaunty.

"Like big trouble," she says. "You better get in."

Reluctantly I pull open the passenger-side door. The car seems to stink a little less than it did last time. Ann's wearing white cotton slacks and a pink alpaca sweater that stretches too tightly across her breasts. The henna has faded a bit from her hair. Her lipstick, rouge and mascara have been brought under some measure of control. She looks almost attractive, a Sally-Ann version of Elizabeth Taylor in *Who's Afraid of Virginia Woolf?*

"I need to make this quick," I say, "I've got…"

"I know, I know," she interrupts me. "You don't want to be seen in public talking to trailer trash like me."

"It's not that at all. It's just that I've got…"

"Well, trouble's what I've got," she interrupts, "and maybe you do too. And maybe others even more." Gloomy premonitions seem to cling to this woman like the stench of her cheap perfume. She drums her painted fingernails nervously on the steering wheel.

"What do you mean?" I ask her. "What's happened?"

"Susan's found a corpse up at that goddamn place."

"A corpse?" She's caught me off guard and I'm not sure I've heard her right. "You mean a real corpse?"

"Yes, a real corpse." Ann's barely disguising her impatience with me. "Somebody dead and buried under—what do the cops call it?—suspicious circumstances."

Christ. Just what we need right now. "Did she tell you this?"

"Nope. Read about it in her diary again. Just today. I woulda brought it along only she's home from school already by now and I couldn't risk it. But she says the weird guy she sees up there led her to a spot where the body's buried."

"Did she dig it up? I mean, how does she know it's a corpse?"

"I guess she dug enough to find a human foot, poor kid. Then she musta freaked out and ran home. I would too."

"And she didn't say anything to you?"

"Not a word."

Talk about a great mother–daughter relationship. "And she hasn't told anyone else? The police or anyone?"

"Well, she hasn't told the cops for sure, or they'd be all over us by now. I don't know for certain, but I doubt she's told anyone else."

Christ. Maybe this explains what Susan's doing on the stage, the manic energy of her acting.

"Look," Ann says, shifting in her seat to stare directly at me, "I may not be the greatest mother in the world, but I love that kid and I do my best by her." This accompanied by a poorly practised concerned-parent look.

"I know you do," I agree, almost gagging on the sentiment.

"I don't want to see her get hurt, and I don't want a bunch of goddamn cops and social workers sniffing around looking for reasons to take her away from me, see?"

"I understand completely," I sympathize. More completely than she probably knows. "But I don't really think that's going to…"

"I don't know what the hell to do!" she cuts me short. "I guess I'm asking for your help." I guess you are. "I know Susan likes you and trusts you," she continues, looking right at me, honest and forthcoming as all get-out.

"What would you like me to do?" I ask her.

"Maybe you could go to that damn ranch with her," she suggests, disingenuously as though the idea has just occurred to her. "Find some excuse, see what's going on. Maybe there's not any corpse at all. She could just be making the whole thing up, like she's writing a story or something. She's like that, you know. A little soft in the head. Bit of a dreamer. Or maybe she's figured out I'm reading her diary and she's just trying to fuck my head around, er, I mean…"

"And if there is a corpse?" I ask her.

"Then I guess we have to tell the cops, right? But at least if you're there it won't be all on Susan, there won't be a whole lot of questions about why she was trespassing at the ranch and her visions and all that. We can keep that part of it to ourselves. Otherwise there'll be psychiatrists and every other kind of asshole poking at her for the rest of her life. And poking at me too."

Right. Me being the important bit. This whole scenario stinks like old garbage. I have the sense of being dragged into something over which I have no control. I'd just as soon not touch it, but I feel already complicit. Plus I am concerned about Susan.

Both Ann and I stare out the windshield, waiting. A pair of mongrel dogs come tumbling across a lawn and take to humping on the boulevard right in front of us. The male, a mangy white terrier cross is pumping away grotesquely, its mouth open, its long pink tongue slobbering out of the side of its mouth, the little black bitch wobbling unsteadily under him. Ann watches them disinterestedly.

"Alright," I say at last, wanting to get away. "I'll see what I can do."

I find Mother sitting in a Cape Cod chair on the flagstone patio out back. The sun's hanging theatrically off in the west, glowing through riverside cottonwoods that cast long shadows across the lawn. Mother greets me and pours me a single-malt whisky, which helps rinse off the foul taste left by my encounter with Ann Slater. My attention's only half on Mother's chatter, the other half turning over what Ann's told me. There's probably nothing to it. The kid's stumbled over a deer carcass and freaked herself out.

I snag my attention back to what Mother's telling me and just then we're interrupted by a stranger, a black woman, emerging from the house, a coat over her arm. "Excuse me," the woman says in a lilting voice, "I'm about done, Mrs. Cooke."

"Oh, Lavina!" Mother exclaims. "Do come and meet my son." Mother introduces us. The woman's hand in mine is soft, warm and strong. My first impression is of someone who exudes a cheerful power. "Lavina's a midwife by training," Mother explains, "but she's unable to find work in her chosen profession." Mother invites Lavina to join us for a drink, but she declines.

"Mr. Cooke is resting comfortably," she tells Mother, "but he did speak to me just now."

"Could you make out what?"

"Same thing. 'Memory.' He just says 'memory.'"

"I do wish we knew what he was trying to tell us."

"I know you do. But try not to fret yourself. We'll know what we need to know in good time."

"Yes, I suppose so," Mother says.

"So I'll see you tomorrow morning. So nice to meet you," Lavina beams a radiant smile at me and leaves.

"She's a treasure," Mother says when we're alone.

"Where did you find her?" Mother hadn't even told me she was looking for help.

"Charlie cooked it up somehow. Through colleagues of his down in the city. And I'm ever so grateful—I think she's an absolute find."

"What's your arrangement?"

"She'll come in nine to five, six days a week."

"Perfect."

"I asked if she wanted to live in, but she said no, she preferred to rent a room in town. I suspect most of what I'm paying her is going back to Jamaica to feed her family."

"She good with Dad?"

"Seems excellent. A great amount of bustling, jovial efficiency. It really has taken a great weight off my shoulders." She smiles at me now in a way she hasn't smiled in a good long while.

"I'm glad," I smile back, "I think it was really smart of you to bring her in." Here I overlook the wrangling and cajoling that both Charlie and I have been doing, trying to get Mother to agree to any invasion of her privacy. "How's Dad?" I ask her.

"Same as ever," she sighs. "He has moments when you think he's coming back—Lavina's very good for him that way—but then he sinks away again. I'm afraid I no longer believe he's ever going to improve."

"I guess I don't either," I agree. "Though we can always hope."

"Oh, yes, hope," Mother wrinkles her nose as though the word itself had a disagreeable odour.

"Mother," I decide to tackle her directly, "can you tell me what went on here after I left for school?"

"Whatever do you mean, darling, what went on here? The same things that have always gone on and probably always will go on. You know dear old Shallowford as well as I do."

"I mean about Gabriel."

"Gabriel? Oh, the great mystic? Yes, of course, I'd almost forgotten about him. Well, if you really want my opinion—" she picks a tiny flake of lint from the sleeve of her cardigan "—I think in many ways that particular summer was the beginning of the end for all of us." She looks toward the river, posed exquisitely against the westering sun, a classic tragic heroine. She's wearing a rayon dress of pale mauve with a light buff cardigan thrown over her shoulders against an evening chill that hasn't yet begun. I've taken off my schoolteacher's corduroy jacket and tie.

"What was?" I prod her.

"Oh, that awful summer! It robbed us all of something very precious. We'd been extraordinarily blessed up until then, your father and myself and you. We had everything anyone could ever want. Now look at us." She sips her Glenlivet and turns to me, wistful and forlorn. I'm not accustomed to seeing her this way. Usually she plays the martyr with a hint of mischief, as though she doesn't take it all that seriously and doesn't expect me to either. But not today.

"Well, of course it's awful what's happened to Dad," I tell her, "but it's hardly because of anything that went on that summer."

"Isn't it?" A tartness in her tone challenges my comment. "I'm glad you're so sure of that, Dexter darling, because I'm not. No, not at all."

"What do you mean?" I think I know. But I also think I don't want to hear it.

"I mean we had a lovely family life until those dreadful people got you under their spell. They ruined what could have been a brilliant career for you, a truly distinguished career, and they broke your father's spirit as well. I see I've shocked you, Dexter, and I'm sorry. I'm sorry to have to say these things; I've refrained from saying anything in the past, you'll grant me that much, darling. And I don't hold you responsible in any way. You were very young, after all, and it's easy to see how you'd be beguiled by them. But there's no denying that they ruined your life and our family life as well."

"I hardly think my life's ruined, Mother."

"Oh, Dexter! Teaching high school to a pack of bumpkins. Married to poor frigid little Deirdre. No children of your own and no prospects of having any. Your father like he is and me sitting here being pitied by everyone in town. How can you call it anything but a ruin? Of all the careers you might have had! You could have been someone very important, very special. You've settled for far less, darling, but I don't blame you in the least. I do, however, blame those dreadful people. Without their interference I'm certain everything would have turned out differently."

Mother pours us each another Scotch, as though to atone for what she's said. But her manner betrays no atonement. This is harsh criticism from Mother. Normally she's given to insinuations or sly ironies. "I'm sorry if I've offended you, Dexter, but you do insist on asking, and some things simply must be said."

"Yes, they must," I agree. And I know she's at least partly right in what she says. Of course my life's a bit of a cock-up. Teaching's never been my thing. I admire my colleagues who genuinely like their students and are passionate about seeing them succeed. I just go through the motions. I don't take particular delight in kids who excel or the ones who struggle and manage to do better than anyone expected them to. I no longer look for the flash of insight in my students, the light of awareness blinking on. No, I'm largely indifferent to the moving parade that passes through year after year. It was Deirdre who'd nudged me down the path of becoming an English teacher whereby, as she said, I could indulge my love of writing while still bringing home a steady paycheque. Dear, sweet, practical Deirdre. At least she got the paycheque bit right.

Could I have done better for myself? Several of my classmates who were total groaners at school went on to far more impressive careers than I have. Carson, the young lawyer who's taken over Dad's practice—the young lawyer I was supposed to be—has done extremely well and is now a force to be reckoned with in town. There's talk of his running for mayor. Even Georges, the Gauloises-sucking misfit of the creative writing department has scored big. His new novel, *Pterodactyls*, has been sitting on best-seller lists for months and has rights sold into a dozen countries. I haven't read it, and don't intend to, but the reviews describe it as a graphic tale centred upon a group of grotesquely disfigured psychopaths who live hidden in the bowels of the New York sewer system. Yes, Mother's right about that much, my erstwhile career is a comparative flop.

"Tell me what happened," I ask her again. "Tell me what you know about what happened to Gabriel and the others."

Mother sips her Scotch and pulls the cardigan around her shoulders. I can see she's calculating how much she should tell me—it's plain that she knows more than she'll disclose, that I'll get only a selected portion of the story. What's the big mystery, I wonder?

"Mother?"

"Alright, darling, if you must," she says with an edge. "But don't blame me if you don't like what you hear."

"Of course I won't."

"The trouble began," Mother starts decisively, "when that filthy little bitch came to see your father."

I'm shocked at Mother's language. "You mean Angela?"

"That's exactly who I mean. She of the angels," Mother sniffs derisively.

"I remember she wanted to see Dad. I was there in the office when she made the appointment."

"I want you to understand, Dexter, that your father never, ever, disclosed to me anything that occurred between himself and a client. It was a point of honour with him and one I supported entirely."

"I know that, Mother."

"But in this case I admit he deviated from that principle—not at the time, mind you, but only later, after you'd become…" she pauses, searching for the right word, "entangled with that wretched girl."

"So he told you then why she'd come to see him?" My eagerness to know is blunting my resentment at how Mother's slagging Angela.

"Later on he did, yes, after you and she had begun living together."

"And?"

"Dexter, what I am about to say I tell you in complete and utter confidence. It is absolutely never to be disclosed to anyone else, for any reason whatsoever. Is that understood?"

"Yes, of course. Would you please just tell me the big secret? You're driving me crazy with this build up."

"Alright, darling, there's no reason for rudeness." Mother takes another tiny but purposeful sip of her Scotch to reinforce the message that she'll tell me what she wants precisely as she wants to.

"That girl, that Angela, came to see your father to seek advice on procuring an abortion."

"What?" I can't believe what she's just said. "What?"

"Surely that's not so hard to believe. She was in fact no angel, Dexter."

"An abortion? What would Dad know about procuring an abortion?"

"It was not a thing as casually done in those days as it is now," Mother says. "Especially not here. To be done legally it involved a lot of referrals and assessments and panels. That girl was cunning enough to know that a lawyer was both bound by confidentiality and able to open certain doors that might otherwise have remained closed to her."

"And did he do it? Did he help get her an abortion?"

"Exactly what role your father played in the affair I don't know. I do know that she secured the abortion. And that not long afterward she and you became...intimate."

"Are you certain of this, Mother?" I feel stunned with incomprehension.

"Perfectly."

"Do you—" I can hardly ask the question "—do you know who the father of the child was?"

"Well, I thank God it wasn't you," Mother says. "That I would not have forgiven you, Dexter, no matter how young and besotted you were. Every indication is that it was fathered by the cult leader, the one who called himself Brother Gabriel, who was, in my opinion, as perverse as she. Your father thought more so; he had some sympathy for her, at least at the outset. He felt she'd been badly used by that fellow, that he somehow had her under his spell. It's not a point of view I shared. She was nobody's fool, that conniving little bitch; I believe she knew exactly what she was doing. She saw you as you were: a beautiful, gullible boy. She took unfair advantage of you and it's one of the great sorrows of my life that I was unable to prevent it happening."

"I didn't see it that way, Mother."

"Of course you didn't, darling, how could you? First love is a powerful and precious thing. I remember it myself. Being entirely smitten with your father. I'd have sold my soul for his love. Fortunately, he was a man of honour, but he could have been a scoundrel underneath his brilliance and I might not have known it. I might have been deceived, as you were, under the heady influence of young love." Mother looks wistful for a moment, remembering. Then sharpens again. "After she'd had her bit of fun with you, she came back to him, you know."

"What do you mean?"

"Oh, yes, back she came and presumably took up with him right where she'd left off, even though it was apparently his refusal to accept responsibility for his child that had led her to have it aborted."

I feel as though a runaway truck has just smashed through the asylum wall. Was that really all my great love affair with Angela amounted to—a pathetic interlude between bouts of lovemaking with Gabriel? That she'd aborted his baby, been with me, then gone back to him? That I'd let myself go off the rails for something as pathetic as that? Yes, it's possible that's why she left me so hurriedly, why the two of them disappeared. Still I can't get my head around it. It's simply inconceivable, and so at odds with my experience of Angela and of Gabriel. Sure, I was young and naïve. But I know they wouldn't have betrayed me like that. And I don't believe they'd have casually aborted a baby either. Life was too sacred.

Mother carries on with her Gothic tale of how my father's world began to fall apart when I abandoned the family in favour of those "depraved people." And this part I know isn't true because my father was made of far tougher stuff than that, something she knows better than anyone. He was upset about my choices, sure, and eventually grew bitter, but he possessed a strength of character that was hardly about to break over something so trivial. Yes, I tote around a niggling suspicion that I'm in some way responsible for my father's condition, but in the cold light of reason, I know that the tragic hero stumbles because of inner flaws not external circumstances. Whatever its cause, Dad's madness comes from within, not from anything I did or didn't do.

I don't argue any of this with Mother, neither do I hear much else of what she has to say, and I leave her as quickly as I decently can.

ELEVEN

Sitting in my car in the deserted school parking lot, waiting for Susan Slater to arrive, I scan the weekend paper. There's a two-page spread of photographs from Bangladesh. The body count from the killer cyclone is now estimated at ten thousand. I can't look at the photos and turn instead to a piece about how Coca-Cola plans to bring back their ninety-nine-year-old formula. Then I notice a small item under the headline: Nazi War Criminal Found Dead.

> A forty-year-old mystery about what happened to the notorious Nazi doctor Josef Mengele may have been solved with the discovery of a body recently exhumed in Brazil. The remains are believed to be those of the missing SS officer known as the Angel of Death. Forensic pathologists from West Germany and the United States are reported on their way to São Paulo to assist Brazilian authorities in identifying the skeletal remains.
>
> Mengele, who was responsible for the execution of some 400,000 people at the Nazi death camp at Auschwitz, disappeared at the end of the war. The subject of an intense manhunt by the Israeli secret service and by West German authorities, Mengele apparently eluded his pursuers by adopting a number of aliases and moving from Argentina to Paraguay and Brazil.

> It is now believed that the infamous war criminal died from a stroke while swimming at the beach at Bertioga in Embu, Brazil, in 1979.

Interesting. And what body are Susan and I going to discover today? I wonder. No old Nazi, but maybe something equally disturbing. Like Angela's abortion. How ugly is that little bit of history Mother's dug up. But is her story real, or another version twisted through the labyrinth of memory? It's certainly not beyond Mother's peculiar instincts to concoct an elaborate fantasy like the story she told me, custom-tailored to fit snugly into her prejudices. She may even have come to believe it herself. The mind can do this. Mother has her own agenda, that I've never doubted. Even so, her spin on Angela's behaviour may be pure fantasy. Yet, I can feel the seeds of doubt she's sown already germinating in the dark.

And worse. I have to wonder if this aborted child was mine. Mother had said not, and I certainly hadn't slept with Angela when she first came to see my father. But we made love frequently after that, the innocent free love of the time. I could have gotten her pregnant, though the possibility's never entered my mind before. But what more cogent reason could there be for Angela's abrupt and final disappearance from my life? Yes, it's a distinct possibility, and Mother might easily have mixed up her dates and details, or be in denial, knowing full well the child was mine. I can't bear to think of Angela carrying my child and then having it aborted. I have to slam a door shut against that possibility. Mother's got it wrong. Or is crazy. Or both.

I stare through the windshield at a garbage truck inching its way down the street like a huge metallic grub into whose maw two guys in coveralls are hurling bagged garbage. The truck's compacter squeezes the garbage down the grub's gullet.

I've arranged to meet Susan here to go up to Dancing Grasses together. I was surprised at how easy it was to get her to agree. I'd expected a struggle. I called her aside after our last class yesterday. Friday afternoon's never easy, as you feel everyone's energy surging for the weekend. We'd been analyzing Chekhov's short story "The Darling." I was trying to get the kids discussing Chekhov's treatment of the nature of love, but they weren't having any of it. Even though the music most of them listen to all day is the most godawful caterwauling about broken hearts and long-lost loves, the suggestion that they publicly discuss what Chekhov has to say about love set them squirming. At the final bell, they bolted from the classroom like rioting prisoners.

"Could I have a word with you please, Susan?" I called as they funnelled out the door. She stepped out of the stream and stood by my desk, but she wouldn't look at me. She was clutching her schoolbooks against her chest with both arms, her head bent forward so that hair curtained her face. I waited until the last of the others had shuffled out. Their guffawing and shrilling echoed down the corridor outside like the cries of endangered animals. I turned to Susan. How to begin?

"I've been thinking about what you told me the other day," I leaned back in my swivel chair, trying to appear casual. "About your experiences at Dancing Grasses."

"Yes," she said, barely audible. The noise of fleeing students had already subsided to a distant murmur.

"I'd like to get to the bottom of it if we can," I said. "If you want to." A scarcely perceptible nod of her head.

"How would you feel," I pressed on, "if you and I were to go up there together and see what happens?" For a moment she didn't react. Then she raised her head and looked directly at me. What was there to see in her blank face—fear? Distrust? Relief? I couldn't read her at all.

"Okay," she said at last, flatly, and I couldn't read that either.

"Are you sure?"

"Yes." Quietly, nodding her head again, her books clutched like a shield against her chest. "Thank you."

I got no more from her and couldn't tell if this was something she wanted to do or not. I wasn't sure I wanted to do it myself.

She shows up twenty minutes late and climbs into the car with barely a "Hi." During the drive out of town she sits beside me, distant, closed as a stone. I try to make small talk about the play, telling her how impressed I am by her work at rehearsal, but she only grunts in response or answers in reluctant monosyllables. Something about this kid—her wistfulness, the sadness that envelops her—appeals to me in a way I don't understand or trust. As though she embodies the innocence around which most of us learn early to develop a protective shell.

As withdrawn as she is, she seems to be exposed and vulnerable. She elicits an instinct to protect and shelter, as though by doing so I'd protect my own vulnerability. This is what I tell myself as we whistle past the ranches outside of town.

I park the car again outside the gate at Dancing Grasses. Nothing's changed since I was here last. Nothing and everything. We stand in front of the gate for a moment, then I climb over and drop down inside. She follows me. I notice the ripple of young muscles in her thighs as she straddles the gate. I reach to help her down, but she doesn't need help; her lithe body takes the gate with ease. She slips down smooth as a gymnast, her sneakers landing softly on the dusty road. For the first time today she looks directly at me, the trace of a conspiratorial grin on her face. She's wearing a pair of old sneakers, cut-off blue jeans and a lime-green tank top. Again I think of Angela, remembering the excitement I used to feel with her, the thrill and danger of being her lover, hidden from the world in this wild place. We stand there on the gravel road. In every direction, grasses are moving in a restless commotion of green and gold. Small cumulous clouds tumble across blue sky, trolling behind them slanted shadows that skim the landscape and evaporate. It occurs to me that I ought not to be here with this girl.

"Ready?" I ask.

She breathes deeply, exhales, and nods to me. "Yes, ready." We set off down the road.

Susan breaks the silence first. "I always come in following the river from town," she says. "I've never come this way before."

"I haven't been up here for a long time," I tell her, "not till just a while ago."

"Oh? Why were you here then?"

I wish I could be honest with the kid about what I know and how I know it, but I can't, even though I feel far more attached to her than to her wretched mother. I loathe duplicity. "You tell a lie," my father used to say, "and right away it takes on a life of its own; where that lie will travel, and what mischief it will work, you have no idea at the time of the telling."

"Oh, I dunno," I say, thinking fast. "Something had got me remembering stuff from when I was young." Not entirely a lie.

"So you used to come here?" It's fascinating how Susan has opened up, how animated she's now become. As though the place itself has the power to work a change in her, like how she changes on stage at rehearsal.

"Oh, sure," I tell her. "For about a year, my senior year—same age as you—I hung out up here a lot."

"What for? What was going on?"

"Ah, good question. What was going on? There was a bunch of young people, older than I was, for sure, but still young, living up here."

"Were they hippies or draft dodgers?"

"Not really. They were more like religious seekers than anything."

"Like crystals and tarot cards and all that?"

A hint of scorn is in her question. "No, a lot more serious than that. For one thing, their leader, Gabriel, was a very charismatic character."

"Gabriel?" she says, stopping abruptly. "You mean that's the guy I've seen here?"

I turn around to her standing in the middle of the dusty road. "Yes, Gabriel exists alright," I tell her. "Brother Gabriel he called himself back then. He looked and dressed and talked just like the person you're describing. Except that was fifteen years ago, so it doesn't make sense it's the same person."

"Freaky," she says, staring off to where the river glints through trees down below us. Equally freaky is how much this girl reminds me of myself at that age. Absolutely no similarity exists between our life stories, and yet I feel a peculiar kinship with her. She's a bit of a pilgrim, as I guess I was too. Oddly she reminds me of Angela fifteen years ago.

"Yes it is," I agree. "Which is why I wanted to come here with you, to get to the bottom of this."

"Did you see him?" she asks me as we resume walking. With each step we take along the roadway, a tiny puff of dust kicks up and is swept away by the wind.

"Gabriel?"

"Yes, did you see him here?"

"No, I didn't. I didn't see anyone and I didn't see any sign of anyone being around either—no campfire or tent or flattened grass. Nothing."

"You do believe me don't you?" It's obviously important to her that I do.

"Yes, of course, but it's strange that there's no sign of anyone being about." I watch her closely, alert for any clue that she may be fabricating the whole story, an ingenious scheme for attention-getting.

We walk for a while in silence. She seems to be puzzling something through. As we draw near a copse of trees, a pair of ravens lift off from an old snag and flap away croaking what sounds like morbid prophecies. We come into the old Clagg homestead. The girl is staring intently at everything.

"Is this where you usually come?" I ask her.

"No. I've never been in this part before. They lived here, did they?"

"Who? Gabriel and the rest?"

"Yes."

"No. They lived in tipis down by the river. This was the original old homestead from long ago."

"It's beautiful," she says, looking around.

She's right, it is beautiful; nature reclaiming her possessions after the transitory passage of humans. The old house and barn, sagging against the elements, sinking back to earth, seem full of stories that no longer have a voice to tell them. Lovely and sad in their collapse.

"Show me where you go, Angela," I say, "where you see him." I catch myself. "Oh, I mean Susan. Sorry." A slip of the tongue.

"Who's Angela?" she asks me, not moving, still studying the sagging shacks.

"She was one of the commune members here."

"Oh."

We stand there silently a while longer. No question the place still has its old magic, its power to make you forget the world outside, to grow silent and in the silence ponder what's beyond knowing. Maybe it was this place itself that so impressed my adolescent imagination back then, not Gabriel. He just happened to be there with his polished insights. A small bird, perched on the tip of a shrub, is wiping its bill on the branch and fluttering its tail feathers repeatedly while emitting a peculiar squeak. Another bird, deeper in the copse, answers it with an echoing cry. I can't hear anything else, just the plaintive antiphony of two songbirds and the perpetual whispering of leaves.

"Let's go, Susan," I prompt her at last. She seems reluctant, now that we've gotten this close, to go any farther. "Susan?"

"Hmm?"

"Do you want to show me where you see him?"

"I want to show you something else," she says, distracted, as though listening for something in the distance. Or maybe she's just listening to the courting birds.

She leads me toward the river, then along it. The river swirls and gurgles off to our right. I can't help but remember walking this same path with Angela. Watching the girl in front of me, her strong young legs, the casual beauty of her swaying hips and buttocks, her shoulders and arms bare to the sun, the toss of long black hair—oh, yes, Angela who took my hand and led me into an enchanted forest from which I've never found my way entirely out.

"Over this way," Susan says, pointing to the left. She leaves the river path and strikes off through the grass. I follow her. We skirt around a few islands of aspen then onto a flat where ancient cottonwoods stand scattered like the wrecked hulls of old sailing ships. The river must have long ago run through this way with the cottonwoods along its banks, then altered its course, leaving its old companions stranded on the gravel flats. Now the trees stand mostly cracked and shattered, lightning-struck, huge trunks with dark and deeply furrowed bark, their tops destroyed. Some have enormous limbs bent to the ground. "These were sacred trees to the Indians," I tell Susan.

"I know," she says. And of course she does; dim memories of them must run in her blood. "The dead were placed in these trees long ago," she says. "The trees would hold their dead up to the sky."

"Yes," I say, "we are in a cathedral of sorts."

"Or a graveyard," she says quietly.

We follow a game trail, the girl leading the way. This dreamlike landscape with its ancient trees of death creates an edgy atmosphere. I could almost be afraid. And what do I expect to find? What am I afraid of finding? Gabriel is here in some mysterious way, and Angela and my past as an intimate of both. It's as though I'm walking blindly into a destiny somehow embedded far behind me. I feel held up to the scrutinizing sky by forces I don't understand.

"I think it's here." The girl's voice intrudes upon my reverie. She's pointing to the biggest of the cottonwoods we've seen so far. I follow her across to the tree. At our approach a small creature dashes from under the tree and away through the grass in a blur of brown fur. We pause for a moment and look at the tree. It's a magnificent specimen with an enormous barrel trunk, maybe thirty feet high, broken off at the top, and huge limbs bent down all around it, some touching the ground, alive, with a fringe of leathery green leaves. The big limbs form a kind of canopy into which the girl steps then turns back to look at me. Something in her slight figure, her troubled face, the angle at which she stands there, small against the dark bulk of the tree, touches me profoundly. Sadness seems to brood in the air, and I realize the girl belongs here, far more than she's ever belonged in my classroom. I feel bizarrely close to tears as I stand looking at her. She seems to embody the pain of dumb, destructive humankind. Somewhere, vaguely, I'm aware of having seen her before, looking just like this, but in a time and place I don't remember.

"Dexter," she calls me by name and reaches a hand out to me. I walk toward her as through the mists of a dream and take her hand. It's cool and dark under the leafy canopy. I'm swimming through murky water, past blurry and disconnected shapes. In the back corners of my brain a voice is calling: Wake up! Wake up! Danger's here. I feel that something is about to go catastrophically wrong.

"Look," she whispers, pointing to a place on the ground where the soil has been recently disturbed.

"What is it?" I can barely get the words out. I'm fighting to get my brain to click into normal, to pull myself out of this tilting dissonance of sensations.

"A skeleton," she says. She is only inches away from me. I can smell her scent, like the scent of the hiding fawn on grass. "See for yourself."

I let go of her hand and stoop down, then kneel in the dirt. The touch of soil on my hands is reassuring and there's a pungent smell of leaf mold. A shiny black beetle, cold and bright as a chip of coal, scrambles away from my hand. My dizziness begins to clear a bit. A slight mound of soil about six feet long is just under one of the tree's huge bowed limbs. Some earth has been excavated at one end of the mound, and in the shallow hole I can see what looks to be grey bone. I reach down and touch it with my fingertips. The bone feels dry and pitted and light, different from a buried stone or tree root. I scrape away some more of the soil; it's loose and easily pulled away by hand. It takes only a few moments to uncover what looks like a human ankle. Trickles of earth keep sliding back into the hole as though to cover up the bones, as though even the soil objects to their exposure. I can hear the girl's warm breathing close behind me.

"It's a body, isn't it?" she asks me. She knows it is.

"Yes, it is." You can feel the power of death in this dark place. I've never touched a dead person before. I touch the bone again and feel nauseous. I'm remembering the grasshopper's final seconds.

Grounded by the touch of death, I'm already clearer, the strange dream state is beginning to lift. We're coming out of mystery. Now we have a problem to solve, decisions to make.

"What should we do?" Susan asks. And she too has returned to herself, a shy and frightened student.

"I don't really know," I say. "We'll have to think very carefully. How did you ever find it hidden away under here like this?"

"He led me to it," she says. "Gabriel. He led me right to it and then he disappeared." She stops for a moment, staring into the little excavation, at the grey bones in the earth. "Do you think it's him?" she asks me. "Do you think it was his spirit leading me to him?"

What can I say? One thing I'm still sure of is that there's danger here, a danger that requires we tread carefully. "I don't know," I tell Susan, "I have no idea. But, you know, I think it's best that we don't mention anything to anyone about this until we find out a bit more. Agreed?"

"Yes, alright," she says. "But shouldn't we dig it up and see if it's a man or a woman?"

"No," I say, "I think we should cover it up and go home and not say a word about it to anyone until we've got more information. Don't tell anyone we've been here, okay?"

"Okay." She looks at me strangely. "Can we stay here a little while, just you and me?"

"I don't think that would be wise." I need to get away from this place.

"I think maybe he's got something else to tell us," she nods toward the grave.

"Like what?"

"I don't know. I just think there's something missing. Something he wants us to know."

"Maybe there is."

We refill the little excavation, like conspirators or grave robbers, and spread a few branches over it. Then we begin the long walk back to the car.

Twelve

Walking with Gabriel through an old city, talking of transformation. Suddenly, a violent explosion erupts behind us, back in the direction of my home. We race around a corner, manic with anxiety, and see a huge plume of oily smoke coiling above the rooftops. I know instantly that my home's on fire. Angela's there, or Deirdre, in danger. We sprint down the street in that direction, then another explosion shatters a big brick building ahead of us. Then a third explosion, closer still, rips another building apart. People are running toward us, screaming wildly.

"Bombs!" Gabriel shouts, "We're being bombed!"

He runs toward a nearby building and crouches behind a low wall in a cobblestone courtyard. Following him, I see the old brick factory looming above us. If it's hit and the rubble collapses, we'll be killed underneath it.

"C'mon!" I scream to Gabriel and take his hand. We dash together across the courtyard and hunker down in a small depression in its centre. Here there's only sky above us; we're safe from collapsing rubble. I close my eyes and cover my head, awaiting the screaming thud of the next bomb.

The dream comes back to me, vivid as the original, as I'm walking the darkened streets of Shallowford. Gabriel again. I have to wonder if it isn't his corpse buried beneath the big cottonwood. How it came to be there, how Susan came to find it, how the pieces of the puzzle fit together. But there's an inner logic to it, an irrefutable "just so" about the patterning. I don't need a sun dancing in the sky for verification.

The evening air is warm and fragrant with the balm of Gilead wafting from cottonwoods. A hush lies over the town, as though it were holding its breath, awaiting a great revelation.

Just this side of the library, where I'm hoping to hook up with Deirdre, a yellow glare pours out of the office of the *Shallowford Times* and spills across the sidewalk in the way that beams of light shine down from heaven in Jehovah's Witness pamphlets. On an impulse I try the front door. It rattles open. The brightly lit room looks as though a tornado just ripped through, sheets scattered like leaves. In the middle of the debris, Ruthie Bleuler sits at her big wooden desk near the back of the room, wreathed in a blue haze of tobacco smoke. She looks up at me through thick spectacles and blinks like a drowsy owl.

"Dexter!" Ruthie exclaims, plucking up a cigarette smouldering in an ashtray at her elbow and dragging on it. Ruthie's got a voice like gravel being scraped by a grader. "Two packs of smokes and a mickey of whisky per day, that's my secret," I've heard her growl, with just a trace of German accent, "I shoulda been a jazz singer." Instead she became a great old lefty in the Woody Guthrie tradition. Union organizing, anti-war marches, women's rights and general hell-raising. I don't know her all that well, but I like old Ruthie; she's a breath of fresh air in this little buttoned-down town.

"Come on in, Dexter, take a load off," Ruthie gestures to a chair beside her desk. "You just out cruising the streets for hookers or what?"

"I see you're busy." I'm still holding the door half open, not knowing why I'm here.

"Nah, just put 'er to bed; I'm in an expansive mood. C'mon over." I close the door behind me. She pulls open a desk drawer and takes out a bottle of sipping whisky. Ruthie's film noir to the bone. "You'll join me, won't you?"

"Sure," I say, sitting down on a swivel office chair facing her desk. Ruthie heaves herself up and rummages around a counter against the wall where the coffee urn sits. She's wearing battered running shoes and an old blue track suit, though I doubt she's ever been on a track in her life. Ruthie's not the running type. She dresses like a one-person assault team against the fashion industry. Her fag's hanging from the corner of her mouth; she squints one eye to keep the smoke out, and the wrinkled skin on her face is tanned an unhealthy yellow from years of smoke exposure. Fetching two coffee mugs, she splashes whisky into each, then passes one over to me—I notice the inside's stained permanent brown—and proposes a toast. "Here's a kick in the balls to Conrad Black!" We clink mugs together mock-solemnly and I take a sip, the whisky going down fiery as molten steel poured at a smelter.

"That's better," Ruthie growls, "Yes, that's a damn sight better."

"Anything exciting in the news?" I ask her.

"You'd have heard about it long ago if there was," Ruthie says, pushing a tangle of brown hair back from her face. And, of course, what she says is true. The *Shallowford Times*, of which Ruthie's publisher, editor, and chief political correspondent, is published twice weekly. On that kind of schedule it can't hope to compete with word-of-mouth in a town this size. Except for the odd freak event that occurs just before press time, the paper traffics in the faded oxymoron of old news. Its function is less reportage than measured reflection. By far its most popular feature is the Letters to the Editor page which provides a forum for the most extravagant expression of ideas, opinions and paranoias from all sectors of the literate, and not-so-literate, citizenry. Ruthie, to her credit, prints it all, unless a particular rant is so blatantly offensive it will outrage everybody, and maybe even then. Ruthie's a great believer in freedom of expression and freedom of the press. "How many newspapers in this damn country," she'll ask you, "aren't owned by a handful of wealthy bastards whose only interest is in making obscene amounts of money and protecting the privileges they and their friends enjoy?"

Nobody knows how Ruthie ended up in Shallowford; she just seemed to drift in at some point years ago, and never drift out. She lives alone in a trailer on the east side of town. I'd guess her age at somewhere between fifty and sixty-five, one of those ageless babes who pretty much sticks to herself and doesn't take shit from anyone.

Ruthie keeps her finger on the pulse of the town, so she just might have an angle on what happened to Gabriel, something that could give a clue about the corpse.

"Say, how's the old man?" she asks without a drop of the dripping sympathy most people now find essential for discussing my father's condition.

"Same," I say, "except..."

"Hell of a thing to see a man's brain go south," Ruthie shakes her head. "Hell of a thing."

"Ruthie, remember Brother Gabriel?"

"Course I do. Who could forget a piece of work like that fella." Her eyes bulge like cat's eye marbles through her glasses. "You used to hang out with him, when you were a kid, didn't you?"

"Yes I did, before I went to the city."

"Uh huh." Ruthie sips her whisky.

"You know whatever happened to him?"

"Oh, yeah. Lots of commotion back then. You missed most of it, I guess."

"All of it. He was here when I left and gone when I came back, and I don't know where."

"No, I don't either." She stubs her cigarette.

"You know why he left?"

"Sort of. Things started going sour for our communards right around the time you left. I guess maybe the crisis began when the cops showed up and grabbed one guy, what the hell was his name, Drago or something like that he called himself, I forget, weasely little guy with a beard full of lice and very bad teeth."

"I remember him. What'd the cops want with him?"

"Draft evasion, I think. The RCMP were running errands for the FBI in those days."

"What else is new."

"Really. Then there was some local kid started hanging out up there, just like you did."

"Jimmy Sjoberg?"

"The very one."

"Yeah, he was hanging around before I left. Nice guy." From one of the ranch families just out of town, Jimmy was a blue-eyed all-Canadian boy who'd fallen under Gabriel's spell the same way I did.

"Past tense. Poor kid started dropping acid or some damn thing and fried his wiring."

"Not at Dancing Grasses. Gabriel wouldn't..."

"I don't think Gabriel knew anything about it. Word on the street was there was a dealer hanging around there those days."

"There was somebody peddling drugs to the local kids and Gabriel didn't twig?"

"Preoccupied with higher things, I guess." Ruthie rolls her owl eyes and takes another swig from her mug. "That's how I'd read it. Anyways, this kid Sjoberg hits the wall. Major meltdown. Totally incoherent. He'd be wandering the town eating out of garbage cans. Sleeping in the thrift shop drop-off box. The whole wacko scene. Eventually the cops grab him and ship him off to a psych ward someplace. I don't believe he ever came back; I never did see him around anymore."

"Then what?"

"Well, as you can imagine, the kid's family was really pissed and a lot of the good town folk were too."

"I guess. And all roads lead to Gabriel."

"You got it."

"Anything happen?"

"Lots of talk. No action. But Gabriel got the message. He and the rest of them got their asses out of town before the posse could get saddled up. End of story."

"And you don't know where he went?"

"No idea. Never heard another peep about him."

"Do you know if he owned Dancing Grasses?"

"Now that I don't know. Could be. Y'know, if you wanted, you could look in some of the old back issues from that time. Could be there's stuff in there I've forgotten."

"Hmm. How much hassle is it to dig out old copies from that time?"

"None at all, so long as you do the digging. They're all back there in boxes. Just don't tell the goddamn fire chief or he'll shut me down for a fire hazard."

We finish off our whiskys and Ruthie leads me to the back of the shop. She walks with a peculiar wobbling gait, her broad beam sloshing from side to side as she walks. The laces are untied on one of her old sneakers and I think she'll trip and hurt herself. She pokes through a door at the back and flourescent lights blink on in a windowless room. The cinder-block walls are lined with dozens of big cardboard boxes stacked on metal shelves, like corpses in a morgue, with magic marker dates scribbled on the front of each box. "What a system, eh?" Ruthie snorts. "Thank Christ it was only a weekly back then. It should all be on microfiche or one of those goddamned things, but who's got the time or money? So help yourself. Just be sure to put 'em back in the right boxes, and don't stay in here too long. You're apt to catch diphtheria or something sitting in this hole."

She leaves me to the stacks. I find and rummage through a box labelled 1971, July–December. Amazingly, the papers are in more or less chronological order. I'm looking for the last three months of '71 and the early months of '72. I start finding occasional references to Dancing Grasses. Several letters in the Letters to the Editor page, a couple of editorials, a scattering of news stories. None of them tells me anything I don't already know. Every so often there's a picture of my father, sometimes both my parents, accompanying a visiting dignitary—there's one where he's greeting Pierre Elliot Trudeau—my father looking masterful, in control of the situation, Mother radiant with patrician loveliness. How young they still looked so short a time ago. Ruthie's right, this mortuary chamber is creepy, but something stirs inside me from going over these old papers, the pictures and stories of how it was here fifteen years ago when the world was still whole, at least in my imagination. How it was in the town of my childhood in the year I finally left for somewhere else.

When I return to the front office, Ruthie's slumped across her desk, her head on her folded arms. She's fallen asleep. A cigarette's still smouldering in the ashtray at her elbow. I reach to put it out and just then Ruthie lifts her head. Her face is grotesquely distorted, her eyes bloodshot and wild and wet from crying. I've never seen her look so upset before.

"Ruthie, what is it? What's wrong?"

She shakes her head and turns her face from me. "Not now, Dexter," she croaks, her words wrenched with pain. "Not now, please."

Stepping outside into the Jehovah's-Witness light, I spot Deirdre down the block and hasten to catch up with her. We walk hand in hand down the darkened street. The scent of cottonwood swoons through the evening air. I can't stop wondering about Ruthie's unaccustomed tears.

"Let's sit for a bit," Deirdre says, pointing to the Kiwanis park bench along the river.

"So what's going on with you?" Deirdre asks after a while. "Is it just about your father or is there something else?"

I tell her about Ruthie, but even in the telling I'm conscious of how selective I'm being. I can't not tell her about the corpse. But what to say? There are definitely subtexts involved that Deirdre's better off not knowing. I give her a carefully edited version of the whole little melodrama. Put into words it sounds absurd, the product of a mind unhinged from overexposure to Stephen King stories. As I'm telling it, feeling a bit of a fool, I wonder again if I'm not being drawn into some sick and elaborate hoax. That the grave and corpse aren't real; that the kid got her hands on some old bones and tricked me into seeing a human foot. Susan's shown in rehearsal what a compelling actor she can be. Maybe the entire expedition was an act calculated to knock me off balance: her silence in the car, the provocative stretching of her thighs as she straddled the gate, the arousing way she walked in front of me along the river path. But why? And why her silence all the way home? Deirdre sits quietly across from me, watching, her face betraying nothing. Even though I'm hedging my bets here, she's still the one person in the world whom I trust implicitly, that I can count on, no matter what. Notwithstanding our troubled past and the dreary détente we've adopted for dealing with it, we fit together in an oddball way. There's never been a sharp breaking moment between us, some definable fork in the marital road that's bound to lead to muddy dissolution. We've never been rocked by one or the other of us becoming infatuated with someone else, no sneaking around. Although, it's true that residue from Angela was a problem from the outset. I couldn't seem to get that bloody woman out of my system, and Deirdre knew it, in the unfathomable way women know such things. Long after Angela had walked out of my life, she'd suddenly reappear—perhaps sitting at an outdoor café as I drove by, barely catching a glimpse of her, or walking toward me from far along a beach. I swear sometimes I could hear her husky laughter in the noise of a crowded party. Even as Deirdre and I were saying to each other that we wanted to live the rest of our lives together, somewhere in a back alley of my mind Angela was lingering, a knowing smile all over her face. The night before our wedding, rather than roistering at a stag party like Pan with a thickening dick, I lay awake for hours agonizing over whether I was making a colossal mistake in marrying Deirdre.

Not long after we'd lost our third baby, the dream children haunting began. I naturally thought that the three of them were our three lost babies. In my dreams the children never danced or sang or ran about. They just stared at me with a deep and patient sadness. Often I'd wake in the night, just as they'd left me, and feel their sadness draped across my consciousness. I'd lie awake for the rest of the night staring into the darkness and numbed by the pain of losing them, a grief that wafted into regret over losing my father's affection and the light that illuminated my childhood and youth but now no longer shone at all.

I never told Deirdre about these dreams, I don't know why, maybe to avoid upsetting her. Perhaps she had similar dreams and never told me. Whole chunks of our existence we no longer discussed, because we wanted to spare one another the pain; they floated past us, unremarked, and inexorable as icebergs.

We drifted like that in the city for several years, purposeless, vaguely hoping to become whole again. We took a couple of stabs at therapy, but that didn't help. Every once in a while we'd have tentative and awkward sex, but never really making love. A miscarriage of love if anything.

Until one day Mother called saying she needed us. Dad had lost control and she could no longer cope with him on her own. It was a measure of how adrift Deirdre and I were in the world that we could readily uproot ourselves at the end of the school year and move back home. Thus, reluctantly and against my better judgment, we came home to Shallowford with our dreams in tatters. I returned a different person from the cocky eager dreamer I'd left as, years before.

I've come to accept that Deirdre and I are bound together, probably forever, in large part through our shared loss. An overarching sense of postponement is in our being together now, as though we have permanently put off whatever it is we should be doing with our lives. Sometimes I think this is how it'll always be with us, that we'll just grow old, holding onto illusions we can hardly remember anymore, indifferent to their genesis, wishing things were different but powerless to make them so.

After listening attentively to my farcical saga of corpse and ghost—Deirdre's a rare and wonderful listener—she considers for a moment before saying anything. "Do you think it was wise going up there with that girl?" she asks.

"Why not? Her mother asked me to, after all."

"Yes, I know, you told me that. But I'm not sure—from what you've said about her, how stable that girl is—or the mother either for that matter. You need to be more careful, Dexter."

"Maybe so. I wish to hell I hadn't gotten involved with them in the first place. What do you think we should do?" Deirdre's expression lets me know, without her saying a word, that she has marked the shift from this being my private adventure to our joint problem.

"Well, it's obvious, isn't it, that you have to report it to the police."

"But what if it's a lark, if there isn't a body at all, I'll look like a complete idiot dragging the cops all the way out there because of a kid's practical joke."

"Well, first you'd better make up your mind: is there a corpse or not?"

"Yes, I believe there is."

"Well then, you should inform the police."

"We could just ignore the whole thing. Pretend it never happened."

"Not with the mother and daughter in on it. Neither one of them seems the least bit reliable, and the mother sounds plain devious. You can't pretend what happened didn't and expect it to just go away. If you're not careful the whole thing could blow up in your face and cause some real damage." Deirdre's being no-nonsense.

"True enough. But how's it going to look when it comes out that I was wandering around up there with a teenage girl? Yes, I can see the headlines now: Psychic Girl and Teacher Discover Mystery Corpse Under Remote Tree. Terrific."

"You should have thought that through before you went." There's a sharpness in Deirdre's tone, a disapproving sourness. "It's going to look like exactly what it is: rather dumb and highly questionable. But you can't pretend it didn't happen. If the girl or her mother say something, and you hadn't reported it, you'd be in an impossible position."

"I suppose you're right."

"Dex, I can't believe you're even thinking about whether or not to report it. Of course you must. There may be a crime involved here; it could be a case of murder for all we know. There's no conceivable reason not to report it, other than the embarrassment around why you were there with that girl."

"Okay, okay, I'll go see the cops on Monday." I'm feeling pushed by Deirdre and I don't like being pushed.

"Is there anything else you'd like to tell me?" Her question has a brittle edge.

"Like what?" The least adequate of answers.

"Like explaining to me why you were there with that girl."

"I've already told you…"

"Like why you didn't mention it beforehand, just snuck off while I was conveniently out of the way."

"I did not sneak off! And I don't like these kind of insinuations."

"I'm sure you don't," Deirdre doesn't back away an inch. "Any more than I like having a husband who doesn't trust me enough to disclose what he's up to."

"Don't talk to me about trust." Hurt and resentment are welling up inside me. "At least I don't have suspicions about you every time you're out of sight."

"I don't do anything to warrant suspicion, Dexter, like you've done with this dumb stunt. What were you possibly thinking, trotting around that place like some moonstruck teenager?" Deirdre's pointed at me like an anti-ballistic missile. When she gets this way there's no sense in discussing things further. She won't back off whatever it is, no matter what.

Okay, I fucked up. Sure she's got a right to be mad. But I've got more than enough shit going on already without having to deal with her attitude on top of it all. This is not a new sensation for me, nor a new situation for us. But whenever one of these occasional conflicts arises, we tend not to resolve them so much as eventually abandon them. I end up simply excluding Deirdre, blaming myself as much as her, repeating to myself that her abrasiveness forces me to exclude her, to find my way alone. Which is what I start doing now, unplugging from our conversation and mulling over in private whether I should talk to Susan or her mother before I do anything else. What a cock-up; and it's my own damned fault for getting mixed up in it.

The river glides past us in the dark, the secrets of its movements pitched too low for human hearing. "Let's go home," I say to Deirdre at last and we walk in silence through the ghostly pools of light cast by the street lamps overhead.

THIRTEEN

I step out of the comatose school at lunch hour, relieved not to be stuck in the staff room with Danielson, Louise and the rest of them. Mondays are often the worst. Pots of acidic coffee are drunk, the weekend's hockey and football scores analyzed, trays of sugary donuts consumed and a terrible ennui settles like volcanic ash on the grizzled heads of the teaching staff.

By contrast, it's a short and pleasant walk from school to the police station. Most of the old institutional buildings in town—the post office, courthouse and high school—were constructed at around the same time, just before the Great War when this area boomed with optimism and cattle. Built of red brick, done in a hybrid Second-Empire style with mansard roofs and dormer windows, they are still used for their original purposes. Together the grand old structures impart a nostalgic symmetry and unity to the town, an atmosphere of good order. Striding along under a canopy of elms, I prepare myself for the impending encounter with the police.

The air inside the station is cool and quiet. My Rockports squeak against polished hardwood floors. The ceiling's at least twelve feet high, the walls shortened by old wooden wainscotting, and the room has a sense of resonant emptiness. A young constable looks up from behind the front desk. Not someone I recognize. The RCMP supplies officers to the town, and regularly rotates them through to other postings around the country before a cop has time to gather much moss.

"Can I help you?" the officer asks in a tone of impeccable neutrality. He's younger than me, fresh and clean cut, and I'm startled, as I've been before, to encounter a cop who looks like a kid.

"I'd like to speak to whomever's in charge," I say, "on a very important matter." My voice echoes in the room, bouncing off the wainscotted walls.

"The officer in charge is Inspector Reisler. I'm not sure if he's available. May I tell him what this concerns?" The guy talks like a recorded message.

"You may. It concerns the discovery of a dead person under what might be considered suspicious circumstances." I'm sounding very in control of the situation. Plus I know Reisler slightly, and that's sure to help.

"I see," the officer scrapes back his chair and rises. "I'll check with the O.I.C. and be back with you in a moment." He first taps on, then disappears through, an office door with frosted glass.

It's not surprising that the station's quieter than a morgue: maintaining law and order in Shallowford's a pretty perfunctory matter. Traffic violations, a smattering of domestic disputes, an occasional case of cattle rustling and a few chronic drunk and disorderlies are the standard bill of fare. Lately drugs have become an issue and the B and Es that trail behind like diseased dogs. But the cops have it pretty cushy here. I'm sure my mysterious corpse will hop to the top of the agenda pretty fast.

Sure enough, within a minute or two the young cop emerges with his boss. "Good afternoon," the senior officer says in a sledgehammer voice, "I'm Kurt Reisler. Now, we've met before, if I'm not mistaken. Mr. Cooke, isn't it?" This one's polished, the spit-and-shine image of the upright Mountie.

"That's correct. I teach at the high school and you've visited several times. And I believe you've been kind enough to escort my father home a time or two."

"Ah, yes." The cop's tone and his intense grey eyes betray nothing. Do they teach them this at the academy, I wonder. This capacity to absorb data as dispassionately as a mollusc filtering sea water. "Do come in please."

He and I go into his office and he closes the door behind us. He gestures me to a chair and sits in his own behind a big mahogany desk that's impeccably neat. He's a heavy-set guy, fiftysomething I'd guess, bullet head and marine-style haircut, bull neck of a linebacker, with a look of athletic bulk reluctantly curdling to fat.

"Now tell me, Mr. Cooke...er, excuse me: what's the first name?"

"Dexter." He writes it on a pad.

"And your address?" I give him my particulars. "Very good. So you've discovered a corpse, is that correct?"

"I believe so. A skeleton, actually. It's buried and I didn't see it all, but enough to convince me that it was the remains of a human."

"Hmm. Interesting." He writes something more on the pad. "Where was this discovery made?"

"On the conservancy lands west of town."

"The place they call Dancing Grasses?"

"Correct."

"Can you describe approximately where on the property?"

"I'd probably have to show you. It's well upriver from the old homestead, under a tree on some cottonwood flats."

"I see." Again he scribbles on his pad. "When did you make this discovery?"

"Saturday afternoon."

"Just you?"

I hesitate only momentarily before answering but I see he instantly picks up on my hesitation. "No, I had one of my students with me."

"I see. And the student's name?"

Again I hesitate for a split second and again I see him register it. This bloody cop's good.

"Her name is Susan Slater. She's one of my grade twelve students."

"Susan Slater." He speaks the name out purposively as he's writing it down. "And where can we find her?" I give him the Slater address. "You were on school-related business were you?"

This is beginning to feel like an interrogation, but I'm able to answer calmly. "Of a sort; the girl had been having some personal difficulties and her mother had asked me to help her out." No sooner have I said this than I regret it. Not only am I breaking my pact with Susan to say nothing for the moment, I'm also disclosing her mother's involvement.

"I see," the cop scribbles some more. But just what does he see? There's more subtlety to this beefy inspector than you'd expect. A bit of caution's called for here. There's no way, for example, I'm going to say anything to him about Susan's visions or my relationship with Gabriel long ago. I've given them the bones, that's enough. Let them find out for themselves whatever else they need.

"How do you proceed in a case like this?" I ask him, shifting the spotlight away from what I was doing and refocusing on the body.

"Well, standard policy when a body is discovered and we don't know the cause of death is to treat it as a homicide."

"A homicide?"

"Correct. We'll consider this a murder scene and proceed with our investigation on that basis."

"Do you guys exhume the body? Or who does it?"

"First off, before we do anything, we put a team in place. We'll get the local coroner in and we'll bring up the bugs and weeds people from Vancouver."

"Bugs and weeds people?"

"Yeah, experts who specialize in insects and plant life. Amazing really, what they can tell us in a situation like this, about how long a body's been in the ground. Fascinating stuff."

"So we should know fairly quickly how long a time the body's been there?" My questions are casually put, so as not to betray that I've got an angle on the discovery that I'm not disclosing.

"Oh, I should think so. Depending on their workload, of course. But if there's any evidence of foul play, we can have the testing prioritized and get it done in two or three weeks thereabouts."

"Great."

"Well, we'd like to get on this right away, of course." He puts his pencil down and leans back in his swivel chair, surveying me. "What's the earliest you could show us the site?"

I don't especially want to go up there with the cops without telling Susan first. "I've got a rehearsal after class today that I'd rather not miss," I tell him.

"Today's not good for me either. Plus I'd like to contact the coroner and our forensic people in the city. And I should notify the landowners. Could you arrange to be free tomorrow afternoon?"

"Yes, I think so; that should be fine."

"Good. Let's say tomorrow at one, then. Suppose I pick you up at the school. Will that suit?"

"Yes, that'll work alright. I'll see you then." This is terribly convivial, fellow professionals pooling resources to resolve a problem. But, leaving the police station and walking back to school, I feel no relief at having made the disclosure. Quite the reverse. I can't escape a sensation of foreboding. I feel as in a dream sequence where the will is powerless and one is hurtled forward through a kaleidoscope of events out of my control. Toward what I don't know. An animal instinct, a tingling at the base of my skull, tells me I'm being followed. I turn quickly around and catch the back side of shadows disappearing into doorways.

The sensation ratchets up a notch back at school when I realize that Susan's absent. Where the hell has she gotten to now? I don't even ask if anyone knows where she is. We get on with attempting to discuss William Blake's "The Tyger," but I'm floundering in deep waters and the kids are mystified. When I was these kids' age I'd been enthralled by the mythic world of Blake's interior visions. I'd read and reread his poems and studied his paintings for hours.

Like so much in those days, Blake's was a new world that Gabriel had revealed to me. "Wouldst thou love one who never died / For thee, or ever die for one who had not died for thee?" Gabriel would look right at me, asking questions like that from "Jerusalem" as casually as though he were talking about the weather. I remember one time I'd said something sophomorically contemptuous about my classmates. Gabriel smiled in reply and quoted Blake: "'Every kindness to another is a little death / In the Divine Image, nor can Man exist but by brotherhood.'" That's what was exhilarating about being around Gabriel; I was constantly being gently guided toward a higher, better plane. He engaged the best part of who I was. But remembering the depressing account Mother's told me about Angela and him, I feel something pinch my heart.

"Is he talking about a real tiger, sir?" Paul Koslowski asks, and I have no idea what to say to him.

After classes, our theatre group assembles in the gym. Little Marni Walsh, who's been understudying all the female roles, takes Susan's place. Marni's as skinny as a stick and unabashedly bucktoothed, but she's got a memory most computers would lust for. She's an absolute whiz at any course requiring rote memorization but a klutz at original thought. She can memorize Shakespeare by the page, but ask her what any of it means and she wilts like last week's lilacs. The whole cast could come down with ptomaine poisoning and Marni'd be able to do the entire show by herself. Unfortunately—and this is a considerable drawback—she can't act to save her life. She stands immobile on the stage, stiff and wooden as a two-by-four, and the lines pop out of her, letter perfect but emotionless. For a perverse moment, I consider recasting the whole production into an absurdist romp with Marni as the star.

Suddenly Danielson's head protrudes through the gym door and croaks at me: "Mr. Cooke! May I have a word when you've got a moment?" This is Danielson code for "Get your ass over here pronto!" We're near the end of rehearsal, so I dismiss the cast and follow Danielson back to his office. I can tell from the way he's walking—he's slightly ahead of me, his head bent forward as though facing into a bitter wind—that this is going to be ugly. He's hardly got the door to his office closed behind me before he asks, "Now, Mr. Cooke, what's all this about the police?"

I'm not quite sure what he means, and tell him so.

"A police officer just called here a few moments ago. Wanted to know if you'd arrange for the Slater girl to come along with you tomorrow. This is an assignation about which I know nothing. Would you be so kind as to tell me what's going on?" Danielson's in a real state. The whites of his eyes are cross-hatched with infinitesimally fine red lines, like miniature road maps etched in blood.

"I've been intending to have a word with you today," I explain to him coolly, "but between one thing and another, I haven't had an opportunity."

"Just as you haven't had an opportunity to provide me with a copy of your play, as you'd promised to do."

Oh, hell, I'd forgotten all about that. "Yes, I..."

"I know," Danielson cuts me short, "between one thing and another. You seem to be a very busy fellow between one thing and another."

"I've got a lot on the go right now."

"That I don't doubt for a moment." Danielson sprinkles his sarcasm like vinegar. "But I can't have my teachers and students involved in police matters without knowing anything about it."

"You're absolutely right." I decide to placate him. "I've today reported to the police the existence of a body buried up on the conservancy lands. I discovered it with Susan. I'm taking the police up there tomorrow afternoon, if we can get a substitute in. I guess they want Susan to come along too, but unfortunately she's not at school today." Danielson is not pleased.

"A body?" he says, as though he hopes he's misheard.

"The remains of a body," I clarify. "A skeleton."

"Human?"

"I believe so." As though we'd be going through all this for a dead racoon.

"And the Slater girl was with you?"

"Correct."

"Anyone else?"

"No, just the two of us." After rehearsing the scene with the cops, it's easier now. I answer his questions deadpan, like Marni Walsh delivering her lines.

"A bit irregular, isn't it?"

"What, finding a corpse? Yes, I'd say so." I couldn't resist it.

"Don't try my patience, Mr. Cooke." Anger flashes across Danielson's response and this too I'm accustomed to. "Why possibly were you prowling around up on that property with one of your students?"

"I wasn't prowling around, as you put it. I was counselling her, the good and simple reason being because her mother requested that I do so." That's three times I've fallen back on this as the only legitimate reason I have for being in that situation. I'm remembering cowardly Peter and the cock crowing three times. I'm going to have to square it with Susan before she hears it from anyone else. And with Ann too. Jesus.

"Her mother asked you to go wandering around up there with the girl, looking for corpses?" There's Danielson again, lacing his irony with contempt.

"Susan's been experiencing some personal difficulties," I answer him, cool and resolute as a glaciologist. "Her mother specifically requested that I accompany Susan up to Dancing Grasses to see if I could help her with her problems."

"But why there? Why not talk to her here?"

"The nature of the problems demanded that we go up there. I'm sorry, but there is an issue of confidentiality here and I'm constrained against disclosing more than I've already told you." This is the sort of pompous blustering Danielson relates to.

"Yes, yes, alright, I understand," he gives ground grudgingly. "But we can't afford any whiff of scandal. Do I make myself clear, Mr. Cooke?"

"Of course."

"We have an aroused public on our hands these days, as I'm sure you know. They'll tolerate nothing untoward, especially from members of our profession. Position of trust, you understand. Nothing unseemly—nothing, however innocent, that might give the appearance of unseemliness—is tolerable. Is that understood?"

"Completely." But I'm hardly feeling the sang-froid I'm projecting to pacify Danielson. Not at all. Fearful symmetry isn't the half of it.

"And you won't forget the play copy will you, between one thing and another?"

I smile weakly at Danielson's triumph.

The Sunrise Trailer Court squats on a godforsaken lot on the east side of town and on the other side of nowhere. Up front there's a battered old Silver Arrow trailer dented like a tin can that kids have kicked down the street. A cardboard sign saying "Office" hangs askew on the door and a tiny dog yaps maniacally at one of the trailer's windows. Two forlorn lilac bushes cling to life in the dust out front. In back, about a dozen derelict-looking trailers are lined up in opposite rows, knotted together by a web of sagging hydro lines. Almost every trailer has a huge satellite dish alongside, staring up into the heavens like one-eyed Titans awaiting another order of forged thunderbolts from Zeus. I can smell frying sausages and taste dust on the dry air.

I spot Ruthie Bleuler emerging from one of the trailers. "Hi Ruthie!" I call to her as the little dog's yapping escalates to near hysteria.

"Howdy, Dexter," Ruthie says, tottering over to me on a pair of absurd red high heels. She's got her trademark cigo in the corner of her mouth, but she's dressed up, at least by Ruthie's standards, in an outfit straight off the racks at the hospital auxiliary thrift shop. Lots of black splashed with hideous yellow triangles. I think she's even permed her hair, which happens about as often as a total eclipse of the sun. "Out slummin'?" she asks me.

"Visiting the Slaters," I tell her, "though if I'd known you were getting all dollied up, I'd have come see you instead."

"Can the corn, Dexter," Ruthie's impervious to flattery. "You find what you were lookin' for yet?"

"Not really."

"Well, we'll have to phone the pope if you find it here, 'cause it'll be a bloody miracle. About the only thing anyone finds in this dump is despair. Say, I didn't know you did house calls."

"A bit of business came up that needs to be dealt with right away."

"I'll bet it has," Ruthie snorts. Then she leans toward me confidingly. She's drenched in powerful perfume. "Say, Dexter, do yourself a favour, will you? Be real, real careful with that one in there." She angles her head in the direction of the Slater trailer.

"Who, Susan?"

"Nah, fer Chrissakes, the girl's off in la-la land. No, watch the mother. And don't turn your back, not while she's in the vicinity." Ruthie sounds like she's been watching too many spy movies by satellite, but still her warning's got a sharp ring to it.

"Why do you say that? What's going on?"

"I wish I knew," Ruthie says, hitching up her pantyhose by pinching it through her dress. "Now, Dexter, about the other night..." She looks uncomfortable, stares away across the trailer court, then back to me.

"Yes, I felt weird leaving you there so upset, but I thought you wanted to be on your own." It's hard to even imagine Ruthie near tears as she was that evening.

"Thought it was the Jack Daniels turnin' me to mush, didya?"

"Well..."

"I'll tell you what it was, and this is something I don't tell very many people and I'd appreciate your not tellin' anyone either."

"Of course." Distracted as I am by my impending visit with Ann, I'm intrigued by what made Ruthie behave so out of character.

"I'll tell you what happened. While you were rummaging around in the stacks, I happened to glance at the *Globe and Mail.* They had a story in there about Josef Mengele—you know who he was?"

"Only that he was a prominent Nazi during the war. And that they just found his body down in South America someplace."

"That's him. That's the one. Mass murderer and sadistic butcher bar none. The Angel of Death they called him." Ruthie's completely abandoned her customary Borscht-Belt schtick.

"He disappeared at the end of the war, didn't he, and was never traced?"

"Hiding out down there with his old SS buddies I guess. Been dead a few years apparently, though nobody knew. Or at least nobody said. Well I'm glad he's dead, the murderous son-of-a-bitch, but I wish he'd died ugly and hard, the way all them women and kids did that he butchered." There's a tough relentlessness in Ruthie's tone.

"You mean he was worse than the rest of them?"

"That was a time and place," Ruthie says, "when the sadistic bastards got to run the whole show. They're always around. Hell, half the countries in the world are run by the same kind of tyrants. Any population's got 'em; we got our allotted share right here in Shallowford, you dig deep enough. Sociopaths, psychopaths, call 'em whatever you want, they're always around. But usually they're hidden away and only their wives and kids get to see how sick they are. But back then they got to run a whole country, and Mengele was maybe the sickest of the pack. He'd stand at the ramp in Auschwitz when a train load of Jews or Gypsies came in and he'd look them all over as they filed past. Aristocratic son-of-a-bitch, all spit and polish right down to his white gloves. He carried a riding crop and if he flicked it to the right, it meant you got to live for a while, but if he flicked it left, you were off to the gas chambers right away. And maybe they were the lucky ones."

"What do you mean?" I don't think I've ever seen Ruthie so wound up about anything. Usually she laughs stuff off in her cynical way, but she's not laughing right now.

"Mengele fancied himself a geneticist. He was at the camp to do research, in between having people slaughtered. He got into this thing about twins. Wanted to try to isolate what genetic pattern caused twins to have identical features. He figured if he could find that clue, how the features were inherited, he'd have the key to genetically engineering for racial purity. His so-called research wasn't worth shit, but the things he did to people, kids especially, would make you vomit. He'd strap 'em onto a slab of marble, then cut into their eyes or their spines, no anaesthesia, no nothing." Ruthie's staring at me hard, bug-eyed behind her thick lenses. Her whole body is shaking. The horrors of the camps seem a universe away from this derelict trailer park. But Ruthie's there, not here. I realize in a flash that she must have had family there, perhaps even been there herself.

"Ruthie," I reach out to her, but just then a cab pulls up at the curb. Ruthie looks disoriented for a moment, but then flicks the butt of her cigarette into the dust and grinds it under the toe of one of her red shoes. "Gotta run, Dexter."

"Ruthie…"

"Don't waste your sympathy on me, Dexter, I got out of there, unlike most. I'm meeting up with my old pals the Albrecht sisters over in Centralia. We're gonna drink a lot of vodka and dance on that bastard Mengele's grave tonight." But her bravado sounds empty, betrayed by a sadness in her eyes. She wobbles to the cab, leaving me in the dervish dust.

Turning, for a split second I catch a glimpse of Ann Slater watching me through the front window of her trailer before she disappears behind the drapes. I head in that direction and she meets me at the door. A smell of boiled cabbage wafts out around her. "Hello, Dexter," she says coolly, "come on in." She seems not at all surprised to see me, though I've never visited here before. The trailer's dark and musty and cluttered with cheap knick-knacks. The carpet's a sickly beige high shag, the furniture's in Naugahyde. A pile of recently washed dishes is drying in a perilous stack beside the sink. Milton Gorman should have tested out his trendy fascination with Skid Road in a place like this.

Ann motions me to the little Formica table in the kitchen. It holds a bouquet of red plastic roses in a wide-mouth Mason jar that's half full of water. The water takes the plastic roses from tacky to pathetic. I sit down at the table and Ann slips into the plastic chair opposite.

"Shall I have the maid fetch some tea?" she asks, smirking.

"Nothing for me, thank you," I can't tell if she's being funny or bitter.

"Very well, let's get down to business, Dexter. What the crap is going on?" Definitely not funny.

"Is Susan here?" I ask her. Incongruously I remember my father advising me on the strategic merit of sometimes answering a question with a question.

"No, she is not. She hasn't been here for two days. She disappeared yesterday morning and I haven't seen her since. What went on up there Saturday? I've never seen her more upset, poor kid." Ann's growing handsomely into her new-found role as concerned parent.

"Well," I answer calmly, "it was just as she'd written in her diary. Without my saying anything about it, she led me to a spot where there's a body buried under a tree."

"Jesus Christ, I was hoping she'd made it all up."

"So, was I. But she didn't. It's as real as you or me."

"So then what happened?"

"We left it undisturbed and came back to town. I reported it to the police this afternoon."

"The police? Without talking to me first?" Her anger rises, sudden and full. "Why'd you do that? I mean, what right do you have to go running to the cops when it's my daughter that's involved, eh?" Ann's glaring stonily through the plastic roses.

"You asked me to help," I reply calmly, dismissing her hostility. "I'm helping. You don't go finding the remains of dead people hidden under trees and not tell the police."

"But you coulda talked to me first, dammit. And Susan. I don't know what's gotten into the kid. Now if the cops show up and find she's run away the shit'll really hit the fan."

This concerns me too, but I keep it to myself. Control is power. "I assure you I would have spoken with her today, had she been at school. She wasn't. Nor was there any message from you as to why she wasn't there." The silly cow quickly pulls in her horns a bit, sensing she may be vulnerable. "It's why I'm here now. You asked for my help, remember. Now where's she gone?"

"Fucked if I know," Ann says, no longer bothering to hide her vulgar underside.

"Did you look in her diary?"

"She's taken the goddamn thing with her. That's a bad sign. Christ, I need a drink; you want something?"

"No thanks."

From under the kitchen sink she takes out a plastic bottle of cheap Alberta rye and splashes a couple of inches into a water glass she's somehow extricated from under the stack of dishes. She gulps the amber liquid like water. "Damned if I don't need a cigarette."

"You quit?"

"Yah, three weeks ago and it's fuckin' near killin' me."

"Good for you," I say by way of soothing troubled waters, knowing that to a smoker in withdrawal nothing is as critical as the loathsome craving. "Listen, Ann, can you think of anywhere Susan's likely to be, someplace she'd go at a time like this?" I'm sure she can't. It's obvious she doesn't know much at all about her daughter. Ann begins moaning again about how the cops and court-appointed psychiatrists are going to come storming in and wreck her life. I wonder what is left to wreck. I really want to get straight with Susan before this thing goes public and gets completely out of hand. I don't want her to think I've pulled a fast one on her. But it's not going to happen today. We leave it that Ann's to call me at home if Susan shows up. By way of a final gratuity I again congratulate Ann for kicking the habit and escape from the wretched trailer.

FOURTEEN

"It's so lovely to have you both here," Mother smiles disarmingly at Deirdre and me as she places her teacup on its saucer. She looks smashing in a teal linen suit and lavender silk kerchief. "Sunday afternoon tea with the family."

I can feel Deirdre beside me, willing herself to smile, to be civil and supportive to Mother, and I appreciate her trying. At this point I appreciate us all, because it's been a hell of a week. Last Tuesday, as arranged, I accompanied Kurt Reisler and one of his constables to Dancing Grasses. We were met at the gate by the coroner from Centralia, a no-nonsense woman named Maynard wearing hiking boots and jeans and a black leather bomber jacket. Reisler had gotten a key to the gate and we all drove together in his cruiser, the two cops up front, Maynard and myself in back, making small talk about the weather and the property. I filled them in on its history, not that they seemed all that interested in prairie sagewort or bluebunch wheatgrass. We drove as far as the old homestead, parked the cruiser and set off on foot toward the river. I led them, as Susan had led me, along the river path and onto the old cottonwood flats. By then Reisler and Maynard were puffing from exertion. I was watching keenly to see if maybe I'd spot Susan in here, this being as likely a place as any, though she wouldn't be seen if she didn't want to be.

We found the big tree without much difficulty. Reisler, Maynard and I crowded into the grotto formed by its limbs and I again felt that strange sensation when I was there the other day with Susan. The place still had a peculiar resonance, though the coroner and cops seemed unaware of it. Working carefully with a small hand tool, Maynard scraped away enough dirt to verify that these were in fact human remains. Using a high-powered flashlight, she and Reisler examined the ankle closely, as Susan and I had done. "No question about it," Maynard said, "we're looking at ankle bones that once upon a time supported a *Homo sapien.*" Moving to the opposite end of the mound, she gingerly exposed enough of the skull to confirm that it was a full corpse. Away went any lingering thoughts I'd had about this all being a trick played by Susan. It was a human skeleton alright. And more. Even with the eye sockets full of soil, now I knew for sure that it was Gabriel. I could see him looking at me with his penetrating gaze, the way he'd do, as though he could see inside my soul. I could almost make out his knowing smile breaking through the dirt over the half-uncovered skull. It was him as sure as Yorick. Seeing him there like that, a lifeless heap of dirty bone, I felt cold and nauseous. I wanted this not to be real.

"Well over two metres tall," Maynard was saying, extending a tape measure. "Almost certainly a male."

"Any sense of how long it's been here?" Reisler asked.

"That's a tough one." Maynard let the tape recoil with a snap. "Sheltered under the tree like this, low moisture, maybe acidic soil—I don't know—it could be that it's a well-preserved skeleton a lot older than you'd expect. But I kind of think not. I'm guessing here, but I'd say not dead long enough to have been an Indian corpse from the old days."

"No," Reisler agreed, "looks like we've got ourselves a homicide to solve. Hey, are you okay?" This addressed to me; I must have looked as pitchy as I was feeling.

"I'm alright," I told him, "it's just I've never seen anyone who's been murdered before."

"Well, it's different alright," Reisler nodded, "different from someone who's died in a bed of disease or old age. And different from a smash-up on the highway too. That's got its own energy, but a murder victim seems to have all sorts of secrets to tell you, none of them pleasant." At that point I knew far more than he did of the secrets buried with this particular corpse, knowing it was Gabriel. But which Gabriel? Mother's "awful man": seducer, betrayer and hypocrite, the architect of our family's downfall? Or the enlightened Gabriel I knew?

Reisler and his constable set about cordoning off the area with yellow tape printed with POLICE LINE: DO NOT CROSS and recording pertinent details.

Watching the cops in a sort of daze, I mused on Gabriel's fate. How did he die and come to be buried here, deliberately hidden? By whom? For what reason? I supposed I should be feeling sad, but I wasn't. I seemed caught in a sort of curious bemusement, dense and impenetrable. Then, from out of nowhere, as I stood aside, half watching the police and coroner go about their rituals, the words of an old Sufi poem came back to me. Gabriel himself had quoted them long ago and I'd been so impressed by it I'd borrowed his book and memorized the passage. Dormant and forgotten all these years, the words returned to me with perfect clarity:

When my bier moves on the day of death,
Think not my heart is in the world.
Do not weep for me and cry "Woe, woe!"
You will fall in the devil's snare: that is woe.
When you see my hearse, cry not "Parted, parted!"
Union and meeting are mine in that hour.
If you commit me to the grave, say not "Farewell, farewell!"
For the grave is a curtain hiding the communion of Paradise.
After beholding descent, consider resurrection;
Why should setting be injurious to the sun and moon?
To you it seems a setting, but 'tis a rising;
Though the vault seems a prison, 'tis the release of the soul.
What seed went down into the earth but it grew?
Why this doubt of yours as regards the seed of man?

Staring at the smudged skull, I wondered. No, I didn't feel like lamenting or crying, nor did I consider resurrection and release of the soul. To me, the shallow grave seemed more a furtive attempt to hide incriminating evidence than a curtain hiding the communion of Paradise. Is it really a rising, this final lying down in the dirt? A seed that surely sprouts? Or just an ingenious heap of carbon from which the spirit has been not released but snuffed out. I remembered my vision of the grasshopper, the moment the spark of life had died in its eye. The hollow sockets in the skull stared back at me, providing no clue as to whether their former occupant was now subsumed into Paradise, illumined in eternal bliss, or simply gone forever. I realized that I wanted Gabriel's spirit to endure, to be alive and thriving, caught like falling leaves in the endless swirling circle of eternal life. I wanted Susan's apparitions to be real, his resurrection to be real. But did I believe it?

"Now tell me this great mystery you're involved with," Mother says, bringing me back to Sunday afternoon tea in her parlour. "Or is it so secret you can't even tell your own mother?"

I'm struck once again by Mother's fantastic capacity to realign whatever's happening around her so as to place herself at the centre of events. I still haven't decided just how much I should tell Mother.

"How's Dad?" Deirdre asks now, ignoring Mother's query about the great mystery.

"Well," Mother sighs and lets her gaze wander across the room and out the parlour window to where a white lilac is in full bloom, "Lavina has certainly helped immensely. She seems to be able to draw something out of him in a way I can't really. He spoke to her a number of times this week, but nothing coherent, at least not so's she'd say."

"Has he spoken to you?" Deirdre asks in a way that leaves me uncertain whether she's being solicitous or hurtful.

"Just a word here and there. He wants to tell me something I'm quite sure. But the words won't come out. I can't imagine how awful it must be for him, how frustrating. It's so brutally painful seeing so brilliant a man reduced to that."

"Mother, we know how difficult it's been for you these last few months," I begin, steering the conversation back to what I must tell her.

"Oh, darling," Mother interrupts, "don't worry about me, I'll be fine. I've had a wonderful life; I can't complain about a smidgeon of suffering now in my twilight years." I notice that the book lying on the coffee table is Willa Cather's *Death Comes for the Archbishop*. And that we're talking about Mother again.

"But there is something we thought it best you should know about before you read it in the paper," I continue. Mother misses nothing in the local news and is never caught short of an opinion on whatever's going on. She pays less and less attention to what's occurring in the rest of the world. But the comings and goings of Shallowford, the accomplishments and humiliations of the families she's known all her life—in these she maintains a keen interest. She has a prodigious capacity for recalling the factual details and subtlest nuances of town life over the years. None of this by way of gossip—Mother never gossips—but more the considered fact-gathering of a social historian. Given Mother's sensibilities, Deirdre and I have agreed that she'd be deeply hurt if others heard about the skeleton before she did, and that we'd best fill her in on developments.

"There have been some odd things happening in the last little while," I tell her.

"No surprise there, darling," she interrupts again, "I've never known this town to shy away from oddity." Deirdre smiles her own wry smile but says nothing, leaving it to me, as we'd agreed beforehand.

"There's been a body discovered at Dancing Grasses," I tell her.

"A body," Mother echoes. Is it my imagination or is there something different in her voice? As she moves her head, glancing sideways, her complexion seems to change, or perhaps it's just the angle of light on her face. "Well, that certainly is news," she says, normal as ever, so that I'm not sure if I imagined her reaction just now. "How do you come to know of it?"

"I found it." I'm conscious of Deirdre silent beside me on the couch. "Well, me and one of my students."

"Did you now," Mother says. "And has it been determined who this person is?"

"Not yet. Not officially."

"What on earth do you mean, not officially?" Mother picks her teacup up again, but puts it down without taking a sip.

"I'm fairly certain who it is."

"Dexter," Deirdre cautions.

"You are? And who would that be?" As far as Mother is concerned, this is a dialogue between herself and me in which Deirdre plays no part.

"I'm quite sure it's Gabriel."

"Oh!" The exclamation pops out as though in shock or surprise, but she quickly recovers. "I thought we'd done with that wretched fellow. Do you mean he's back again to haunt us further?" Mother allows herself a small smile, but now it's less clear what is acting and what isn't.

Haunt may be the right word. I still can't quite believe it myself, that we've found the mortal remains of Gabriel buried all these years in a secret grave. There's been no confirmation of anything yet, and the cops and coroner's office are being secretive about the whole case. I called Reisler on Friday to find out if there'd been any progress. "No, nothing to report yet," he told me. "It's far too soon to expect lab results yet. Plus the thing's complicated because the area's an old Native burial site. We can't exhume the corpse and ship it off to Vancouver as we'd normally do in a case like this."

"Do you have any idea of a timeline?" I asked him.

"I'll certainly let you know when we have something substantive to report," he told me, placing me diplomatically but firmly outside the investigation. Part of me still clings to the hope that the body may prove to be somebody else. Or that it's so old, so long buried, it no longer matters. But that's the will at work, hoping; everything else in me—intellect, instinct, emotion, spirit—knows it's Gabriel. That's obviously why I had that blackout, or whatever it was, the first time I saw the grave with Susan. Call it paranormal, I knew it was Gabriel because in some way he was telling me it was. I felt his presence when I looked into those eye sockets. Then the poem coming back to me, a poem he'd recited to me. No matter what the pathologists end up saying in their report, I know it's Gabriel.

I said so to Deirdre last night, while we were discussing visiting Mother today. "What makes you so certain it's him?" she asked me. She was curled up on the living-room sofa, wrapped in her fuzzy blue housecoat.

"Intuition. Instinct. Something like that. The kind of things you're always telling me to trust."

She pondered for a moment. "Do you think maybe you're projecting a whole lot onto this that isn't really there? I mean if you take away all of Susan's talk about her apparitions, would you have any reason to think it's him? I doubt it. I'd wait to see what the pathologists have to say before I went leaping into conspiracy theories."

"I'm not leaping into any kind of theories," I replied calmly, though I resented her know-it-all tone, "I have a certain history with all of this that you don't have, darling..."

"I'll say you do."

"And that's why I'm certain it's Gabriel," I finished lamely.

"There's been no positive identification of the remains yet," Deirdre tells Mother, no doubt thinking I've already gone too far. But I haven't. I know I haven't.

"Well, I do so hope they aren't identified as the remains of our holy man," Mother says dryly, gathering up teacups. "Would you care for another macaroon, darling? No? That fellow was wearisome enough in life, I can only imagine how tiresome he'd be in death."

We leave it at that. At least Mother's been told.

I stop in to visit Dad for a minute before we leave. His room is almost dark, the drapes having been drawn to keep the afternoon sun from washing out his TV screen. There's an old rerun of *Three's Company* on. Lying in his bed, propped up on a heap of pillows, Dad's staring at Suzanne Somers as though she were the Blessed Virgin appearing in an aura of blue and white light. I sit down on the edge of the bed but he doesn't acknowledge my presence at all. His eyes stare raptly at the screen, its light shining on his gaunt, immobile face, so that he looks like a ghost or a corpse himself. What does he see, I wonder again, what registers in his brain? Does he recognize Suzanne Somers but not me? Love her but not me? The laugh track shrieks.

I sit and watch him for a little while and then, unexpectedly, my father turns toward me. Do I imagine it, or is there a glint of recognition in his eyes? His hand—thinner now, wrinkled with sinews and veins bulging under mottled skin—reaches for the remote, fumbles with it a moment, then finds the mute button. In the suddenly silent room my father speaks to me. "Forgiveness," is the only word I can understand in his garbled sentence. He looks at me pleadingly. Is he offering me forgiveness or seeking it? I don't know what to say to him. I smile and say "Yes, Dad," in a reassuring voice, but he replies with only a single word—"memory" I think—and his eyes close.

It comes to me then, unbidden, unsuspected, in the peculiar intimacy of the room, that what's befallen my father and what became of

Gabriel are entirely connected. Of course! The thought has not occurred to me before, why would it? But now it comes with the impact of revelation. The enmity between the two of them. Gabriel's sudden and unexplained disappearance. My father's inexplicable resentment festering all those years, the disillusionment that seemed to come out of nowhere, his loss of interest in almost everything, then his rapid and premature descent into dementia. My father a murderer. Or somehow complicit in murder. It's inconceivable, obscene. But could it be true?

I tell myself this kind of thinking's crazy. There's no proof the body's Gabriel's. No evidence yet of foul play. Not a wisp of anything real to connect my father or anyone else with this death. And yet the traitorous suspicion of my father possesses a morbid coherence. I replay the few scenes I witnessed of my father and Gabriel together. A time or two when I saw them meet by chance in town, and that afternoon when I first brought Gabriel home. There's no question my father disapproved of Gabriel and of my infatuation with Angela. Mother took a more tactful approach, never losing her composure, never being anything but loving and solicitous toward me. She became mediator between my father and me. Skilled though she was in diplomacy, she might as well have been mediating between bull elk in rut.

It remained inexplicable to me that my father and Gabriel disliked and distrusted one another so intensely, for they were both, in their way, profoundly moral men. At least that was my experience of them. I had no inkling in those days of anything like what Mother's told me about Angela's abortion and Gabriel's role in it. It doesn't fit at all, any more than my father conspiring to do violence. Both notions are preposterous, but neither will release its grip. I wonder if this is how my father began his slide into dementia, with things not quite fitting into place the way they once did, with everything slightly off focus, the needle on your moral compass quivering, unable to settle on a direction.

Somers is down to her underwear now, absurd in the silence without the laugh track's screaming. No wonder Mother reacted as she did when I told her just now about the corpse. She knows. She's known all along. I look at my father lying there asleep, his numbed mind consumed with forgiveness, and once again I wish that we could rewind the tape to before all this started and do everything differently.

Fifteen

"Oh, Dex," Deirdre says, standing behind me, massaging my neck and shoulders as I slump in an easy chair, "I can't bear you're going through all this. You don't need this. Neither of us needs this."

"No kidding." I'm feeling grateful to Deirdre for just being here, but as her fingers press against the knotted ropes in my neck, I'm conscious that I haven't been entirely forthright with her. Nothing new in that, of course. Almost from day one, when the loss of Angela still haunted me, I disclosed only certain things, left out elements she wouldn't want to hear, or wouldn't understand, feathered the edges a bit, had highly selective remembering. But this is what we habitually do to one another, isn't it?—create a comforting pastiche that we know from experience the other person will be inclined to accept. As Mother likes to say, it's "creative managing." I don't believe, for example, that Deirdre has any idea how preoccupied I've been of late with Gabriel and Angela. Of course I've said nothing to her about Mother's version of events—Angela's abortion and Gabriel's role in it—and I'm sure Mother hasn't either. Mentioning such details to Deirdre is like playing with matches at a gas station. Nor does she have the full script around the Slaters. She never saw Ann at eighteen, when half the men in Shallowford would have mortgaged their lives to mount her. I certainly haven't given Deirdre any sharp details about Susan—her uncanny analysis connecting Lamb's dream children with miscarriages and abortions, or her appearing in my dreams, for instance. I've not mentioned how much Susan reminds me of Angela, nor the disturbing sensations I experienced that afternoon with Susan at the grave. I've told Deirdre more than anyone else about what's going on, but certainly not all of it. I think that's why I'm feeling weary now, from the effort of carrying too much weird stuff in my head. I can't love Deirdre any more than I do and yet it seems a furtive and dishonest love, lived among deceptions. This isn't diplomacy; it's fraudulence, brought into sharp focus by events, and I'm finding it bloody exhausting. I'd like to go to sleep somewhere and not wake up for a month.

Behind it all, our childlessness moves like a dark creature through the shadows of the room. After losing our three babies and the hope of ever having another, we tried our best to get on with our life. But every so often we'd stumble into a "maybe we should consider adoption" conversation that brought the pain back into focus, reminding us that some things can't be put behind. That some things are as much a part of us as skin or sinews.

Not long after our third miscarriage, Deirdre and I went to Greece for a holiday. A change of scene was in order, so we booked a flight to Athens and spent two weeks on Corfu. One day we visited the monastery at Paleokastritsa, then hiked up a mountain footpath through terraced olive groves to the little village of Lacones, then on to the ruins of the clifftop castle of Angelokastro. Descending the hillside below the old fort, we encountered a donkey tethered on the trail. It wore a saddle-like contraption for packing firewood or barrels of olives. The wind was warm and fragrant with the scent of herbs. Slender cypress trees towered over the billowing olive groves. Deirdre reached out and touched the donkey's head, tenderly, stroking it while the animal looked at her through enormous liquid eyes. Then Deirdre began to cry, and would not stop, could not stop, crying all the way back down to Paleokastritsa.

The donkey wasn't to blame. The two old ladies from whom we were renting a room in Kekira, the Panos sisters, had asked us on the first day of our stay, in broken English and much gesturing, if we had children back at home. When we told them no, their old creased faces fell and pity welled in their eyes. A tragedy. Each time we encountered them thereafter, they smiled at us with pained smiles of condolence. They knew nothing of our loss and grief—it was our being barren that elicited pity. Seeking to get away from the memories of home, we'd stumbled into a temple dedicated to procreation, the old black-robed Panos sisters its vestal virgins of begetting. No wonder Deirdre wept.

Pity over our childlessness carried on long after those two old crones had hobbled away forever down the narrow alleys of Kekira. "Do you have kids?" The question would come at us suddenly, like an attack dog, at dinner parties, informal gatherings, chance meetings. Then the awkward silence, the not knowing what to say, the groping for a not-too-obvious topic switch. As though we had a disease that shouldn't be mentioned. After a while we felt like wearing a button that said "No, we don't have kids so don't ask." And spare us your sympathy. Please.

But the things I'd say to myself, or not say, are the worst. Standing in an art gallery one time, at a show of Australian painters, I was transfixed before an oil on canvas by Russell Drysdale titled *The rabbiter and his family*. Four cartoonish kids and their outback parents stared at me from the fields of their homestead. The mother held her baby, the swarthy father gently touched his oldest daughter's shoulder; everything about the group of them said, "We don't have much, but we have each other." I don't know how long I stared at the picture before I was interrupted by a gallery attendant asking if I was alright. My face was wet with tears.

Another time getting off a plane at Vancouver airport, I saw a young family just ahead of me. The mother was fashion-model pretty, perfectly groomed and smartly dressed. The father had the carefree swagger of a young buck on top of the world. Their twin daughters, maybe seven or eight years old and miniature copies of their mother, held his hands and chatted with him gaily as we walked the long corridor to the terminal. I trailed after them like an astronaut in zero gravity, connected to a space station by tenuous lines. I envied that father the affection that flowed to him from his daughters. I wanted to be him; I didn't want to be myself anymore.

Just as I'm beginning to float away under the healing touch of Deirdre's hands, the phone rings. Deirdre answers it and calls across the living room to me, "Dexter, it's Ruth Bleuler. She says it's urgent."

"Hello, Ruthie," I say into the phone, sharing a grimace with Deirdre. "What gives?"

"Dexter," Ruthie's voice rasps down the line, "there's something I need to discuss with you right away. You able to come over here for a minute?"

"Sure." Dammit! "You at the office?"

"Yeah, I'd appreciate it, Dexter."

I take the car over, even though it's not far, because I don't have the energy to walk. I find Ruthie exactly as she was last time: alone, sitting behind her cyclone-tossed desk, wearing her blue track suit and smoking a cigarette.

"Dexter," she croaks, "c'mon in and take a chair. Thank you for coming over."

"No problem." I'm remembering my last conversation with Ruthie, at the trailer court. I have a hundred questions I want to ask her.

"Dexter, I'm gonna cut right to the chase here."

"Please."

"I just had Ann Slater in here. Told me a long story about her kid seeing a spiritual being—that's what she called it, 'a spiritual being'—at Dancing Grasses and that the ghost led the kid to that body, the one the cops've got. A'course the bloody cops won't tell me anything about it yet. The case is still under active investigation, blah, blah. She wants to sell me her story, exclusive rights, she says, and if I don't take her up on her offer, she says she'll peddle it to one of the big dailies in Vancouver and make a bundle. I'm bettin' she already tried and they told her to take a hike."

Bloody Ann Slater. Bloody stupid cow. How much has she said, I wonder. "Did she say if the girl's back yet?"

"Oh, yeah, girl and diary both apparently. She told me all about the diary. That's what's she offering to sell."

"She's going to sell you the kid's diary?"

"Yep."

Jesus Christ! Now what? "So you showed her the door, I assume."

"Told her I'd talk to you and get back to her. So that's what I'm doin'."

"Well, I'll tell you, Ruthie, it's a long story."

"That's okay, I got all night." Ruthie leans back in her chair, hands behind her head, her owlish eyes magnified behind the thick lenses of her glasses. "So you came poking around in those old back issues because of this girl's story, didya?"

"That's what got me started, yes."

"And?"

"And I don't know what, Ruthie. The girl's in my class. She was having some kind of hallucination or vision or something and the mother found out by reading her diary. The mother freaks out, comes to me and asks if I'll talk to her daughter. Naturally I say yes. Next thing you know the kid's leading me to this buried skeleton. Says Gabriel's ghost led her to it. Then she disappears and I report the body to the cops. The coroner's supposed to be conducting an autopsy to determine cause of death and they're trying to trace who the body is. End of story."

"Not so long a story after all."

"No, I guess not."

"What do you think?"

"Off the record?"

"Of course."

"The mother's entirely untrustworthy—you just got through telling me so yourself. I wouldn't give credence to anything she says."

"And the girl?" Ruthie's watching me closely.

"I don't know, I really don't. She's not cut from the same cloth as her mother, that much I am certain of…"

"But?"

"Yeah, the but's the killer. I don't know what the but is." My suspicions—I'm almost ready to say "convictions"—run deeper and more dangerously than anyone could guess. The other players know nothing about my father and Gabriel. Nothing about Angela. They have no idea of how explosive the device is they're playing with. Nor does Ruthie.

"So what are you going to do?" I ask her.

Ruthie looks at me in a peculiar way, then takes off her glasses and rubs both her eyes with the heels of her hands. "Dexter," she says at last, "Remember I told you the other day about Mengele?"

"Yes, I just saw in the paper that forensic experts from the States and West Germany are on their way down to Brazil to confirm that it's really him."

"Oh, it's him alright," Ruthie says, not looking at me.

"How can you be so certain?"

Ruthie picks up a small box of staples and turns it slowly from side to side so that the staples make a steady sound like faraway jackboots on cobblestones. "They came for us in the middle of the night," she says, still tilting the box back and forth.

"Who came?" I already know.

"Soldiers. Large men in black with guns and swastika insignia. I was only eight years old. They'd come once before and taken my father away. We never heard from him again. It was just my sister Judith and my mother and me that night they came for us." It's nighttime outside the office now, its big plate-glass window a dark hole into the unknown. "We were on a train, stuffed into a boxcar with other mums and kids and some old people. It seemed like we were in there for days being shunted this way and that. Other trains came thundering past us. There'd be sounds of men shouting, sometimes troops marching, noises from trucks and tanks. We couldn't see anything. We just sat in the dark with no food or water, people pissing and shitting themselves. The stench was dreadful. My mother held onto us tight the whole time, my sister and me, one on each side of her, and told us it would be alright, over and over, everything would be alright.

"After, I don't know how many hours or days, the train came to a final standstill. Everyone in the car seemed to know we'd finally arrived at wherever it was we were going. The door of the boxcar rolled open and we were blinded in the light of hell on earth. 'Auschwitz!' somebody said out loud and the word ran through the crowd like vermin. 'Auschwitz!' A woman who'd been beside us most of the way was trying to explain something to my mother, telling her I should go with this other woman, not stay with my mother and sister. 'They can't be seen together,' she kept saying. But my mother was crying and clasping us tight. She wouldn't let us go. 'My babies,' she kept sobbing, 'my babies.'

"We stumbled out of the boxcar down onto a wide platform. There were hundreds of us all milling around, all soiled and dishevelled. The woman who'd been next to us was still trying to pull me away from my mother and two other women were saying to my mother to let me go but she wouldn't. She just held onto me and my sister and was crying and crying.

"Suddenly there's an SS officer standing right in front of us. The other women backed away, as though from a hot fire. He grabbed me roughly by the shoulder and Judith too. '*Zwillinge*! *Zwillinge*!' He shouted across the platform."

"What does that mean?" I almost whisper, not wishing to intrude on Ruthie's macabre narrative.

"Twins. It means twins. That's why the other woman had been trying to separate Judith and me. We were twins. Identical twins. I guess the women had heard stories about what happened to twins in that hell hole. Maybe my mother had heard them too, I don't know, but she still couldn't let us go out of her sight." Ruthie's rattling the box of jack-boot staples again. "Then suddenly there he was, standing on a ramp right in front of us, smiling down at my sister and me."

"Mengele."

"The Angel of Death himself. Of course we didn't know it then, we had no idea who he was. But I'll never forget how he looked that day—young and handsome, perfectly groomed, his uniform immaculate right down to spotless white gloves. Then two soldiers pried my mother's arms away from Judith and me. She was screaming and crying and we were trying to hold onto her. Then Mengele flicks his riding crop and the soldiers dragged her away, we didn't know where. Turned out it was into the line going directly to the gas chambers." Ruthie's got an unreal, spectral look about her now, and the image of that awful scene has sandblasted away all my worries of the moment.

"We were taken to the showers," Ruthie goes on, "but our hair wasn't cut off like all the rest, and we could wear our own clothes instead of uniforms. We had our own special barracks, just for twins. Judith and I cried and cried for our mother at first, but eventually we cried ourselves out. It was strange and, in a funny way, wonderful living there with all those other twins. We started to make friends with some of them. We started to think that, past the pain of losing our parents, this wasn't so bad after all. We had classes and were allowed to play games. Every morning Mengele came to inspect us. But we weren't afraid of him, at least not at first. He'd bring us candies and chat with us, sometimes even play games with us. We called him Uncle Mengele like he was our kindly uncle. Every morning each kid would have blood drawn, from our fingers or arms, sometimes from our necks. Then the trucks would come and certain kids would have their numbers called and they'd be taken away to the laboratories. Some of them never came back and some came back but you wished they didn't.

"Finally my sister and I were taken away one morning in one of the trucks. We didn't know what to expect. We were marched into a laboratory where we were made to undress and lie down side by side. Every detail of our bodies was carefully examined and measured. The doctors or whoever they were wore surgical masks and didn't speak to us the whole time. Judith and I didn't speak either—we just lay there like small terrified animals. The first thing they did was take a huge transfusion of blood from Judith and pump it into me. Then they didn't do anything else for a while. Next time they poured a bunch of chemicals into my sister's eyes, but not into mine. Judith was blind after that; I'd have to lead her around by the hand. Her eyes got infected and she'd weep this horrible pus. I don't know what else they did to her after that.

"I learned later that some of the kids were given injections into the spine or spinal taps, all of it without anaesthetic. Some were castrated or had other organs amputated. And some of the girls were impregnated with their twin brother's sperm. Sometimes one twin would be innoculated with a disease like typhus or tuberculosis and when the child died from the disease, its twin was killed to compare the two. In the end almost all of us were killed as a final experiment: stabbed in the heart with a hypodermic full of chloroform."

"What about Judith?"

"They took her away one day and she never came back."

"But somehow you were spared?"

"Yep. I don't know how or why. There were very few of us ever got out of that hell hole alive. I spent a lot of years asking myself: Why me? Why was I the lucky one, when all those others died such excruciating deaths? I couldn't talk about it for the longest time, not to anyone. And it still hurts like hell remembering it. But them finding Mengele's body brought it all back clear as yesterday's evening news."

"Ruthie, I don't know what to say..."

"I don't know what to say either, Dexter, other than the dirty truth of what happened. You want to go on believing in truth and goodness, all the virtues my parents taught me and yours taught you, then you run smack up against something like that. Or Angola. Or Thailand or Christ knows where else. You stare into the face of evil and you wonder where it came from and why."

Neither of us says anything for a while. "What're you going to do about Ann Slater?" I ask at last.

"Yeah. Ann Slater."

Ruthie and I sit for a long, long time, each with our separate thoughts.

SIXTEEN

I half expect Susan to be back at school today but she's not. Hell, I'm hardly here myself. A rotten taste is in my mouth this morning, like the residue of too many beers and cigarettes from the night before. I'm sleepwalking through my classes. Somehow the abrupt shift in point of view employed by Willa Cather in "Paul's Case" doesn't strike me as all that relevant just now. I don't know if the kids even notice. I remember when I sat in class as a student, it never occurred to me that any teacher was a real person, someone who might have a headache that day, or be going through hell from a sloppy divorce, or have a sick kid at home. To us, teachers were caricatures, one-dimensional mannequins whom we'd long ago categorized as bitchy or boring or cool or whatever, and we drifted semester after semester, vaguely aware of individual teachers living up, or down, to stereotype. What I've discovered in the meantime is that it works from the other side of the desk as well. As a teacher you can have a million other things on your mind but still have a part of your brain conducting class, like a subconscious substitute, while your attention's someplace else entirely. It's an unspoken but perfectly understood compact between class and teacher that we can each wander off on our own at times so long as proprieties are maintained and a general course of academic advancement advanced.

So this morning, while we're officially engaged in grinding away at the finer points of point of view, I'm engrossed in darker themes. The bodies of Gabriel and Mengele are performing the dance of the dead in my mind. I keep trying to force my thoughts back into the tidy categories of the lesson plan, but can't. Meanwhile, who knows what the kids are thinking about; that's this morning's joke of the day, I guess. In earnestly discussing point of view nobody knows what anybody else is really looking at.

At morning break I telephone the Slater place and Ann answers on the third ring. "Good morning, it's Dexter Cooke," I try to sound upbeat. "How are you?"

"Fine."

"I understand Susan's back home."

"Yeah." Ann's monosyllables are worth a thousand pictures.

"Well, that's a relief. May I speak with her?"

"She don't wanna talk to you."

"Oh? Why not?"

"What d'you think?"

"I'm sure I don't know. But I do want to speak with her about her school work. If she's upset about my going to the police before..."

"It ain't about that and you know it." Now there's real antagonism in her voice. Venom.

"What then?"

"As if you didn't know."

This is like having a session with a subnormal sophomore at school. The same inarticulate resentment brooding under every exchange. Nothing, and everything, being spoken through grudging innuendo. I have no idea where it's coming from. Ann's a strange confusion of predator and cornered prey, both vulnerable and dangerous. Her danger lies in her unpredictability, moving by rules she alone understands, or by no rules at all.

"Look, Ann, I'm not sure what's going on here but I'd like to clear up any misunderstanding."

"That's what you call it, is it? Never heard that one before."

"What do you mean?"

"Don't play the innocent with me. You know damn well what I mean."

"No, I don't actually."

"Well, you will soon enough."

A warning shot. By some process I don't understand I've now become the enemy, the one to be taken out. I have no doubt Ann can inflict real damage and that I'm in a badly exposed position. Pathetic as she is, in a certain way she has me at her mercy. And I'm conscious of Danielson circling overhead like a vulture.

"Ann, I'd really like to..." But she's hung up on me. What the hell has gotten into her? I fish another quarter out and call her back, but no one answers. This is bloody frustrating. I want to find out what game Ann's playing. And I have to at least see Susan, get things sorted out between us and get her back into school before anything unravels further.

The little mutt's still on guard in the office trailer window and breaks into hysterical yapping as I pass. I do an old soft-shoe routine in front of its window, wondering if I can incite the little bugger into a coronary. I rap on the aluminum screen door of the Slater trailer. Radio sounds squawk from inside. Talk radio. Ann opens the door scowling. She's wearing an oversize sweatshirt and jeans, none of her usual makeup, hair all over the place. A talk show host is shouting in the background about country-club prisons. Ann seems startled to see me. "What the fuck you want?" she snarls.

"Ann, what's going on? What are you so angry about?" I remain entirely calm against the sudden squall of her rage. My dad's example stands me in good stead here. "Don't ever buy into other people's anger," he used to tell me. "An enraged person is someone who has lost their power. Their anger is about themselves not about you. The worst thing you can do is answer their rage with your own. Let them rage all they want, just don't buy into it." Good old Dad and his sage advice.

"These cretins should be locked up for life!" the radio shouts. "And if they want to play rough with one another, let 'em; it'll mean a few less mouths to feed."

"You think you're so goddamn clever, don't you?" Ann sneers at me, folding her arms across her chest, attempting a little tactical repositioning of her own. "Mr. Big Shot." Now I begin to discern a long compilation of grievances behind her bitterness.

"Ann, I think it would be best if we sat down and tried to work out whatever's bothering you."

"Your kids and my kids have a right to walk down the street without being afraid one of these perverts is going to leap out and snatch them!" the talk-show guy shouts.

"You'd like that, wouldn't you?" Ann sneers again. "A chance to fancy-talk your way out of it. Like we're just dumb trailer trash you can have your bit of fun with and then fuck off. Well, I'll tell you this, asshole: you ain't getting away with it. I don't give a shit how important your family is or how clever you think you are, you're going to fucking pay for this, believe me!" And she slams the door shut so violently the whole trailer shudders.

Talk about unstable personalities. Jesus. I have no idea what this is about. Should I knock on the door and try again? I don't think so. "Let them blow," my dad'd say. "You can't do much with them in that state, but they can only blow hard for so long; then, when they've blown themselves out and gone slack, you've got something you can work with." I turn away from the trailer and past the yapping sentry.

The instant I step into Danielson's office I smell trouble. The principal's lined face hangs more morosely than usual. He stands by the window and glances out of it as though awaiting the first signs of an imminent apocalypse. This looks ugly indeed.

"Please sit down, Mr. Cooke." Danielson gestures me to a chair and sits down himself. He's wearing his standard-issue grey suit and blue tie, though there's an uncharacteristically dishevelled look about him this afternoon.

"What's going on?" I ask, forcing lightness into my voice.

Danielson clears his throat and looks as near to directly at me as he can. "Mr. Cooke, it's my unpleasant duty to have to inform you that there has been a very serious allegation levelled against you."

Impervious as I am to Danielson's machinations, the grimness in his tone this time unnerves me. I feel the floor under me shift slightly, as though a minor tremor had rattled the building.

"Allegation? What sort of allegation?" I'm determined to appear indifferent to his morbid solemnity.

"About as damaging an accusation as can be levelled at any teacher," Danielson lets the tension build.

"Well?" I prod him.

"You've been accused," he bears down on me hard, each word hurled like a stone, "accused of sexually molesting one of your students."

Now the building does rattle and tilt and I'm thinking we should sound the fire alarm, get everybody out before the tremors worsen, before bricks and glass start flying. "Say that again," I ask him in disbelief.

"Ann Slater has accused you of molesting her daughter, Susan." Bang! A couple of windows blow out and disintegrate into shards of falling glass.

"You gotta be kidding!" This I don't believe. Not even from Danielson.

"I assure you, Mr. Cooke, we are most certainly not kidding." His gaunt manner tells me that's true. "This is not a kidding matter."

"No, I guess it isn't." The reality of the accusation seeps like spilled blood into soil. "Tell me what happened." I'm reaching to find my balance.

"Mrs. Slater came to see me this morning. I interviewed her at length. She informed me, as I already knew, that you recently accompanied her daughter to a remote area in the nature conservancy. She alleges that you had sexual relations with the girl there, without her consent."

A hot rush of anger flashes through my body, the indignation of the wrongly accused. I feel an instant urge to counterattack, to denounce Ann Slater as a hysterical nut and a venomous schemer, determined to wound me for sick reasons of her own. But again my father's advice against responding with anger serves me well. I take my time in replying, giving nothing away to Danielson, searching through this accusation for clues as to where it came from. My immediate instinct is it's some sick game Ann's playing. But what if she actually believes in the accusation she's making? For sure it explains her anger when I was at her place. The crucial question quickly settles out; is this her accusation, or Susan's?

"Did she tell you that Susan had accused me?" I ask Danielson. He looks nonplussed for a moment, but recovers.

"She simply stated to me the facts as she knew them to have occurred."

"Knew them because Susan explicitly told her so?" I press him. Maybe more clandestine diary reading. Taking the kid's fantasies for reality.

"She didn't say so explicitly," Danielson doesn't like being pressed. "But how else would she know?"

"Good question! How else indeed? You can't possibly give this allegation any credibility at all until we hear Susan's version. And I know there's no way in the world she's going to corroborate it."

"So you're telling me categorically that nothing of the sort happened?"

"Absolutely. It's pure fiction. And malicious fiction to boot. If it were true, why wouldn't she go to the police and file a complaint instead of coming to you?"

"She told me she didn't want to cause a scandal, for her daughter's sake."

"Oh, right!" My mocking tone laughs back at me. It's becoming obvious that Danielson doesn't necessarily disbelieve Ann's story. "So what did she want to cause, if not a scandal?"

"Two things actually," Danielson ignores my tone. "She wanted you suspended from your position and she wanted Susan to graduate with honours."

"I see. So, it's blackmail we're dealing with, is it? Well, I understand the second. Susan's missed a lot of school and she's shaky on certain subjects at the best of times. But why does she want to have me suspended?"

"Well, Mr. Cooke, it's not all that hard to understand that she doesn't want her daughter being taught by a man whom she's accusing of sexual misconduct, is it?"

"But I didn't do anything with her daughter and she knows it as well as you do! I think you've got to talk to Susan and you'll see there's absolutely no substance to any of this." As the reality of this accusation seeps in, I'm getting pissed off. I can't believe Ann Slater would be so goddamn stupid. But it's cunning stupid, I've got to hand it to her. And what's Susan's part in this? I can't imagine she's behind it and I wonder if she's even aware of what her mother's up to.

"I certainly hope so, Mr. Cooke, for all our sakes. The Governor General's visit is imminent and the very last thing we need is to have the school embroiled in a sordid sexual abuse scandal. Not exactly how I'd like to make the national news."

"There was no sexual abuse and there is no scandal, as you'll find out as soon as we talk to Susan."

"I sincerely hope that's the case, for all our sakes. But even were that to be the case, it's my duty to tell you that your recent conduct has fallen well below the standard expected of staff at this, or any other, school."

"What's that supposed to mean?" Despite my best efforts, Danielson's succeeding in getting under my skin.

"I mean all this business with the police and corpses and you wandering around the back woods with your female students. And now this. Something like this was bound to happen sooner or later. I knew as much. I gave you fair warning, Mr. Cooke; I was very specific in warning you that scandal must be avoided at all costs."

"With all due respect, Mr. Danielson, there is no scandal. A body was found and the police are conducting their investigation. Period. Ann Slater's accusations are entirely separate and frivolous. And, if you don't mind my saying so, it's normal procedure for a person in your position to stand solidly behind their staff unless and until substantive proof of wrongdoing has been brought forward."

But Danielson's dug in. "You'll see how frivolous they are if charges are laid. I don't need to tell you that more than one promising teaching career has been destroyed by accusations of this sort, whether true or false. This is not a laughing matter, Mr. Cooke, believe me. It's all very well for you to dismiss Mrs. Slater out of hand and proclaim your innocence. But there's more than enough people ready to take accusations of this sort as true, whether proven or not. Careers can be ruined. Lives can be ruined. Communities can be torn to pieces. And none of it, Mr. Cooke, absolutely none of it is frivolous!" Danielson's hard as a flint striking sparks. I don't blame him really. I know this is a land mine that could easily blow up under us, maiming and crippling all sorts of people. Yes, Danielson's right. This mess has got dynamite sticks and blasting caps wrapped all around it.

"You're right," I tell Danielson, partly by way of placating him. However repulsive he might be, the principal is not someone I need against me right now. I'm equal parts outraged and mystified by Ann's move, but, disconcertingly, in the farthest dark corner at the back of my brain there's a small tingling sensation, a disturbing insinuation, like the insistent whistle of a kettle left too long on the boil in an adjoining room. An insinuation that maybe, just maybe, there's the tiniest shred of truth to this disgusting allegation. It's indistinct and unfocused, but unmistakably there, and vaguely unnerving. As though I'm guilty of gross indecency in my dreams. The charge Ann's making must relate to whatever occurred under the tree where the corpse lay buried. I remember again the dark and urgent secrecy I felt in that peculiar room of roots and limbs. Susan taking my hand. A tingle of fear in the air. Her breathing close beside me, the warm animal scent of her. And yes, if I'm honest I'll admit I felt sexual arousal. Partly it was circumstances—the isolated place, the hushed expectancy of discovering the corpse, how much Susan had reminded me of Angela—the whole scene straight out of *A Passage to India*. Sentimentally, I'd been carried back to being seventeen, when all the world was young and pantingly in love. But it was all in my head, nothing more. I'd remember—how could I not? It didn't happen. But still.

"Where do we go from here?" I ask Danielson, chastened into treating him more civilly.

"Mrs. Slater and I agreed that this matter need not be brought to the attention of the police at the present time. She has requested that you be relieved of your duties in the interim. However, I'm not inclined to take so serious a step until I've determined the veracity of her story." I hear between the formal lines of Danielson's pronouncement the ragged fact that he believes Ann's accusation is true but requires verification. "I believe, as you've pointed out, the next logical step is to interview Susan and determine whether or not her version of events supports the mother's. I've determined it would be best not to draw undue attention to the matter by having Susan come here, so I've arranged to meet her this afternoon at a neutral location well away from prying eyes."

It occurs to me that this situation, as much as he deplores it, might represent for Danielson an unexpected opening toward the checkmate he's long wanted to trap me in. Maybe he sees it as his chance to finally knock me off my pedestal and scramble up there himself, the ultimate triumph of the outsider who's never gotten the respect he imagines he deserves. Left unwatched, Danielson might easily manipulate this situation toward his own advantage, just as I suspect Ann's doing.

"I'd like to come along," I say, "then we'll quickly get to the bottom of this." I want to see Susan. I can't imagine she's going along with this mischievous fiction. But I'm remembering how withdrawn she became that afternoon at Dancing Grasses. How she wouldn't talk to me all the way home. I thought at one point she was crying. Now I wonder, did she imagine a passionate encounter with me that she wanted to have happen? Has she convinced herself that it did? Maybe told her mother that it did, so Ann's outrage is genuine, and this whole fracas is Susan's doing, not her mother's at all. Maybe Ann's only responding as any mother would at her daughter's violation. Jesus, what a mess.

"I don't believe that would be appropriate," Danielson replies, "given the circumstances at play here. I shall certainly inform you as soon as I return as to what the girl has to say. We can only hope," and here his caustic gaze flickers out through the window, "that the girl does not have the same sordid version of events as her mother."

Sitting alone in my homeroom after leaving the principal's office, I know Danielson's right: this thing could turn ugly fast. As he said, allegations don't need to be true to be destructive. If this situation goes public—and there's no reason why it wouldn't, given Ann's recent call on Ruthie—I'd almost certainly lose my job and have to leave town. I could end up doing time. Mother would be doubly punished, humiliated at her golden son's disgrace and left on her own to deal with Dad. And it could be the final straw that snaps the back of my marriage. Deirdre might simply decide enough was enough. How ironic that I've been harbouring suspicions of my father as a potential felon only to be blindsided by the possibility of being convicted myself. Suddenly our mystery skeleton and all my projections about it seem considerably less significant. A real and present danger's stalking me now and it is a shock to realize that I'm feeling an emotion whose acquaintance I've never truly made before. I'm feeling afraid.

Seventeen

A telephone's shrilling from inside the house as I walk up my front pathway, but I'm not rushing to answer it. The oriental poppies Deirdre planted along the path last year are blooming for the first time, holding their enormous vermilion chalices up to swarms of feeding bees.

As I step onto the porch I hear Deirdre talking on the phone, and coming through the front doorway I see her gesture to me, mouthing "the police." I could pretend I'm not here—Deirdre's waiting for my cue—but I decide I'd better get it over with and signal her I'll take it. "Here he is now," Deirdre says brightly, handing me the receiver.

"Hello?" I say, as though I don't know who's calling.

"Yes, good evening, Mr. Cooke. Kurt Reisler here." I don't respond for a moment, steeling myself for the worst, not wanting to hear that charges have been laid, that the nightmare is about to commence. "RCMP," Reisler adds, mistaking my silence for my not remembering who he is.

"Yes, yes, I'm sorry. I was expecting a call from someone else and you caught me off guard."

"I apologize for calling you at home this late in the day." Reisler sounds excessively civil for someone who's about to dismantle my life.

"That's fine." I try to strike a casual tone. "What's up?"

"I thought you'd be interested to know we've just received the coroner's report on the remains you discovered."

I exhale with relief and surprise. A brief reprieve anyway. Truth is, I'd just about given up expecting that progress would ever be made in their investigation. The few times I called Reisler to enquire how it was coming along, he politely but firmly put me off. He told me what a tough case is was. First the bug and weed experts took forever to get here and even longer to poke around the site. Then the cops went over every square inch of the ground with a metal detector, looking, Reisler told me, for bullets, teeth or other evidence. They found nothing, at least nothing they were willing to discuss. Then they painstakingly removed each of the bones and carried them off to the coroner's office. There was some talk of shipping the remains to Vancouver for examination by a coroner who specializes in such cases, but the bones came from an old Native burial ground, and a recent protocol signed with First Nations prohibited them from doing so. They couldn't get a match through dental records. They couldn't even determine the cause of death—no sign of violence, no trace of toxins, nothing. They seemed to be concluding that a crime may not have been committed, other than unlawful disposal of a body. The case plainly had no impetus—no grieving relatives sobbing on the evening newscast, demanding that the perpetrators of this heinous crime be tracked down and punished, nothing like that. I got the impression that the cops, having run through their standard routine and come up with nothing, would just as soon have the bones reburied and the case closed.

But now here's Reisler at last with something fresh. Perhaps to tell me that they've finally made the vital connection to Gabriel. As the investigation dragged on, I'd been tempted several times to tell Reisler what I know about Gabriel's last days here and about Susan's visions; that would've stirred the pot for sure, but likely caused more problems than solutions, so I kept out of it. Now with the assault stuff simmering like a toxic stew, any disclosure is out of the question. Like the guarded suspects in TV crime dramas, it occurs to me that I ought to be getting a lawyer before I say anything to anyone.

"What's the coroner concluded?" I ask Reisler.

"She's determined that the bones are of Native origin, a male, buried for at least fifty years, with no obvious cause of death evident. They're being returned to the reserve over near Centralia and the case is officially closed."

So there goes Gabriel's ghost, like a puff of smoke in the wind. A brief illusion, a chimera. I don't know if I'm more relieved or disappointed. Illusions occur for the soundest of reasons and seldom die easily.

Reisler thanks me for my co-operation and hopes the next time we meet it will be under less morbid circumstances.

"I hope so too." Reisler can't know the irony involved. We say goodnight and I hang up.

"Well?" Deirdre asks.

"End of the mystery," I try to fake a smile for Deirdre's sake and repeat to her what Reisler's just told me.

"That's a relief," Deirdre says, exhaling upward across her face so that her bangs flutter up.

"It is." And it isn't. "You know, I was completely convinced those bones were Gabriel's."

"I know. It was a side of you I don't think I've ever seen before. Sort of irrational, superstitious, almost paranoid. Not who you normally are at all."

"The worst part of it was the suspicions I had about my dad. I mean, I can't believe I convinced myself of that."

"A peculiar instrument, the human mind."

"Exactly. But you always think it's somebody else's mind in question, not your own." Like Susan's for example. This news about the corpse has brought me full circle. Since they aren't Gabriel's remains did Susan really encounter his spirit there, or did she dream the whole thing, the way she's maybe concocted sexual contact with me? I'm left groping for the invisible place where fantasy begins and ends.

Deirdre and I don't talk much over dinner. The CBC radio news rattles along in the background about the latest bout of sleaze in the Mulroney government, but I'm barely paying attention. My brain feels like those images you see of lava bubbling in a crater, hot and toxic, seething for escape. Sensing my mood, Deirdre doesn't intrude and seems far away in musings of her own. By the end of the meal, I don't even know what we've eaten.

Just as I'm clearing the dishes, the phone rings again. Danielson this time. "I thought you might appreciate hearing the outcome of my conversation with Mrs. Slater and her daughter this afternoon."

"Mrs. Slater?" Antennae up instantly. " I understood you were going to talk to Susan. We already know her mother's opinion."

"Yes, we do." Danielson's as dry as a tight martini. "But the mother turned up as well and I was scarcely in a position to ask her to leave, was I?"

"Of course you were."

"Well, I didn't."

"You were supposed to be getting an unbiased account from Susan, which you'd hardly get with the mother hovering overhead."

"You must understand, Mr. Cooke, this is a woman whose daughter has made a serious allegation. And if she chooses to come along in order to support her daughter through a potentially difficult interview with the immediate superior of the person against whom the allegation is being brought, I, as the person in that position, can scarcely tell her that she's not welcome, can I?"

It must have been an interesting matchup—Danielson and Ann. I couldn't think of two people who deserved each other more.

"And you must understand, Mr. Danielson," I'm not backing off here one bit, "that Susan herself hasn't made any allegations against me, serious or otherwise, at least none that I've heard yet. So did you or did you not get a statement from Susan corroborating the mother's accusation?" I know he didn't or he wouldn't have called.

"Well," he pauses, and now it's obvious he's made a cock-up of it, and that's the thing about Danielson: he manages to be devilishly shrewd and hopelessly inept at the same time, "not precisely, no."

"What do you mean, not precisely? It's either yes or no. Either the girl's making the accusation or she isn't."

"It's not exactly that simple, Mr. Cooke. Would that life were that simple, but it seldom is. As I'm sure you remember Oscar Wilde putting it: 'The pure and simple truth is rarely pure and never simple.'" This is what I mean about Danielson. "In point of fact," he continues, "the mother did most of the talking." Big surprise there. "The girl was very quiet and withdrawn, which I'm given to understand is not unusual in cases of this sort."

Cases of this sort! Jesus, give me strength. "You're saying you never did get a clear statement of accusation from Susan?"

Danielson hates having his feet held to the fire. "No, I did not. Not in so many words."

"Well, we're hardly going to accept a wink and a nod, now are we? Words are what it has to be in." As furious as I am over Danielson's bumbling, I'm also hugely pleased that Susan isn't party to the plot, that it's her mother, not her, who's doing the dirty. At least I think so.

"Mr. Cooke," Danielson needs to reassert his authority, "this entire situation puts me, as you realize, in a very difficult position. I'm thinking it might perhaps be best for all parties concerned if you were to take a leave of absence, with full pay of course, for what's left of the school year. We could bring in a substitute to mop things up for these last few weeks."

"Well, you might be thinking that, but I'm not. And I'm certainly not about to take a leave of absence just because Ann Slater's made up this cock-and-bull story. I'm telling you categorically it's not true and you've just discovered for yourself the girl won't verify it..."

"It's not as though she won't," Danielson interrupts.

"But she didn't, did she? Because she can't. Because it never happened. What more do you want?" I know exactly what more Danielson wants—he wants this whole thing to go away, to avoid a public scandal which could, among other consequences, ruin his precious visit from the Governor General. The thought of which instantly gives me a bright idea. "I should also let you know, while we're talking, that the drama group will not be proceeding with the play and certainly can't have it be part of the graduation celebrations." Truth of the matter is, Danielson's incessant meddling in the production—wanting script changes, fretting over what might or might not offend somebody—has turned everybody off. Plus Susan hasn't been around, and her part's pivotal to the play.

"But the programs are at the printer already; we must proceed!" Suddenly a note of pleading slithers into Danielson's tone.

"I'm sorry, that's final," I tell him. "For one thing, Susan Slater was a key player in the piece, but she's withdrawn and we have no satisfactory understudy."

"But surely someone can be put in place!"

"Well, maybe you can bring in a substitute drama teacher who can mop things up in these last few weeks." As far as I'm concerned, Danielson's fair game at this point.

"Mr. Cooke, I'll thank you not to take that tone with me. This situation..."

"Let me guess," I interrupt him, "it's put you in a very delicate position. Well, let me tell you exactly what I think about the delicacy of the position you're taking. How about cowardly and reprehensible, that would cover it nicely, don't you think? You know as well as I do that your first obligation is to stand by your staff until you have a legitimate reason to do otherwise. All you're doing is covering your own backside because some disgruntled broad has got it in for me. Well, speaking bluntly, Mr. Danielson, that's moral cowardice, and it's completely repugnant to me." I swear I can hear his blood vessels bursting over the phone, but he doesn't say a word. I flash again on the time I stuffed Milton Gorman's sarcastic guff back down his throat. I feel strangely exhilarated, better than I have for weeks. I press my advantage. "I can't believe you'd ask me to quit at this point in the school year solely on the basis of Ann Slater's gossip. But I'll certainly take a leave of absence," I give him a dramatic pause, just to mess his head up a bit, "the minute charges are laid. But not a minute before. And if you try to force the issue, there'll be blood on the tracks, believe me. I'll have the union all over you like a burst sewer. So you let me know, why don't you, once charges are laid. Meanwhile, as far as I'm concerned, it's business as usual. And that, I believe, is all I have to say for the moment, so I'll bid you a fond good evening." And I hang up. There: I've called Danielson's bluff and Ann's too.

As I put the receiver down a jubilation of larks rises singing in my brain.

"Dexter, what on earth is going on?" Deirdre asks me from the kitchen doorway. She's wearing an apron and holding an immaculate spatula. "I couldn't help but overhear some of that, and I've never heard you talk to Danielson that way." In an instant the larks plummet to earth.

"Oh, Christ, it's a mess like you wouldn't believe."

"What's all this about resigning and charges being laid? Are you in some kind of trouble you're not telling me about?"

"Not at all. It's just weird Danielson's paranoia."

"And the Slater woman? What's she accusing you of?"

"Oh, she's just blowing smoke, it's nothing serious." Somehow I can't tell Deirdre.

"It sounded pretty serious to me."

"I'm sure I can straighten it out."

"Dexter, what are you being so secretive about?"

"I'm not being secretive!"

"Yes, you are. Would you please tell me what exactly is going on?"

"Alright!" I stare at her fiercely, my anger at Danielson and Ann still simmering. "Ann Slater has accused me of sexually molesting Susan."

The look on Deirdre's face curdles into something almost hideous. She doesn't say a word, just stares directly at me, her eyes large and glowering, eyebrows arched.

"There's absolutely nothing to it, of course," I hurry against Deirdre's glower. "And Susan herself isn't even saying it's true. It's all her wretched mother's fabrication."

"Has she gone to the police?" she asks in a constricted voice.

"No. She's told Danielson and they've agreed to keep it quiet. He wanted me to take a leave of absence, so there'd be no trouble, but I refused. Told him he'd have to fire me and take the consequences."

"And why haven't you told me any of this?" Deirdre sits down across the table from me.

"I don't know." I do and I don't, but I can't explain it to her.

"You just don't get it, do you, Dexter?" Deirdre's got me clearly in her crosshairs, "that we're supposed to be in this together. That we tell each other what's going on. It's inconceivable to me that you'd be accused of violating one of your students and not say anything to me about it. What sort of a husband does that make you, what sort of a partner, a friend? How am I supposed to have any faith in you, any confidence at all, when you behave that way?" This isn't Deirdre being bitchy. She's hurt and offended and disappointed, and I don't blame her. I would be too. I don't even try bluffing my way around it.

"Deirdre, I'm sorry. You're right, of course, I should have told you. You have no idea how shitty I feel that I didn't. But the thing is I thought I could deal with it. The whole situation's so preposterous, I thought I could deflate it right away and there'd be no need to drag you into it."

"These are misplaced sensitivities, Dexter."

"I'm not trying to exonerate myself. I can only say I'm sorry. I really am. I'm so fucking sorry about everything." Then suddenly tears come spilling out of my eyes, hot and urgent.

Deirdre makes no move to comfort me. I'm on my own. She places her joined hands on the table in front of her, as though she were praying, "I'm only going to ask you this once. I want you to be absolutely and completely truthful. Is there anything, anything at all, to this accusation?"

There we are again: in that dark and disorienting place under the sagging limbs of the cottonwood. The smell of dirt and rotting leaves. Gabriel's ghost, and Angela's too, somewhere near. The scent of the girl's body in the heat, her breathing close beside me. Nothing happened there. Nothing happened. Deirdre's looking at me hard as I try to regain my composure.

"I don't think so." Trying to force these tears to stop.

"You don't think so?"

"Something strange did happen, something I can't quite remember, like a dream you can almost remember but not quite."

"A dream?"

"I never touched that girl. I wouldn't. You know that."

"That's what I would have thought."

"And if I had—for whatever reason—I'd hate myself afterward. There's nothing like that here."

"You're sure?"

"Absolutely. I'd tell you, Deirdre, if there was, I swear."

Deirdre doesn't say anything for a long time. Then "Dexter," she says at last, "it hurts me to see you like this, it really does. But you know what hurts even more? To be shut out of your life the way I am."

"I don't try to shut you out."

"Well, try or not, you do it. You have too many secrets, Dexter. Too much keeping me in the dark while you go around taking care of business that I don't know anything about."

"You're right. I do that."

"I love you, Dexter, I really do. But I think we've reached the end of the line here. I'm not willing to put up with being treated this way any longer."

I can't look at her as she's saying this, but every word registers.

"I'm needing some changes in you, Dexter. You're going to have to decide: either you want to live with me as fully loving partners or you don't. If you don't, fine, we'll say we've gone as far as we can go together. If you do—if you want to save this marriage—we're going to have to start doing things differently. Am I being perfectly clear?"

I nod in agreement, unable to speak for fear of more tears. But Deirdre's adamant. "Dexter, I want you to tell me you're willing to take a good long look at yourself and change those things we both know need changing."

I force myself to look into her eyes, which are burning with a blue intensity. My "Yes," is muffled under thick layers of shame.

EIGHTEEN

The aluminum screen door on Ruthie's trailer squeals open and Ruthie growls for me to come in. "Seen you over there at the Slater place. No answer, eh?"

"No, they seem to be out. Or else just not answering." I've come determined to confront Ann and Susan, only to find them not around. I am now left dangling without direction.

"Seen the mother go out with a suitcase a coupla hours ago," Ruthie says, motioning for me to sit on a sagging couch. She lowers herself into a frayed armchair opposite. "Not the girl though. Ain't seen her since she supposedly got back. What the hell's goin' on, Dexter?"

Something's given way inside me since my conversation with Deirdre, descending to an older layer of consciousness where instincts and emotions scuttle through subterranean chambers. I keep sliding off the hard shiny surface of practical affairs, unable to determine the proper coordinates where this or that detail might be placed. All of it a formless seething.

"Ann Slater's accusing me of sexually molesting Susan."

Ruthie inhales noisily through her nose, as though she'd been squeezed. She looks old to me today, a scarred veteran of battles nobody remembers anymore. "And?"

I'm too weary to explain the ambiguity of my position: that the charges are false but that I'm far from an innocent man. Instead I tell Ruthie I've come over to see Ann, to try to discover why she's doing this.

Ruthie's studying me carefully. "Y'know, Dexter, it's seldom a wise idea to rush to the defence of anyone facing that particular accusation. You know as well as I do how much of that shit goes on and how little of it is even reported, much less punished." Ruthie reaches for her smokes and lights one with a clunky silver lighter shaped like a rooster. "But I'm having a hard time seeing you violating that girl."

"I didn't."

"Wouldn't a thought so. Say, you want some coffee?"

"No thanks."

"You know I been so tied up in knots over that bastard Mengele. I mean, it's brought up all kinda shit for me, stuff I thought I'd left behind long ago that I've not been..." She's wracked for a minute with a smoker's hack, a rasping of throat and lungs in phlegmy revolt, and shuffles to her kitchen sink for a glass of water. After gulping some, she drops the smouldering cigarette into the half-empty glass. It hisses and disintegrates. "What was I sayin'? Oh, yeah, you remember I told you that Ann had tried to peddle her kid's diary to me?"

"Right."

"Well, what I didn't mention at the time..." Ruthie flops back into the overstuffed chair. "The nickle really didn't drop for me until later, when I got to thinkin' about it, because at the time I was so preoccupied with Mengele, but I started askin' myself: now why would Ann Slater be pullin' such a stupid stunt?"

"I thought she was looking for money."

"Sure, sure she was. But whenever it's about money, it's always about somethin' more than money."

"Such as?"

"There was somethin' in the whole set-up that told me what she was really interested in was getting at you. I had no idea why she'd want to do that, you bein' such a sweetheart and all, but I definitely had the impression she had you in her sights."

"I have the same feeling. But she's got no reason. I've had nothing to do with her, other than teach her daughter. She and I have no history at all."

"That was my impression, too. But history's a bitch with more pups than you can count. So I asked myself: could it be someone other than Dexter she's after? But close—like family."

"What do you mean?"

"That's when the light went on!" Ruthie slaps the stuffed arm of her chair and a little poof of dust puffs up like spores disgorged from a fungus. "Your dad."

"My dad? What's he got to do with any of it?"

"I remembered somethin' that happened, it must be a dozen or more years ago. Back then, Ann was shacked up with a genuine psycho, guy named Sprungman. They had a house just down the road here, on one of them vacant lots. He had a big Harley, you'd see him comin' and goin' up the road all the time. They were together maybe two or three years and she had a kid by him. Poor little kid cried all the time. Susan was probably four or five by then. Big, mean son of a bitch that Sprungman was, thought nothing about knocking Ann around when he was pissed. He was crazy with rage, one of those guys, and he damn near killed her a couple of times. Finally she charged him with assault. It turned into a real circus: screaming matches, cops, restraining orders, the whole scene. Your old man represented Sprungman; you know what your dad was like, always defending the underdog, making sure the wretched of the earth got a fair deal."

"I never heard any of this before."

"You musta been down in Vancouver at the time."

"I guess." Remembering my father's visit, our scratchy talk at the hotel, how distracted he seemed.

"So, sure enough, your dad got Sprungman off on some weird technicality. Something about how the cops screwed up in arresting him, I don't remember. Sprungman disappears, but not long afterward there's a fire at Ann's house one night. She gets out and gets Susan out alright, but not the baby. Burned to death. Beyond recognition. The investigators said they couldn't be sure, but they wouldn't rule out arson. It wouldn't be that much of a stretch for Ann to believe it was Sprungman set the fire."

"What happened to him?"

"Don't know. I don't think he was ever seen around here again."

"So Ann blames my father for her baby's death."

"It kinda adds up. I can see her figuring if Sprungman'd spent some time in the slammer he never would have come after her and her baby wouldn't have died in that fire."

"Christ, what a mess."

"A mess and a lot of guessing. It might have been Sprungman set the fire—suppose he was stupid and crazy enough to kill his own child—but for all anyone knows it might have been mice chewing on electric wires, or some kids fooling around with matches out back. But if Ann's convinced it was Sprungman who killed her baby and she blames your old man for getting him off and setting him free to do it, I can understand her wanting to take you down."

"Revenge."

"Sins of the fathers. I can see it. If Mengele's kid lived in this town, and he was on top of the heap and I wasn't, it's not that big of a stretch to imagine wanting to hurt him."

As I can imagine some of what Ann must have felt with a baby burned to death. Haven't I lost three babies of my own? Yes, I can understand Ann Slater's rage, her misguided need for vengeance. Suddenly I see her, not as a repulsive schemer, but a mother holding a dead baby in her arms. As for my father—is this one of the memories he's struggling to remember or to forget? One of the reasons his numb brain swims helplessly through a black sea toward forgiveness?

"Jesus," I say, more to myself than to Ruthie, "I had no idea."

"I'm just kickin' myself that I didn't think of it sooner, Dexter. Might have helped for you to have known about it."

"Well, I'm glad you've told me before I confronted Ann. I was so mad at her I'd probably have said things I'd later regret."

"Yeah."

Now I don't know what I'll say to Ann. The air's completely leaked out of my righteousness. And I'm fully aware of the irony of having just seen my father exonerated in the fantasy murder of Gabriel, only to find him complicit somehow in the death of Ann's baby. What can you touch in this world that doesn't turn to death?

I need some breathing room so I shift the topic by asking Ruthie, "How was the party?"

"What party's that?"

"Last time I saw you, you said you were going over to Centralia to celebrate with friends."

"Oh, right. Just a barrel of laughs. I was with the Albrecht babes—that's what they call themselves. They were at Auschwitz too. Lost their parents there. They knew Mengele, not like I did, but they knew who he was and saw him plenty of times."

"They're not twins?"

"No. Or triplets—there's three of them—that would have really given him something to work with. Just sisters. So they weren't part of the bullshit 'research' like Judith and me. They were in another part of the camp, totally separate from us."

"So you didn't know them?"

"Never laid eyes on 'em till I got here, back in the Stone Ages. It was the damndest thing. I was sittin' in a coffee shop over in Centralia one day and the place was packed and these three women asked if they could sit at my table. They hadn't been sittin' there for more than five minutes when I knew there was something different about them. Partly their accents, for sure, but more than that. Something about the way they talked to each other and how they looked around, as though they were watching for something. We got talking somehow and within a couple of minutes it came out that we'd all been in that hellhole at around the same time. Imagine that, out here in the middle of nowhere. And it's not like I ever talked about it, especially not to strangers. It became something I didn't even admit to myself had happened. I didn't have any photographs of my family. I can't even remember what my mother looked like. I used to try think about her, but the only way I could remember her was those last few minutes on the platform when the soldiers dragged her away screaming. Then her face would be replaced with Mengele's smiling down at us. So I stopped trying to remember her because I wanted to forget him. Forever. And my dad? I can't remember him at all. Just a sense of absence. That he was there one day and then he wasn't anymore. Nope, never talked about any of it for years. Not till I met the Albrecht babes, then it came pourin' out of me like a burst pipe. I tell you, Dexter, I just about went crazy back in those days. I'd just lie on a couch or a bed screamin' and cryin' for hours and they stayed with me, they'd take turns, those three sisters, and I'll never forget 'em for it."

"What did you do at the party?"

"We didn't go back, that's for sure. I'm through with that. You have to go back at some point to really escape from the prison—most of us got prisons to escape from, Dexter, even bluebloods like you. But once you've escaped, you don't have to keep goin' back. You wanna go forward. You want to see who's building the prisons today and who's gettin' locked up in 'em. There's always someone at it, I don't know why, but there is. So, no, we didn't go back to the camp. But I'll tell you we gave that bastard Mengele one hell of a send-off. We danced on his grave and drank way too much vodka and laughed our fool heads off that we'd outlasted him, that that monster who'd tortured and killed our families had ended up living for years in fear and loneliness and had finally died like a jellyfish on the beach. Death comes to the Angel of Death. Ha!" Ruthie slapped the chair's arm again.

"I feel like I should offer congratulations or something, though it doesn't seem quite right."

"Nah, the hell with him," Ruthie snorts. "Oh, say, didya see the *Globe and Mail* last Saturday?"

"No. Haven't been in relaxing-with-the-paper mode this week."

"Guess not. But something of interest to you, I would think." Ruthie shuffles over to a stack of old newspapers lying on the floor in a corner of her kitchen. She rummages through them, scans a couple of sections without finding what she's looking for, then says, "Here she is." She brings me over the review section folded open to a page. I don't know what I'm supposed to be looking for, when suddenly a photo stops me cold. It's her. Angela. It has to be. That peculiarly oversized face. Yes, it's her, unmistakably. The photo shows her standing, dressed in a simple blouse and skirt, sandals, her hair tossed by a breeze, pointing off camera as though giving directions. A chain-link fence stretches behind her and clinging to it, like wind-driven plastic bags, are dozens of Third World peasants.

To Hell and Back in Borderlines, reads the headline, and under the photo the caption: Award-winning documentary filmmaker Angela Lang shown on location shooting a segment of *Borderlines*, her latest film which premiered at the Organism Theatre last night. The accompanying story reads:

> A who's who of left-leaning celebrities and social activists packed the Organism Theatre on Thursday night for a premiere showing of documentary filmmaker Angela Lang's latest production *Borderlines*. Shot along the US–Mexican border and in the

infamous maquiladora zone, Lang's film is a harrowing examination of the brutal life many Mexicans, especially young women, endure.

At the film's end, when Lang was introduced, the overflow crowd gave her a standing ovation and there's no doubt the film lived up to expectations. Lang developed something of a cult following with her first two films—*Red is the Colour of Your Neighbourhood Rez* and the even more controversial *How to Kill a Porn Star*. Her new release, like its predecessors, probes deep into the dark underside of society, but with such wickedly savage wit that viewers are willing to endure the pain.

Moviegoers won't be seeing Lang's film at the local Cineplex any time soon, as it does not have a major distributor. "I expect it will do the festival circuit and a few art-film houses, maybe a specialty channel on TV, then disappear quietly," the enigmatic director told the audience.

I glance again at the photo while a thousand old emotions simmer in my blood. My first real lover, a woman I loved with a reckless, poetic, ridiculous abandon. I'd changed the direction of my life on her account, broken with my parents over her. The last time I saw her she'd left me shattered. Though I've seen or heard nothing of her for years, the memory of her has lingered with me like the faint and acrid aroma of smoke from a long-extinguished fire—long gone, but far from forgotten. Looking at her photo now I realize again just how much an unfinished piece of work Angela is in my life.

"Thought you'd be interested," Ruthie says slyly, "what with all this talk of old prisons and escape routes."

"Yes." Ruthie's touched a nerve. And now it's me looking backward at old ghosts and memories I don't want to remember or forget.

NINETEEN

"I'm sure you don't want to hear this, Deirdre, but I've decided to fly to Toronto next weekend."

Deirdre looks up from her plate, rests her fork on it and peers at me quizzically. "Toronto? Whatever for?"

"I have to talk to Angela." There, that wasn't so hard after all.

"Angela?" The spectre of my long-lost lover, Deirdre's nemesis, wafts through the dining room like toxic fog.

"Yes, Angela. I know what you're thinking—that I still carry around some romantic delusion about her, but it's not that at all."

"No?"

"No."

"What then?"

Good question. Ever since seeing her picture in the paper, seeing her name in black and white rather than the pastels of memory, I knew I needed to see her. I couldn't say why. I've known instinctively for weeks there's a reason Gabriel has re-entered my life after all these years, even if only through the volatile medium of Susan Slater's visions and his putative corpse which was not his corpse at all. But there he was, there he is, a presence as real as anything else. Now Angela steps forward too, unexpected and unbidden, with something to tell me, I'm certain. And beyond them both, as behind sheer curtains, my stricken father lying in his bed mumbling about forgiveness and reconciliation.

After leaving Ruthie's place, I sat for a long time on a bench down by the river. I studied the newspaper clipping she had given me. Ruthie dancing on the grave of her old ghost while unearthing another of mine. I looked at the photograph again. Hair blown back from her large, coarse face, the athletic grace of her body, how the single gesture of her pointing off-camera contained an indefinable but unmistakable power. Then an intuition flashed in my brain and I realized in a moment of perfect clarity that Angela knew something that I needed to learn from her. Perhaps something about Gabriel and those final days at Dancing Grasses. Perhaps about my father. Or Susan's visions. I sensed intuitively that she would be the guide I needed to unlock my muddled history, to throw an illuminating light onto this shadow world of blurred fantasies and facts. Yes, I must go to see Angela straight away, to learn the truth. I wouldn't do it by phone, I'd see her face to face. She would give me what I needed.

I didn't mull it over at all; straightaway I called directory assistance for Toronto. They had no Angela Lang listed but eleven different A. Langs. Great. Next morning I called the Organism Theatre and got the artistic director. "Angela? Oh, yes, of course we all know Angela!" he answered my query with a lilting sarcasm that implied only a naïf would suppose that he might not.

"Do you know how I could reach her?" I asked.

"Well, she doesn't have an office, dear thing, she wouldn't, would she? And naturally I can't give her home phone number or address out to just anybody. You understand, I'm sure."

"Of course. Is it possible to get a message to her?"

"Well, we're dreadfully busy at the moment, you know, with a new production of Benny Margaret's *Now I Lay Me Down With Layton*. Frightfully cutting edge. But I do suppose I might drop a word in Angela's ear. Who, if you'll forgive the Leonard Cohenism, shall I say is calling?"

I gave him my name and number, thanked him for his help, wished him well with the new production and hung up with a billowing relief that, notwithstanding all the crap that was happening in my life just now, at least I wasn't dealing with that level of blasé pretentiousness on a daily basis.

Angela called the next day. Just hearing her voice over the phone, as husky and playful with mischief as ever, I felt seventeen again and almost as awkward as I'd been that first time I'd talked to her in my father's office. I didn't tell her my reasons for wanting to see her. I simply said I'd be in Toronto on the weekend after next and would like to meet with her to discuss something of importance. I'd feared she might be flying off to some exotic locale, but she wasn't and readily agreed to meet. We set a time and place. All that remained was for me to tell Deirdre what I was up to.

Deirdre's not making it easy and I don't blame her. We've been tiptoeing around one another ever since I told her about Ann Slater's accusation. Just as Danielson and I are doing at school, edging past one another like cartoon characters on a high ledge. But there too everything's hanging in suspension; neither Susan nor Ann have been heard from for days and it's obvious Danielson now doesn't know what to do. He huddles in his office with Louise, a pair of co-conspirators whose schemes have come unstuck.

"Well, go if you must," Deirdre says. "But I think it's extremely unwise. That woman treated you so shabbily before, I can't imagine why you'd want to see her again, how you can even bare to see her."

"It's not about that."

"Isn't it? You can't tell me, surely, that you're not still at least a little bit in love with her, can you?"

My hesitation tells her all she needs to know. "You know, Dexter, it can be a very fine line between functioning normally and losing it completely. And it seems to me you're getting closer and closer to that line every day. Despite what you might think, I'm not jealous and I'm not angry about this latest crackpot move you're proposing. But I am really concerned about you, how close you are to the line. You've got a lot going on right now, and an awful lot to lose."

Deirdre's right, as usual. Uncannily right considering I haven't told her the hidden half of my reasons for wanting to see Angela: to ask her about the abortion, about her love affair with Gabriel, her real reasons for leaving me. Though I'd thought I was over it long ago, I realized the moment I saw her picture in the paper, that the end of our romance has been festering within me all this time. I can surely trace my loss of faith in myself back to that sudden rupture. Without my even noticing, a filthy little cynicism crept into my soul years ago and I accommodated it, so that it grew, like a malignant tumour that remains undiagnosed. But it's been there all along, I know, slowly choking off any opportunity for joy, any possibility of real love. How brilliantly I would have shone if I hadn't been sabotaged. Abandoned. So, failing to shine brilliantly at all, instead I nurtured my abandonment, coddled it and kept it close as a sick man's talisman. I've been stuck for fifteen years, ever since that watershed summer. What should have been a lovely coming of age, unfolding into my own person, became for me instead a snare that's held me all this time without my even knowing it. I'd put real life on hold in favour of what?

"Well, it may be a mistake," I tell Deirdre, "but for better or worse, I have to untangle these knots in my head and I think Angela can help. If she can shed some light on things—and I'm sure she can—then it has to be done."

"Well, you do what you have to then," Deirdre says, standing up, "and I'll do what I have to do as well."

Part Three: Flame *of* Separation

The child was lost
Before I awakened
In time
I saw her disappear
Through an unknown aperture
One sunny afternoon
I called to her
Not knowing a name
To which she might respond
And imagined for a moment
That she turned to me
And smiled
Or were those tears
That glistened
Had I been awake
To the pain of separation
The pleasures of her moving
Through sunlight and shadows
Perhaps in India or Bahrain
Jostled by crowds
Veiled strangers
Her slender arms wrapped around
The brutish neck of a bull
I could not look upon
Her kissing the wild boar
Come away I cried
Come away with me
Then surely she turned
Startled as a wading bird
And in an instant
Was gone.

TWENTY

A fire is roaring through an old wooden house. Flames slither up the walls like incandescent eels hissing and curling. A fierce heat strikes my face, malignant as a desert wind, hot with the wrath of prophets, and black smoke coils into the sky. Somewhere a woman is crying "My baby! My baby!" but I cannot see her anywhere. I think she must be Ann Slater but the voice sounds like Ruthie's. "Can no one stop this fire?" I'm trying to shout. "Can no one stop this fire?" But there is no answer. Only the unseen woman's wailing and the fierce roaring of the house collapsing into flames.

I'm awakened, disoriented, by a flight attendant asking me to please fasten my seat belt and straighten my seat back. The boundless sprawl of Toronto stretches beyond the horizon of the jetliner's window. Losing speed and altitude, we bank smoothly over the slate-grey lake, the city tilting sideways, so that the jumble of Tinker-Toy vehicles crawling along the streets and expressways could be tumbled into the lake and eaten by fish with enormous eyes and ghastly lesions on their flesh. As we level out, I'm struck again, as I usually am on leaving Shallowford, by how frenetic and crowded the rest of the world appears. How small and narrow life in Shallowford seems, how insignificant our bush league melodramas, set against this vast cartography of frenzy. Does anyone in that insane arterial congestion along the 401 even know where Shallowford is, much less care? Even the extreme events of recent weeks—the skeletal discovery, Ann Slater's machinations, the threatened collapse of my erstwhile career—seem awfully trivial. All of them together would scarcely register on the Richter scale amidst the bafflement of motion below me. How could you even stop traffic long enough to investigate something that may or may not have happened fifteen years ago? From this perspective, floating down across the industrial parks and troglodytic towers of Rexdale, the operatic themes of life and death in Shallowford are muted to insignificant whispers. By the time we're skidding on the runway, the huge jet shrieking against further motion, my mission here seems irrelevant to the throbbing entanglements of this imperial city. As we taxi toward the terminal, a sudden knot of anxiety tightens in my stomach. Deirdre was right: I never should have come. What could I possibly accomplish by rooting out Angela this far removed in time and space from those few months of adolescent tenderness in the disappearing world of old Shallowford?

The chaos of the airport intensifies my misgivings. I jostle to claim my luggage, then to catch a cab in the bedlam of languages and foreign faces, my head still floating somewhere through the cumulus clouds high above Saskatchewan. The cabbie wears a turban and a fabulous mustache. We don't speak to one another. Instead we listen to the staccato directives of the dispatcher crackling over the radio. Every so often I almost catch the driver's brown eyes observing me in the rear-view mirror before they look away. The city floats past in a meaningless blur of hanging blue-grey haze, billboards, an ocean of posters, old brick buildings, streets packed with people, a thousand languages, beggars on the sidewalks, black Seventh Day Adventist conventioneers solemn in black suits, ancient streetcars rattling and clanging with the traffic.

We're stalled at a busy intersection downtown when something in the blue electric air, the pulse and roar of this exorbitant city, its thrumming energy and towers of wealth, jolts me into wondering again about my choices. Instead of a half-hearted pedant stagnating in a backwater town, I might have been one of these confident, striding city hotshots, prestige to burn, hustling toward my next Rolex appointment, laughing in farewell to perfect, departing colleagues. Imagine being a lawyer here, maybe by now a junior partner in one of the town's top firms. Power like an instrument at your fingertips. An impact player. What might have been.

I check into a downtown hotel on Front Street. From my room on the seventeenth floor I overlook a broad silver river of railway tracks flowing westward past a vast construction site where a new sports stadium's being built alongside the CN Tower. Beyond, the grey lake extends as far as I can see till it finally smudges into horizon, so it's impossible to tell where sky or lake begins or ends.

I have several hours to kill before meeting Angela. I know I should go out and explore the city but I have no interest in it. Truth is, I don't want to be here. Standing in the green marble bathroom, stripped of the veneer of the familiar and reflected back in the gilt-edged mirror, I see myself in a harsh light. I do not want to be who I've become. I'm embarrassed of Angela seeing who I've become. I hang the "privacy please" sign on my door, strip off my clothes, climb into the king-sized bed and pull the feather duvet up over my head, disappearing into darkness.

I awake swimming through the backwash of another dream. I've dreamt of the children again. I see a fading image of them still: silent, plaintive, unspeakably sad. One of them is Susan, I'm sure of it. The other two, much younger, are clinging to her. Slowly she unbuttons her blouse and holds it open, displaying her lovely girl's breasts. She is crying as she does so, erotic and forlorn. I cannot look at her, nor the others. Their sadness is my doing, I don't know how, but it is; a sadness for which I'm responsible. And yet I don't know what they want; I don't know what I can do. Trains are shunting back and forth. I realize with horror that I'm holding a riding crop. Faint tremblings of terror run like wild children through the building. The membrane separating the dream world from the waking world stretches thin and permeable.

Gradually the hotel room pieces itself together and I remember where I am. The bedside clock glows in electric red: 5:47. Time to get up. Time to go face Angela.

But I lie in the bed, catatonic. I've fantasized about this day for years—the day when I'd meet Angela again and reclaim from her whatever it was she took away with her that rain-lashed night long ago. Looking back, I truly believe I'd had a muse guide me until then, a guardian angel perhaps, who arranged the pieces on my karmic chessboard. So that only good things, extraordinary things, happened to me. Yes, I was blessed in a way I didn't understand at the time. I thought that was what life was, not the repeated kick in the teeth it became and then the extended treading water it settled into. My muse, my guardian angel, deserted me, when Angela walked out into the November night. This is really why I'm here: to finally set things right between Angela and myself, to find some closure. After seeing her I'll find myself again, whole and unscathed and mad for the jubilant rush of just being alive. Real life will resume. That's what my reptilian brain must have planned, anyway, without my being aware of it.

But now, with the moment of meeting Angela bounding toward me, I wish to Christ I was anywhere but here. Rather than setting me free, won't meeting her again just reopen old scars that have scarcely healed over? Or worse. It could reignite old passions. She might bewitch me all over again. Yes, she could easily. I'd laughed off Deirdre's concerns, but I'd been a fool to do so. It's not at all impossible that Angela could seduce me as completely as she did before, and lure me from Shallowford. Unlikely as it seems, I could abandon Deirdre and Mother and my demented father. Be rid of Ann Slater. Danielson. The whole milling herd of them. I could just walk away and wipe them from the map of the world. The way Angela herself did years ago. And what then? Sweet freedom from the grinding trivia of every day! A chance to start again, fresh. Maybe travel the world; go to Prague and Bangkok. Do theatre. Be insanely in love once again with the only woman I've ever truly loved.

The shower's hot water washes off my torpor and I take to belting out a few lines of Springsteen's "Dancing in the Dark." By the time I'm towelling off I feel invigorated. No question it's important to me that I look my best for this encounter. I select a pair of seawater-green cotton slacks and ecru-coloured linen shirt that accentuates my musculature. My blown-dry hair looks good. Dammit, I look good! Enough with the whining and doubting already. I descend in the elevator alone, pause for a moment in the bustling lobby and emerge onto the wide and crowded sidewalk.

We've prearranged to meet at a Greek restaurant that's only a short walk from the hotel. The sky has cleared off in the west and a marvellous evening light gilds the city so that the old brick buildings glow like polished copper through a haze of illuminated hydrocarbons. Toronto as Byzantium. I'm wafted along the streets by a warm breeze. The air is rich with the savoury odours of roasting meats. I find the restaurant without any trouble, a nondescript little place called Zakinthos, tucked between old warehouses. Inside it's dark and intimate. Only a few tables are occupied; the dinner crowd's not here yet, if they ever come. Angela said on the phone it's a place awaiting discovery. Aren't they all? The maître d'—a handsome character with a roguish smile lightly etched on his chiselled Balkan face—leads me to a small alcove by the front window. Private and discreet. He seats me with a slight bow, equal parts deference and amusement.

Angela arrives before I know it, catching me by surprise as I'm gazing out the window. I turn instinctively and there she is, standing slightly behind me, looking at me. "My God!" she exclaims, "It's really you! I don't believe it!" No awkwardness now, no holding back, no mumbling to myself: What if? Should I? I stand up quickly and we hug the hug of old lovers. I feel the strength of her body, catch the musky scent of her that I don't think comes from any designer fragrance, feel the brush of her coarse hair on my face. "Let me look at you!" she cries, stepping back, taking my hands in hers. "Oh, you're as beautiful as ever!"

"And you're as sassy as ever," I laugh in return as we sit down. Neither beautiful nor pretty, Angela radiates a captivating energy. She's outstanding still, just as I remember her. All my apprehensions evaporate; I feel completely at ease with her already. We order a bottle of retsina to begin because it was our favourite back in the days when we were young and poor. "Just look at the two of us," Angela says happily, leaning across the table toward me.

"It's weird to be seeing you now—" I'm grinning too "—after so many years."

"It seems another lifetime, doesn't it? How are you, Dexter, really; I want to hear everything about you." I believe she really does.

"I had no idea where you'd gotten to, until I saw your picture in the *Globe* a few weeks back. That's how I tracked you down."

"For everything there is a season," she says with mock solemnity, "so we were meant to meet again. I think I knew it when we parted…"

"Yes, I remember. You said, 'It's just farewell, not goodbye forever.'"

"And it wasn't."

"No."

Then a silence, as when an angel passes over. We look at one another and decipher a thousand stories. The waiter interrupts with the wine and two chilled glasses. We go through the tasting ritual as though sipping something far grander than rot-gut retsina. With a glass of the cold clear wine in hand, I propose a toast to old times.

"You always were a hopeless sentimentalist," Angela laughs. "Alright, to old times then, and new times too!" We clink glasses and sip the astringent wine. "That's nice," Angela says, putting her glass down and peering at me, just the way she used to: scrutinizing, faintly mocking, coyly inviting, all at once. "Now what mischief are you up to, Dexter?"

Trust her to skip polite preliminaries and cut to the bone straight off. I remember it perfectly, this way she had of slipping inside my head, as though I were talking to myself rather than another person. She did the same thing that first day in my father's office, chatting to me as blithely and happily as though we'd known each other all our lives. It's amazing how she can pick right up again, as though the last fifteen years never happened, as though our love was never lost. And in a way, I realize, it wasn't. Not completely. Because I'm already feeling a tingling warm tenderness toward her, that particular distillation of sweet feelings reserved for a long-lost lover. "You want to hear my whole sordid tale right away?" I ask her.

"Dexter, you know I've always adored sordid!"

The waiter arrives for our order, and I'm reminded that we only have a few short hours together. "Probably all of what I have to tell you," I begin, after we've ordered, but then looking at Angela, her peculiar large face framed in that wild tangle of dark hair, I stop, unable to continue, cast back to the days when we were indeed lovers, the days I wanted never to end. Then the remembered stab of hurt for the ending that came, how she walked out on me, the darkness that descended. I suppose she's recalling the same things because there's a damp softness in her eyes, a wistful tenderness that reflects how I feel. As though our souls were twin mirrors. The candle between us gutters. A mournful tinkling of mandolin and bouzouki in the background.

"Tell me how it is for you, Dexter, how it's been for you."

"Well, how it's been is in many ways different from how it is for me now, because of what I have to tell you. I'm hoping you'll be able to clear up some of the mystery around it."

"So, it's a mystery we're dealing with, is it? I'm intrigued."

"There was a corpse discovered at Dancing Grasses a little while ago. At first the police couldn't establish an identity but I became convinced it was Gabriel's remains." I cannot read her response to this news, other than a sudden turning inward, as certain flowers close up in the evening. But it's only for a moment, and now she emerges again.

"Why did you believe it was Gabriel?"

Shall I tell her everything? I've told no one else, not everything. Not Deirdre or Mother. Certainly not the cops. Not Ruthie or Danielson. Shall I tell my story for the first time in its entirety? I feel compelled to do so. On some unfamiliar primal level I need to confess and be given absolution. Washed in the blood of the lamb. I'm just about to start, but where to start? With Angela's leaving? My father's dementia? Then Angela, noticing my hesitation, says with a rueful smile, "Well, you can at least rest assured that your corpse isn't Gabriel."

"Yes, I know. They finally identified it as a Native person dead for some years."

"Hmm. Well, meanwhile our old magus, rather than mouldering in a cold, cold grave, is alive and well and living in New York City. Of course he's dropped the Brother Gabriel affectation," Angela laughs. "So '70s, wasn't it? He's reclaimed his real name. Edgar Froom."

"Edgar Froom?"

"Still the same old bullshitter, though," Angela shakes her head, "only now he's being paid big bucks for spewing it out. He's a professor of comparative religion at Columbia. Several books to his credit. A couple of TV specials. I'm surprised you haven't heard of him."

"I wouldn't have paid attention to that name."

"No. Apparently his students adore him. And of course they would. Gabriel—or I guess we should say Edgar—was never lacking in the charisma department. Are you alright, Dexter?"

I'm not sure if I am. The calamari we've been nibbling suddenly taste as though they were raised in an oil spill. I feel like I'm going to vomit. I take a sip of water and close my eyes for a moment. My brain does not want to let in what Angela's just told me. I force her words back, as though they were a gang of bullies pushing against a door I'm trying to hold shut. I don't want her version of Gabriel. For me he'll always be our wild prophet walking beside the river, the breeze flirting through his long hair, his words brilliant as bluebirds in aspens. I don't want a Professor Froom charming starry-eyed undergraduates with impeccably polished lectures. How bizarre—I'd rather have Gabriel dead and buried at Dancing Grasses than alive as somebody else.

"Are you okay?" Angela asks again.

"Yes. Fine. Fine." I dab my lips with my napkin. I take another sip of wine and glance again at Angela, trying to process what she's just told me. The maître d' is watching me with an amused look. "You have no idea how foolish I feel at this moment." An adequate explanation is impossible.

"You were never foolish, Dexter, it's not in your gene pool."

"But if you only knew what I went through these last few months; I've been tied up in more knots than Harry Houdini."

"Over this dead person?"

"In part. For a while I was convinced it was Gabriel."

"What convinced you so much?"

"Well, that's a long story too. One of my students…"

"Ah, so you're teaching now too?"

"Yes, at Shallowford High."

"How lovely. I'm glad." I don't know why she would be, but I think she is.

"Anyway, this girl began having paranormal experiences in which she claimed to encounter a spirit man at Dancing Grasses. He called himself Gabriel and eventually led her to where this corpse lay buried."

"Fascinating." Angela's leaning forward, absorbed in what I'm telling her.

"It took the coroner and the cops forever to establish that it wasn't."

"But you were certain it was Gabriel?"

"Absolutely convinced of it."

"Because of the girl's visions?" Angela obviously sees nothing extraordinary about schoolgirls having visions.

"In part. But more than that. I looked at the corpse lying in its grave and it seemed to speak to me in Gabriel's voice."

"Wow." An inscrutable glance across her wine glass. "You want to hear that voice for real?"

"What do you mean?"

"Edgar—Gabriel—is in town this weekend."

"He's here?"

"Yes, he's come up for the opening of Benny Margaret's new play."

"*Now I Lay Me Down With Layton*?"

"The very one. He wasn't planning to come up for it, but plans changed and now he's here. I'm meeting him at the theatre tonight. If you'd like to come along, I know he'd love to see you. I told him you were visiting this weekend. If you're free, that is."

Am I free? The waiter bustles over with our entrees. Of course I want to see Gabriel. And don't. "Yes, I'd love to go with you," I tell Angela. "Do you think I can still get a ticket?"

"I'm sure Edgar'll have a few comps from Benny; I'll go phone right now." She strides over to the public phone by the cash register, giving me a moment to process this new reality, and returns in a moment smiling. "All looked after," she says, "there'll be two comps waiting for us."

"Great." At this point I'm just holding onto the roller coaster, screaming inside.

"Edgar is thrilled that you're coming. And so am I." A crooked grin, heartbreakingly lovely. "Let's just hope the bloody play's alright. Benny's work is not exactly my cup of tea."

"I don't know his work at all."

"Not a huge void in your life, believe me, though he's a lovely man himself. Are you still writing?"

"No, I gave that up long ago." A sudden shift of mood. Back to old wounds. I want to say: I gave it up the night you walked out on me. You were my muse, damn you, and my fountain ran dry as soon as you left.

"Mmm." It's unclear what Angela thinks of this. "And are you with someone?"

"Yes."

"And…?"

"I met her some time after…after us."

"Well, I hope not before, and certainly not during," she teases. "Kids?"

There it is again. I half expect the Panos sisters to emerge from the kitchen, smiling dolefully, with a tray of baklava. "No. We..." I don't finish.

"And are you happy, married and teaching?"

"As happy as the next person, yes. You?"

"Oh, I've got two wonderful sons!" She's instantly animated.

"You do?" She's caught me by surprise again. Somehow I'd pictured her on her own. I'd imagine she'd mention her films first.

"Yep. Seven and nine. Mad for playing hockey, I think just to spite their pacifist mom. They're teaching me all sorts of things about boys, things I never knew before." Does she mean me, the boy I was in her arms? Maybe not.

"Your husband?" I don't really want to know.

"A lovely man. Really. You'd like him. Alden's his name. He's wonderful with the boys, which is great because I'm away a lot making these preposterous films."

"What does he do?" I don't want to know that either, but in a way I'm intrigued by whatever man has managed to settle down with Angela.

"He's a lawyer. Just like your dad, come to think of it." Yes, come to think of it. As I would have been myself, come to think of it, if it hadn't been for you. "He practises environmental law. Really good at it. And, of course, he makes a few shekels, which helps a lot, because all I do is spend money making films that everybody approves of in principle but nobody wants to see."

"I keep reading that your films are brilliant."

"Well, I don't know how brilliant they are, but I think they're important to make. You know that old line from Hollywood: If you want to send a message, call Western Union. Well, I do want to send a message, you know, about what life's like in the maquiladora slums, the reservation prisons. And the truly amazing part is, working with people in those situations—I loathe the term "the oppressed" but that's who they are—I invariably get far more back from them than what I give to them. It's astonishing really, how much courage and patience and compassion you find blossoming in those hellholes. So, yes, I believe it's crucial to tell the stories they tell, not just because there are so few voices telling them, but because we need to hear those voices, really hear them, for all our sakes, if we're not to go completely insane. Oh, my God, I think I'm preaching!" she finishes with a faux apologetic laugh. But what she's said is close to what Gabriel told me long ago. Like why I abandoned the predestined practice of law for the revolutionary dream of telling stories.

"I'd like to see them." I'm being honest here.

"I'd like you to. Though I don't suppose they make it to the Shallowford Cinema. Truth is, they don't make it to almost any cinema. They do the festival circuit and end up on obscure television channels that nobody watches. It's a really perverse lifestyle choice." Angela laughs a self-deprecating laugh.

"But you've done well."

"Yes, I have," she replies, serious now. "Far better than I ever dreamed I would."

"Like if you'd stayed with me, you mean?" The words just blurt out.

"Oh, Dexter," Angela reaches across the table to touch my hand, "you don't really feel that way, do you? We were only kids. There's no way in the world we could have or should have stayed together."

"I loved you." I say it without hesitation, not even caring how vulnerable I sound. It's obvious that my role in her life was nowhere near as large as hers in mine.

"And I loved you too, Dexter, God knows I did. You were beautiful. So young and beautiful. You were the first man I ever truly loved. But we couldn't stay together. Surely you knew that."

"No, I didn't. Why couldn't we?" A sharp blade is inside me, pressed against vital organs.

"Well, for one thing your parents despised me entirely. We were both far too young. And I was helping make a mess of your life."

"Thanks a lot."

"You know what I mean. You had all kinds of wonderful options open to you and you were closing them all off just so you could hang out with me."

"I didn't think of it as hanging out."

"Of course you didn't, but it was. I was getting in your way, whether you knew it or not."

"Your leaving is what fucked me up, not your staying." I can't seem to stop myself from venting these adolescent outbursts. It's like we are back in that ratty apartment again, arguing bitterly about whether or not she should leave. "You went back to him, didn't you?"

"Back to who?"

"Gabriel. Or professor whatever he calls himself now."

"Well, I went back to Shallowford, yes."

"To be with him?"

"Not in the way I think you mean."

"Oh, what other way is there?"

"All sorts of other ways, actually. Dexter, Gabriel and I weren't lovers, if that's what you think."

"I don't know what to think."

"Well, first think about this: Gabriel is, and was, gay. As gay as the gilly-flowers blooming in June. I can't believe you didn't know it."

Another blow to the head. "I didn't." Jesus, it never occurred to me. "So you were never lovers?"

"Hardly. Never even close."

"But I thought that…"

"What did you think?"

"That you and Gabriel…"

"There was no me and Gabriel, Dexter."

"That you'd gotten pregnant by him."

"What?" She stares at me as though I'm mad. "Pregnant? By Gabriel? Whatever gave you that bizarre idea?"

"I…" I stumble for an explanation other than the truth, which was that Mother gave me the idea and I accepted it. I'm conscious that I've already pried too far into Angela's personal affairs, but needing to know, I ask the question I came to ask:

"But what about the abortion?"

"What abortion?" Now there's a definite undercurrent of anger in her tone.

"You came to see my father about an abortion."

"Oh, that!" She almost laughs. "Dexter, have you been thinking all along that I was attempting to abort a child of Gabriel's? That's so far off the mark it's positively comic." Though nobody's laughing.

Here I am again, in a completely unchartered landscape. "Well?"

"Well, for starters, you shouldn't know anything about why I came to see your father. I'm shocked that he'd discuss it with anyone other than me. But I'll tell you, as no harm can come of it now. Yes, I did seek your father's advice about procuring an abortion. But not for myself."

"Who then?"

"There was a girl in town, one of the local girls, had got herself knocked up. The father had disappeared—big surprise, eh? I met her by chance and she ran her whole story on me. And you'll remember Shallowford, for all its Christian piety, wasn't the most compassionate place toward a young girl in trouble. I felt badly for her and tried to help her out. That's all."

"And did my dad help her?"

"I really can't say, but I don't think so. He was less than completely enthusiastic when I came to see him."

"That was before you and me."

"Yes."

"Do you remember the girl's name?"

"Even if I did I couldn't tell you."

I think I already know. "Was it Ann? Ann Slater?"

"Dexter, I can't tell you. I shouldn't have told you this much." There she goes again, just like in the old days, with her secrets. I remember it well, this manner she had of closing within herself, excluding all the outside, excluding me. I'd struggled against it when we were together. She was so wonderfully engaging when she was open, which made it all the more hurtful when she shut me out. It may have been why she left me in the end—my insistence on prying into this private enclave of hers. I wanted no part of her removed from me, fool that I was. It may have been her private self that in the end decided to leave. But she doesn't need to tell me any more; I can see it all clearly now. This whole pulp fiction mystery has nothing to do with Gabriel or Angela; it's all about Ann Slater. Not just the fire, perhaps, and my father helping Sprungman, but this abortion too and my father's refusal to help her abort the child who would later die in the fire. Small wonder Ann's bitter and my dad tormented.

Angela shifts the conversation back to the present. She seems not to want to spend any more time on our Shallowford days. So we're back to Edgar Froom. "He lives with Benny Margaret, you know, that's why he's in town for opening night."

But I'm still not finished with the past. "Did people know, people in Shallowford, I mean?"

"Know what?"

"That Gabriel was gay."

"The ones who made a point of knowing knew. Your father did for sure. I think that's why he despised Gabriel. He was convinced Gabriel was attempting to seduce you."

"He never did any such thing!"

"Of course he didn't. Gabriel was too busy being the brilliant magus of the moment to muddy it up with being a raging faggot. But you were a beautiful boy. And Shallowford wasn't exactly a bastion of gay liberation. It's why they finally ran him out of town. The good citizens became convinced that Gabriel was a sexual predator. A menace to their youth, like old Socrates. Of course, to them any gay man would have been that; so they made life uncomfortable for him and he finally left. That's why I went back to him those final days. Things were very rough for him then. I was afraid they might really hurt him. Frontier justice, 'fetch a rope, boys,' and all that."

Angela reaches across the table again and takes my hand. "Dexter, I hate seeing you all twisted up in this old stuff. It's history. It's over." Like us. She's looking directly at me, her dark eyes fixed on mine. "I'm sorry that these things came between us. And I'm sorry that I hurt you by leaving. It seemed like the best thing to do, the only thing to do. Your father was right in his own wrongheaded way. Gabriel and I were unwholesome influences in your life."

"That's not..."

"Shhh!" she hushes me. "You were too young. So young and beautiful," she squeezes my hand and I feel hot tears close to spilling. "You were losing your family and your future too. I had to leave."

"Angela..." I start, but she presses her fingertips against my lips. There's a cast of sadness on her face, and even though she's looking toward me, I can tell she's not seeing me at all. She's staring into someplace else. For several minutes neither of us speaks. We sit there in the candlelight, remembering.

At last she says, "I'm not being completely honest with you, Dexter."

"I don't understand. About the abortion, you mean?"

"No, not that. What I've told you is true."

"What then?"

She doesn't answer for a moment. I can see she's struggling with something. Miserably.

"Angela?"

"I can't decide if you're better off knowing this or not."

"Knowing what? Please tell me."

She sips her water, our abandoned dinners between us. "I never had an abortion, Dexter, but…"

"Yes?"

"But I did have a baby back then."

"You did?" Another hairpin turn.

"Yes. Your baby."

Bang! "My baby?" I'm utterly stupefied.

"Yes." She looks away again, not sure she should have said it.

"And?"

"I realized I was pregnant when we were in Vancouver together."

"And didn't tell me?"

"No. Even before I found out about the baby, I'd known I had to leave. Then I knew for sure."

"You had my baby without telling me?" Anger, elation, a thousand other feelings swarm like hornets inside me.

"Yes. I knew if I told you, you'd want to keep it, and that would have destroyed everything for both of us."

"Why would it have destroyed everything? Why couldn't we have had that baby?" A sudden fracturing, far worse than the abortion I'd feared.

"We were too young."

"We were in love, dammit! At least I was. We could have raised that child in love."

"I didn't think so at the time, and I still don't. I certainly wasn't prepared to be a parent. And you weren't either, Dexter. We were just starting out; we were still children ourselves."

I can hardly swallow through the bitter taste in my mouth. "So what did you do?"

"Came back here. Made all the adoption arrangements before the birth. I hardly got to see her."

"A girl?"

"A beautiful baby girl. She was gone within a day or two."

"Do you know where?" Every molecule in me wants to see her, my daughter, to have seen her at birth, to have held her and rocked her to sleep, to have been her dad.

"No, I don't. It hurt so much to lose her, if only I'd known how much it would hurt and for how long, I might have done things differently.

But I thought what I did was best for the child and for me and for you too, Dexter."

I'm sure that's what she believed at the time, but now all I can feel is doubly betrayed. She didn't just take my muse away; she took my baby as well. I'm sparking with anger. "You could have written. You could have told me what was going on."

"Not really. Not without making things worse. It would only have started us up all over again. It was the hardest thing I'd ever done, leaving you, and then having to leave our baby too."

"I thought you couldn't wait to leave."

"It broke my heart to go, Dexter, just as it broke my heart to give our baby away. I loved you more than I'd ever loved anyone. You have to believe that. And I don't mean kissy-kissy puppy love." Another squeeze of my hand and a smile so tender we may just both burst into tears. "Much more than that, though. You taught me so much."

"I taught you?" I'm completely numb, unable to focus on anything except the lost baby.

"Oh, yes, just being with you I learned so much about honour and integrity, which weren't exactly second nature to me. You were as beautiful on the inside as you were to look at, that's what was so remarkable about you. It's why I hooked up with Gabriel's dog-and-pony show in the first place. I was totally fucked up and desperately searching for virtue in a world I saw as fundamentally corrupt. I was fleeing Richard Nixon, like so many of us were."

"And you found Gabriel."

"Yes, I found Gabriel and followed him. And he was wonderful up to a point; he helped me turn my life around. His words were brilliant, as you know, but behind the words I didn't find what I was looking for."

"Which was?"

"Purity, I suppose. Yes, I was looking for purity."

"And you didn't find it in him?"

"No."

"What then?"

"What I found in you. Interior beauty. For me, being with you was always like stepping inside a sacred place I'd never known before. You gave me a vision, Dexter, a vision of how I could live my own life, free from all the bullshit games I'd learned to play. You changed who I was and I've never forgotten you for it."

"But you wouldn't stay with me, and you wouldn't even tell me you were carrying my child."

"Because I didn't want to change you into who I was, what I was trying not to be. And that's what was happening. You were too good, too beautiful to be dragged down by my neuroses."

"I would have been gladly dragged."

"I know you would," a single tear trickles down Angela's cheek and she dabs at it distractedly, "that's what I mean; that's why I loved you so much. Why I couldn't see you turning into what I despised in myself. I thought if I left early enough, you'd be able to get on with your life. Can you forgive me, Dexter, please?"

I don't know that I can. I don't know that I want to. My own baby girl, gone. "She'll be fifteen already. Do you know her name? Do you know where she lives?"

"Dexter, please. Maybe I shouldn't have told you. I thought I should."

"Yes, you should. Fifteen years ago."

"I'm sorry, Dexter. I did what I thought I should do, what was best for us all, especially for her. Will you forgive me?"

I don't say anything. I'm lost.

"It took me years to get over you, and the baby, to get myself straight. But I never forgot you, or her, and I never stopped loving you for what you'd given me. Sometimes when I look at my boys, I see you in them, playing your ridiculous football, bursting with life and energy, and I love you all over again through them. And I think of her, out there somewhere, I don't know where. I wonder what she looks like, what parts of me there are in her, what parts of you, how smart she is, how talented. Does she play an instrument? Does she dance? Sometimes I think of finding her, but then I realize I'm wanting that for myself, not for her. That finding her might only mess her up. So I think of her as our dream child, out there wherever she is."

My anger evaporates in the heat of Angela's sadness. Now we're both going to cry, I can feel it. But before the floodgates can open, Angela glances at her watch and exclaims, "Oh, my God, look at the time! We're going to be late for the play!"

Twenty-One

A tumultuous dash from restaurant to cab and quickly across town. Angela and I sitting in the back seat, hand in hand, scarcely saying a word. A theatre's the last imaginable place I want to be, rocked as I am by the shock of what she's told me. My mind feels like a medieval meander convoluted with sinuous windings. I don't need more words right now; I need to put all this in order, to find some pattern that will give meaning to this torment of fragments. But more than anything I want to be with Angela. I can't just wander off on my own, carrying her revelations through the city streets like stolen goods.

We bolt from the cab into the Organism Theatre, an old converted Baptist Church just off the trendy stretch of Queen Street. At the door the artistic director, the fellow I'd spoken with on the phone from Shallowford, greets us effusively and escorts us down to front row seats. The house is full, the crowd young and hip and, I would guess, predominantly gay. I'm moving in two different dimensions simultaneously: one the mad dash to the theatre and to our seats, the other a lovely and dreadful unsettlement of spirit.

There are two empty seats on my left and just as the lights dim, a pair of men slip silently into them. The one alongside me squeezes my forearm lightly and whispers, "Hello, Dexter," in a voice I recognize instantly. Gabriel.

"Hello," I whisper back just as a bearded actor wearing high heels, black veils and a wedding dress enters from stage left.

I can't concentrate on the play at all, my mind's in such a swirl. There's lots of gender-bending going on and rapier flashes of witty repartee. I absorb enough of it to know it's a cleverly constructed puzzle full of intriguing conceits. For sure far beyond anything I could dream up. And that's okay; I don't really care. In my imagination I'm walking down darkened avenues my daughter's just disappeared from. Angela's assertion of her love moves through my body like a warming liquor. Not to mention the coup de theatre of Gabriel-cum-Edgar risen from the dead and sitting beside me chuckling at the whizzing one-liners.

It's all too bizarre to be credible. I could be dreaming that I'm sitting here between Gabriel and Angela. What about the corpse, its hollow eye sockets staring at me, my total recall of the poem rendered in Gabriel's voice. Susan's seeing him as a spirit man. But mostly everything Angela's said. The depth of her love. Her reasons for leaving. Her giving birth to our child, then losing her—a tender spot I can't even touch without wincing. It's all revelations to me: Moses on the Mount, Lord Krishna on his lotus flower, the four horsemen of the Apocalypse riding roughshod across my psyche. What am I going to say to Gabriel? And yet, even amidst this whirlwind of new information, I feel a tremendous calm, as though resting at the cyclone's centre, impervious to the whirling all about.

The play ends abruptly, the lights come up and the audience swells to its feet, whistling, clapping and cheering. The cast bows and swoons, is presented with bouquets, and everyone's terribly pleased. Standing on my right, Angela's clapping with the rest while rolling her eyes in a gesture intended only for me. Edgar's turned away from us at the moment, embracing the man beside him who's obviously Benny Margaret. Cries of "Author! Author!" ring out and Benny untangles himself from Edgar and makes his way up onto the stage. I'd half expected a peacock, but he isn't that at all. Tall and thin, spectacles and mustache, impeccably groomed and conservatively dressed, he looks modest, shy on stage. He waves tentatively to the wildly applauding crowd, embraces each of the cast members, smiles in a slightly bewildered-looking way and quickly disappears off stage.

"Ah, Dexter!" I find myself being embraced by Edgar. "How wonderful to see you!" I return his hug, a bit awkwardly because my left foot's hooked behind the leg of my seat. "Let's have a look at you," Edgar holds me at arm's length, as the audience noise subsides and people begin making their way out. "Yes, it's you alright, isn't it? Still a handsome devil after all this time."

"I can't seem to call you Edgar," I reply, lightheaded and distracted still, "I want to call you Gabriel."

At which he laughs and claps me on the shoulder more jovially and affectionately than Gabriel would have done. Nor is there much of the old Gabriel's appearance left either. His long blonde hair is completely gone, shaved almost down to bare scalp. His beard's disappeared too, the jade necklace, his trademark white cotton clothes, replaced by expensive-looking black slacks and shirt. A face more lined than I remember. But his blue eyes haven't changed, not a bit, nor his wonderful voice. "Listen, come back to the green room with us, will you," he includes Angela and me in the invitation, a hand on each of our arms. "We've got a magnum or two of champagne on ice and Benny would love to meet you."

"Well, just for a minute," Angela says, "I've got an ailing boy at home and I'm feeling the need to get back there." She hadn't mentioned this to me all evening. The mother of my child, with children of her own. I hang like an old tree over a swimming hole, dangling a rope from which no children swing.

"Nothing serious, I hope," Edgar looks concerned.

"Nothing a little loving won't cure."

"Ah, yes, loving!" Edgar leads us backstage with a dramatic wave of his arm. "Our salvation, our undoing, our eternal blissful madness!"

"See what I mean?" Angela says to me irreverently. "Still an incorrigible bullshitter!" at which Edgar feigns looking crushed. This Edgar's decidedly different from the Gabriel I knew who was far too solemn and spiritual for this brand of smart riposte. I wonder if Benny Margaret's lightened him up.

The green room's crowded with cast members and crew, friends and admirers. Champagne's flowing as freely as the fountains at Tivoli. Angela seems to know everyone in the place and introduces me to a blur of people none of whose names I remember for more than seven seconds. I talk to Benny Margaret briefly, enough to be charmed by his modesty and to know I'd like to spend some time with him, but he's too overwhelmed with well-wishers for any meaningful exchange.

At one point Edgar takes me by the elbow and guides me through the crowd into the deserted dressing room next door. We sit on what look like old barbershop chairs in front of the makeup mirrors. The countertop in front of us is jumbled with jars of face paint and cold cream, hairspray, lipsticks and mascara. "Well, Dexter," he says, "it's a marvellous surprise to find you here. Tell me all about yourself."

As if I know enough about myself right now to form a single coherent sentence. I smile in reply and force my mind to focus on the here-and-now. "I'm at least as surprised as you are. And delighted to see you. Really. Doubly delighted, actually."

"You mean with Angela?"

Ah, Angela. What to think about, feel about, Angela? No, I wouldn't say delight's exactly it. "I mean with seeing you. I never expected to see you again. For a while I was convinced you were dead."

"Indeed? How intriguing. Probable cause of death?"

"Murder."

"Ouch," he winces, "that has to hurt."

"It hurt me to see what I thought was your corpse."

"Ah ha." Edgar's silent for a few moments, drilling the fingers of his left hand on the makeup countertop. "Those were not pleasant times, it's true, those final days in Shallowford. The collapse of our Utopian dream. Would it still be a Utopian dream if it didn't collapse, do you suppose? Or would it be a Utopian reality? We only ever hear of the dreams. But the ugliness in some of your good neighbours. Not pleasant at all. They did, however, stop far short of murder."

"So I see. I'm glad."

"Me too." An ironic smile. "It seems very long ago and far away, like all good fairy tales."

"Not to me." I ignore his joke. "It's been on the front burner for me."

"Interesting. It's the power of our history, isn't it?" He's instantly more serious, more the old Gabriel. "The hold it has on us, for good or ill. How much of our time we're compelled to spend coming to terms with our own history. Reliving the events of our earlier lives, as though we hadn't lived them fully, or at least consciously, the first time through. Which, of course, we hadn't."

"Tell me about it." I'm easily the Relived Lives Player of the Month.

"Yes, it's what all the great teachings boil down to in the end, isn't it, this coming to terms with our own life story. Who we are and how we are to live our lives. How we unbecome the people our history tells us we really are. It's what I teach now, you know."

"Comparative religion, Angela told me."

"And you?"

"Teaching too."

"Really? How splendid! You must make a marvellous teacher."

"Not really."

"Oh, come along, Dexter, away with this false modesty. Whatever's become of the swaggering young buck we all knew and loved?"

"I ask myself the same question these days."

"Rubbish. You're so gifted. I'm sure your students adore you."

"No, I can't say that they do." No false modesty here. They don't adore me, why should they? Kids can sniff out indifference as surely as hypocrisy. "I don't seem to have whatever it was you had back in those days at Dancing Grasses, that I'm sure you still have, whatever that elixir is that ignites the student's imagination, sets them mad for learning."

"Ah, yes, the great leap into understanding! It's a marvellous thing to see happen, isn't it? Fireworks in the eyes, wild blood rushing to the brain. It's what I saw in you back then, what I loved in you." He's smiling at me tenderly, and I feel tears well behind my eyes again, remembering the purity of those days. The brilliant run of imagination leaping cleanly from insight to insight.

"I believed I'd see it too when I started teaching." There's a slight choke in my voice. "And I did for a while, but then..."

"Then what?"

"Well, somehow there always seems to be so much bullshit that gets in the way."

"If you let it, yes."

"You can't stop it."

"Of course you can. You can't stop it existing, of course—the world, regrettably, is overpopulated with damaged souls—but you can stop it from getting in the way. Can and must."

"But how?"

"Mostly, I've come to the conclusion, it's a matter of getting out of the way of yourself. Stepping out of your own story. But you know all this, you don't need me telling you."

"Maybe a bit of a refresher course." I smile lamely. I do know it, or did, but it doesn't stick. Dealing with Danielson or Ann Slater, dealing with Deirdre, I go to impatience or contempt, rather than equanimity. I buy into hubris every time.

"You seem not very happy, Dexter. Have you lost the plot?"

"I guess so." I'm sure of it.

"I'm sorry to hear you say so. But it's part of the process, you know?"

"Losing it?"

"Absolutely. Indispensable. A *sine qua non*. You get lost and you get found and you get lost again."

"What about the Divine Oneness, all that you taught?"

"Comes and goes like a travelling salesman. One day you think you've achieved eternal bliss, next day you're just another karmic dumpster diver. It's not a failure when you fall, you know, only when you fail to get back up. It's how you get to the next step."

"Over and over?" We're talking to each other's reflection in the mirrors.

"Nature of the beast, dear boy. Unless the grain of wheat falls into the ground and dies…Osiris…John Barleycorn must die…the Hanged God…it's the same old tale. Dying to ourselves. Being reborn. Again and again. It's the only way we move toward the light. I've started teaching at a prison, you know," he changes tack.

"A prison? No, I didn't know."

"Yes, one night a week, teaching comparative religion to a group of inmates who've done things to other people you don't even want to think about."

"Is this something they have to do or want to do?"

"Oh, entirely voluntary. But the response is unbelievable."

"In what way?"

"They gobble it up, like people who've been starving all their lives, which of course they have. Just last week I had the most extraordinary conversation with one of my felons. Charles Nathan. An enormous black man with a scowl that could break bones at twenty paces. In for life. A couple of punks raped his little sister, I understand, and he quite literally tore them to pieces."

"He comes to your classes?"

"Religiously, if you'll pardon the pun. He said the most startling thing to me last week. He said, 'I always thought it was about being poor and black and whitey whaling on you all the time, but now I see it's more than that. We're not being taught, kids like me, growing up in a shitbox tenement in Bedford Stuyvesant, we don't get taught a damn thing about the world of ideas, of culture, the stuff you're teaching us. We could be learning what the greatest minds in history have thought and taught, and instead we're growing up thinking the latest jive from the neighbourhood crack dealer is wisdom.'

"'It's true,' I said to him. 'Ideas are power. Which is why they're denied to you. They'd make you more powerful than some folks want you to be.'

"'Damn right,' he said, 'It ain't just the power of money keeps us under whitey's thumb, it's even more that we're shut out from the power of ideas.' And that," Edgar smiles into the mirror at me, "is about as gratifying a student evaluation as I've ever had."

"I would think so. Can I ask you something?" He nods. "I'd have thought your being gay would be a real problem in there."

"I was apprehensive about that myself before I went. And, of course, I don't make a point of swishing past the cell blocks. But you know something: if nothing else, the felons have taught me that you have to suspend judgment about your students, about who they are and what they might think, what they've done or failed to do. Even the dullest of them, the most abused of them, has a particular genius buried inside. It goes with being human, with this splendidly elaborated cerebral cortex of ours. It's your job, and mine—our high calling if you will—to search out that tiny spark of genius and kindle it till it glows with an illuminating light. Of course we don't succeed all the time—we may fail smashingly as I did at Dancing Grasses—but that's no reason to stop trying. It's not about your career or mine, our puffed up sense of accomplishment. It's about the future, the triumph of excellence. Or, God knows, in these dark ages, maybe just the mere survival of excellence."

As bewildered as I am from what Angela's told me—and, yes, hurt—here I am now, feeling inspired all over again by my old mentor's eloquence. And it's fascinating that he's talking now about excellence, which is more like what my father would have said in the old days. I have the sensation, as I had fifteen years ago, of wanting to capture some of what he's said, the way you'd net a butterfly, and carry it back home for illumination.

"Are you in town long?" he asks me.

"No, I have to fly out tomorrow morning. Classes Monday."

"Too bad. It would have been fun to spend more time with you. We're sticking around for a couple of days. Benny'll have a million notes for the director."

"His work's really good, isn't it?"

"I think he's wonderfully gifted. Just like you."

"Oh, there you are!" Angela's at the door. "Playing at makeup, are we?" Edgar and I smirk at one another, as though we were Angela's boys caught playing with her cosmetics. "Dexter, I do have to go. My house is only a few blocks away. Would you like to walk me home, or would you rather stay on here?"

"I'd love to do both. But I think I'll opt for walking you home."

"Spoken like a true gentleman, which you always were!" Edgar claps me on the back again as we rise. "I'm sorry our time together's so short, but it's been a real delight seeing you. I don't imagine I'll get back to Shallowford in this lifetime, but if you're ever in New York, do look me up. I'll show you the town."

"Prisons and all?"

"Prisons and all," he chuckles.

"I'd like that." We shake hands a little clumsily, then Edgar clasps me warmly in a hug. We wish each other well. Angela kisses him lightly on the cheek.

"Ciao, darling," he says to her, "I'll call you tomorrow. Goodbye, Dexter."

"Goodbye."

Angela and I slip out a side door into the cool evening air. We walk the near-deserted streets as though they were a dreamscape. There's a million things I want to tell her and really nothing left to say. Mostly I want to talk about our daughter, but know I can't, that it's too hurtful and too long ago. It's a chapter that's over, though I've only just heard the beginning. My desire to know more, hear every detail, entertain every fantasy, throbs in my body like a dull ache. This is all unfinished, but all horribly finished, and it's going to end any minute.

"This is my place," she says, too soon. A tall and narrow brick house with a big verandah, a wild flower garden in front.

"Lovely."

"I'd invite you in, but…"

"I understand."

"Well, Dexter," she says, tender now, "it's been a slice, as they say."

"More like the whole pie for me."

"Me too."

"It means a lot to me for you to have told me what you did. You've no idea how much you've meant to me." This is the best I can manage.

"So you don't hate me horribly, you're not bitter?"

The amazing thing is I'm not, even though I have even more reason for bitterness than I did. "I'd like to know more about our daughter."

"So would I." The soft tenderness again. No acting now.

"Do you think we will? Ever?"

"I don't know. Sometimes I consider searching for her, even making a film about my search for her, finding her, our discovering one another. Part of me would love to do it…"

"But?"

"I'm not sure how fair that is to her. She may not want to be sought out. She may not know anything about me, or be really pissed at finding out. I can't do it now, I know that. Maybe some day. After she's found herself and it won't unsettle her too much. Nothing surprises me anymore."

"So she obviously doesn't know anything about me."

"Nobody knows about you, Dexter. Just you and me. I told the adoption agency I'd been sleeping around all over the country and didn't have a clue who the father was."

"But you're sure it was me?"

"Absolutely. As sure as stones." A pause. She looks away down the darkened street. "Do you wish I hadn't told you?"

"I suppose I should wish that it hadn't happened, but I don't."

"Me neither. I love that she's out there somewhere, a living, breathing, thinking amalgam of you and me."

"Yes."

"But I don't want to trample on her young life the way I did on yours. I'm so sorry that happened, Dexter."

"Me too."

"Bye," she says, giving me a lovely rough hug, like she used to when we were lovers, only this time charged, as though this parting is not just farewell but goodbye forever.

"Thanks, Angela," I can barely get the words out.

"Thank you too, Dexter. For everything. Goodbye." She kisses me softly on the lips, then turns quickly away and is gone.

Twenty-Two

Maybe the best part of going away is coming home again and seeing the place you call home as though for the first time. "Little Gidding" in your back pocket. During your absence the old familiar surfaces have been scrubbed clean of the rime that accumulates through your daily shuffling passages. You return in the guise of a visiting dignitary for whom the city has been, as the news reports put it, "given a fresh face." There's a sharpness and clarity to each line, a depth and vibrancy of colour, so that even a cluster of garbage cans on a street corner seems brilliantly correct. This is how Shallowford looks to me now, barely off the plane, as though it has been washed in a cleansing light.

The tiny connector plane from Vancouver drops me off at the rough airstrip outside town and there, waiting at the terminal, is Deirdre. Seeing her standing there by herself, I am jolted by the realization that she hasn't entered my consciousness once all weekend. The noisy parade of Gabriel, Angela, Benny Margaret, and my lost daughter didn't once include my wife. And had I thought about her, I would have realized she might not come to meet me upon my return. She might have severed the few remaining threads holding us together and walked away for good. I couldn't have blamed her for it. But not Deirdre. She wears a tight smile like a costume ball mask as I approach her in the little terminal.

"Hello, darling," I say and we hug, as reunited husbands and wives hug in airport terminals and bus stations. I retrieve my suitcase and we walk together to the car.

"Want to drive?" Deirdre asks me.

"No, you drive, if you would." I stash my bag in the trunk and slide into the passenger seat.

"Well?" Deirdre asks me, her fingers holding the key at ignition.

My thought exactly: Well? The same question I rose with this morning in my hotel room. Groggy, as though hungover from the night before, I tried to sort through the sleep-blurred clutter in my head. For a moment I thought I was just waking from my nap, before seeing Angela, that none of what I thought had happened—the last supper, our lost daughter, Gabriel among the convicts—had happened anywhere but in my sleeping brain. But no, the June sun blazing through the hotel window like an orange fireball over Scarborough announced morning, unmistakably dawning.

Sitting at a table in the hotel's abysmal café, munching my way through a bowl of Mueslix, I stayed fogged in the same state of torpor. The chattering from nearby tables, the singsong voice of the waitress, came to me like muffled whispers in a darkened wood. How tentative the mind can be in embracing the unexpected. I felt as though all my possessions—furniture, books, clothes, utensils, everything—had been piled in a heap outdoors by the karmic bailiff and I was now faced with the task of sorting through the rubble, deciding what to keep and what to discard. I should take no more than I could carry. But where was I going?

Sitting in the jet winging west I clasped at the memory of last evening. Edgar's eyes, blue and inspired, as he spoke about the sacred calling of the teacher; the single tear that coursed down Angela's cheek as she described the ending of our affair and her giving away our baby. Turning these images over, squeezed into a window seat alongside a twentysomething guy in a rumpled business suit feverishly working with a pocket calculator and a sheaf of balance sheets, I felt myself a soggy lump of mawkish sentiment. I was almost reduced to describing my state as "bittersweet." Straight out of a Hallmark card, as Milton Gorman had once sneered.

Goodbye. Goodbye. Goodbye. A mantra repeated in my mind. I shook Edgar's hand a hundred times, felt the sweet parting kiss of

Angela's lips on mine. Goodbye. Saw my daughter from a distance disappearing down a pathway. Goodbye. I saw myself as a snake shedding its skin. Exhilaration waltzed stylishly with regret as little particles of who I thought I was peeled off and fell away.

Somewhere over the prairies—the calculator kid beside me biting his fingernails down to the quick—my mind came back to real life. I tried to distract myself with the inflight movie, a moronic piece of Hollywood's finest. But that didn't work. So I got a *Maclean's* magazine from the flight attendant and was thumbing through it disinterestedly, when suddenly, there he was again: Mengele. A black-and-white young man in an SS uniform smiling disarmingly at the camera. I thought instantly of Ruthie as a terrified child encountering him on the platform, at her mother being dragged away to die at this man's whim, her sister, Judith, tortured to death by his hands. Even knowing he was dead I hated him intensely. Then I thought again of Edgar teaching his convict murderers. The accompanying story focused on Mengele's son Rolf. Born less than a year before Mengele fled Auschwitz to escape the advancing Russians, Rolf never knew as a child who his father was. No more than my own daughter does. When he was twelve years old, on a family holiday in Switzerland, he first met his "Uncle Fritz" visiting from South America. He didn't know at the time that Uncle Fritz was really the notorious Uncle Mengele, secretly returned to Europe. Later Rolf would learn that this man was his father, and that he was the child of a monster. Twenty-one years later, in 1977, by then a progressive lawyer who despised his father's legacy, Rolf made a clandestine journey to Brazil to visit his father. "I was fed up with written arguments," he said, "I wanted to confront him." I guess you would. Once anyway.

He found the old man, living in squalor and wizened with paranoia about being captured. The Angel of Death with the angel of death on his shoulder. And, amazingly, the old Nazi felt no remorse at all for his atrocities. After torturing, maiming and killing thousands of children, after dispatching nearly half a million people to the gas chambers, the old bastard was entirely unrepentant, unwilling to acknowledge that he'd done anything that should not have been done. According to the article, Rolf was a person with the normal moral scruples his father never possessed. And so he faced a profound question of family loyalty. Do you betray your own father, your own flesh and blood, have him brought to justice for his monstrous crimes? Rolf, the abandoned son, chose not to. "In the end he was my father," he explained in the article. He could not betray him, though justice cried out for his betrayal. Then we began our descent into Vancouver International Airport.

It wasn't until I'd changed to the little connector plane, bounced over the coast mountains again and at last saw Shallowford, nestled in its river valley, surrounded by green fields, shining like Mecca, that I knew I was returning to where I belong. Back down to earth, sitting here in the car alongside Deirdre, I realize with pleasurable amazement how good it feels to be home.

"You are going to tell me what happened?" Deirdre says.

"Hmm? Oh, yes, sorry, darling, I'm still a bit woozy from being up and down in planes all day."

"Did you find what you were looking for or not?"

"I guess I found out that I didn't really know what I was looking for."

"There's a revelation."

"But I did find something I wasn't looking for."

"What was that?"

"A new beginning, I think. I hope."

"For us you mean?"

"Uh huh."

"That sounds promising." Deirdre gives me a real smile this time and starts the ignition.

As we glide past the fields outside of town, then into the valley and through the familiar and strange streets of old Shallowford, I feel a great sense of cleansing. At last I'm rid of Gabriel's ghost. Angela's too, though our daughter's ghost has slipped in to fill the vacancy. "'Pilgrimage to the place of the wise," I remember Gabriel long ago quoting Jalalu 'ddin, "is to find escape from the flame of separation.'" I feel that flame now—the separation from that child of mine whom I wouldn't even recognize if I met her by chance. Wouldn't know that she's a part of me wandering the world, carrying my past into the future. Unknowingly, Rolf Mengele carried the genes of a monster. As maybe we all do. Then Edgar's words came back again: we must lose our way and find it again, and again, and again, while everything within us fights against the losing, sustains the separation, embraces the flames.

As we pull up in front of the house and Deirdre kills the ignition, I feel a sudden letting go. I take her hand in mine. "I'm sorry for how I've been," I tell her, "truly sorry."

"Actions speak louder," Deirdre says, "but thanks." We kiss lightly for a moment then climb out of the car.

Twenty-Three

Susan's alone in the classroom. She's staring out the window, her back to the room. She doesn't turn around when I enter. "Hello, Susan," I say, trying to sound natural, putting my briefcase on my desk. "I'm glad you're back."

She doesn't answer. I can see her face reflected in the window. She's staring at the treetops out along the river. "I'm sorry," she says at last. "I'm sorry for everything that happened."

"Are you alright?"

"I'm fine," she says, turning at last, but with her head bowed so that I can't see her face. "I'm just so humiliated. And I hate my stupid mother."

"Well, there's no need for that," I say, going over to her. "Susan?"

She raises her head and looks at me for a moment with a different face than the one I see in my dreams. The poor kid's dripping with misery.

"You talked to your mother about the allegations she's made against me?"

She nods slightly. "After the principal talked to us." Another pause. "I had no idea she was doing that, honest." A quick glance in my direction. "I tore a strip off her like I've never done before. She just started blubbering like a baby. You know she's gone to dry out?"

"What do you mean?"

"She's down in Vancouver at a drug and alcohol treatment place."

"I didn't know that. Was that the real problem?"

"Partly. She drinks way too much and she gets into speed and stuff with her loser boyfriend. Only this time she kinda went over the edge."

"How so?"

"This whole stupid thing about wanting to get even with you."

"Do you know what that's about?"

"Not really."

"It must come from somewhere."

"She says you're, like, the aristocracy. That people like you walk all over people like her."

"Do you believe that too?"

"Not really." Her head's still turned down and away from me. "Well, sort of. I mean…"

"Yes?"

"It's no fun being poor."

"I guess not."

"And she hates your dad for some reason I don't know. She's hated him ever since I can remember."

"Yes, I know that."

"You do?" She looks up, surprised. "Do you know why?"

"Old wounds that were slow to heal."

"Whenever she'd get really drunk, she'd say how she was going to get even with him some day."

"But she's given it up?"

"What? The booze?"

"The getting even."

"Oh. Well, yeah, she's dropped that stupid sexual assault stuff anyway."

"Do you know where she got the idea for that?"

"I dunno."

"Susan." She squirms. "There's something you're not telling me and I think it would be best if you did. We've had more than enough secrets for a while."

She hesitates, anguished, then takes a deep breath. "I wrote a story, sort of, in my diary." Full stop.

"Yes?"

"And my mother read it."

"Uh huh."

"She had no right to! It was private!"

"I know. She didn't. What was the story?"

"I can't tell you."

"Why not?" No answer. "Look, I don't want to invade your privacy. You've every right not to say. But with all of what's gone on it might be best if we knew where each of us stood, okay? But only if you want to."

After a long pause she says, "I wrote about you and me being at the Conservancy that day."

"Uh huh."

"But the body we discovered wasn't that one."

"What was it?"

"It was…mine."

"Yours?"

"Yes."

"Do you want to explain?"

"I wrote that I was, like, sleeping there."

"Sleeping?"

"Yep. Like…it's really stupid…like Sleeping Beauty. I was lying asleep in the shade under that big tree." She won't look at me.

"And?"

"And you…you kissed me and I woke up."

"Just a kiss?"

"No."

"No?"

"I wrote that…that we made love then."

"I see."

"I didn't mean it really!" She turns to me fiercely, but then wilts. "Well, sort of."

"So your mother read it and concluded I'd seduced you?"

"I guess so."

"Not that big of a leap is it?"

"Guess not."

"No. Well, I appreciate your telling me. And, since we're being honest here, let me be honest with you too, okay?"

"Okay." The poor kid's obviously humiliated over what's she's just confessed. Maybe I shouldn't have compelled her to tell me. I thought I should.

"I knew your mother was reading your diary."

"How could you know?"

"She told me so. She said she was worried about you and asked me to help."

"Like what?"

"Your going to Dancing Grasses. Your seeing Gabriel there."

"Did you read my diary too?" A thread of anger under the humiliation.

"Just that once, yes, I did. I felt rotten and despicable doing it and I apologize for it. I knew at the time I shouldn't have, but your mother can be persuasive."

"Tell me about it. Now I really do feel like I've been violated some way."

"I understand. I can only say I'm sorry. I made a mistake. A lot of us have been molested through this mess."

"What part did you read?"

"Only the entry where you described first encountering Gabriel. Later your mother told me about how you'd discovered the corpse, but I didn't read that."

"And not that later bit…about…you and me."

"No. If I'd known about that, it might have saved us all a lot of hassle."

She's silent for a while. "It was nice though, you know." She blushes furiously.

"I'm sure it was. And you know it was just a fantasy, don't you? That it can never happen?"

"Of course! I knew it then too. It was just a dream, just a story. You're allowed to have dreams, you know."

"Yes, you are. And you're entitled to not have other people spying on your dreams and exposing them to others."

"Especially not your mother."

"Agreed. Especially not your mother." Finally a small smile flits across her face.

"And what about Gabriel? Was that a dream too?"

"Oh, no!" She's instantly animated. "I saw him! I swear I did! Just like I wrote about."

"I believe you. I also believe visions and dreams come to us for a reason."

"I know. I think it's why the world's so fucked. I mean so screwy, why so many people are screwy, because they don't believe in the dream world anymore."

"You're right. It's become a cliché, but it's still true that the dream world's dismissed as paranormal and only personal, irrelevant to the working of the world."

"It's why I like your classes," she says shyly.

"Why's that?"

"Because they're all about dreams and visions and stories, stuff like that. Sometimes I think those poems and stories are the only thing that keep me from going insane. Even your crazy play...I mean, compared to physics or trigonometry, it's brilliant."

"I don't think Mr. Danielson would agree."

"Probably not. But I'd take that as a really good sign. Are we going to continue with the play?"

"We'll see."

"I think we should."

"That cheers me immensely. You know I flew to Toronto on the weekend, to speak with someone who used to live here, someone who knew Gabriel well."

"Angela?" she asks, watching me closely.

"Yes, that's right, it was Angela." I'm surprised she would remember the name; the kid's full of surprises. "And guess what? Gabriel was there as well."

"He was?"

"Yes, I spoke with him. He's a university professor now, living in New York. But he doesn't dress in white anymore or wear his hair long. He doesn't even call himself Brother Gabriel anymore; he's Professor Edgar Froom now."

"But is was him for sure?"

"Absolutely!"

"So it wasn't him I was seeing. But who could it have been?"

"I have no idea." And I really don't. "I don't doubt for a minute what you've told me, but there's no rational explanation for it. It's really important that you don't start writing the experience off as a fantasy or something, just because he's still alive."

"I won't."

"Good. You have to see it as absolutely real. Like Charles Lamb's dream children, you remember?"

"Yes, I remember," she says quietly.

"May I ask you a personal question?"

"Yes." Wary and tentative.

"Were you thinking of anyone in particular when you wrote your 'Dream Children' essay?"

"Yes, I was."

"Would you like to tell me who?"

"My baby brother." She says it as though she has something caught in her throat.

"Who died in the fire?"

"Yes." She gazes out the window wistfully. "He was only two years old. His name was Billy. He was the only thing in the world I've ever truly loved. When he died in that fire I wanted to die too. When the house was burning and my mom and I had gotten outside and I realized Billy was still in there, I tried to go back in to get him. I thought I could hear him screaming over the noise of the fire. But my mother held me back, she wouldn't let me rescue him. I'll never forgive her for that."

"Maybe she knew it was hopeless and didn't want to lose you too."

"Maybe. But I'd rather have died in there with him than have him die alone."

"I know."

"I still see him sometimes, you know. He had the goofiest little face you ever saw. Great big eyes and a funny little mouth that was always twisting off sideways. He was my little darling."

"I believe that's who your mother's been thinking of too."

"Maybe."

"It might be helpful for you to think of her not as someone hateful and stupid, but as a mother grieving over her dead baby."

Susan doesn't reply. In the girl's silence there's confirmation of how it probably is for Ann Slater. A mother still mourning the child she's lost. Her baby son. Not the way it was for Deirdre and me, how we lost unborn and unnamed babies. And not the same as it is for me now, only just coming to terms with the loss of my unknown daughter. Ann had held her child and suckled it, felt its tiny hands cling to her, smelled its swaddled body, kissed the soft moving spot on its head. She was bound to it with the fibres of maternal love. Then lost it. I doubt there were any grief counsellors or expensive therapists to help her through the loss. No mate to cling to when nightmare flames licked up the walls of her house.

"Do you think what happened to my brother has something to do with my seeing Gabriel?" Susan asks quietly.

Good question. It lingers, unanswered. Who or what did she see at Dancing Grasses? How did she discover the spirit of someone who's not dead, but in another way is? I don't believe there was an actual person there, but she surely encountered something. Are Susan's experiences any more or less real than the Angel of Light and the radiant Virgin at Fátima? Or is all of it just electrical currents surging through the brain? It is a mystery, whatever happened to her, how she came to see visions. Just as I'd seen visions of my own at her age. And maybe it all boils down to what Lewis Carroll proposed, that we're all just part of the dream, that each of us makes the whole thing up. Maybe we do breathe the world into existence.

Susan looks young to me now, an insecure child, and I'm ashamed remembering my Lolita fantasies about her. She's barely older than my unknown daughter. The loathsome thought of old men leering at my daughter.

"Are you going to be alright?" I ask her.

"Yes. Fine. Really."

"And it's okay between you and me?"

"It is with me if it is with you."

"It's fine with me."

"Me too." She gives me a lovely shy smile.

"I'm glad."

"Me too."

And as if on cue, a tumult of kids come tumbling into the room, laughing and chattering, and the day kicks into gear as though nothing in the world had changed nor ever would.

Twenty-Four

The Red Stone River slides smoothly across a bed of polished rock. Bank swallows swoop and glide above the shine; unseen trout lurk in deep pools. Standing on a grassy bank just above the water line, Deirdre and I hold hands. Yes, old Heraclitus had it right: you can't step into the same river twice. But I'm wondering if maybe humans need to be rooted in a certain place for centuries, generation succeeding generation, creating Mont Saint Michel and Versailles, the visions of Fátima, horrors of Auschwitz, before we truly understand that while everything changes nothing really changes at all. The Red Stone people hereabouts undoubtedly knew, perhaps still know, the secrets of the place. But not the rest of us. Not yet. We have not been here long enough to meet ourselves on the other side, to see our shadow emerging from ourselves. That's the downfall, and the genius, of living in a historical hiccup like Shallowford, like Canada, where we're still making it up as we muddle along, our history still a preliminary sketch, shallow as the waters of our patronymic ford.

But right now I'm thinking more of Deirdre, of us, than of Heraclitus. It's been a strange week since my return from Toronto: her apprehensions about my seeing Angela, Ann Slater's sudden departure and the evaporation of her allegations, the abrupt return to something like normalcy after the stress of the weeks before. Even Danielson's withdrawn into the narrow crevice of his unrequited dreams, perhaps awaiting redemption at the feet of the Governor General. I told Deirdre about Edgar straight off, to clear the last of those particular old bones from our closet. But I couldn't talk yet about my new-found unknown daughter. I needed to sort it out first, to come to peace with it myself. She sensed, as she would, that there was something left unsaid. A peculiar quiescence settled over us, full of hushed expectancy. We tiptoed around one another all week, careful that nothing be knocked over and smashed in the preternatural silence.

On Tuesday night we went to visit my parents. I was anxious to reassure Mother that the problems of recent weeks had been settled. I never quite know with Mother just how much information she may have in a particular dossier. In any case, there seemed to be no point in attempting to set her straight about her vividly imagined dalliance between Angela and Gabriel, resulting in pregnancy and abortion. When all's said and done, Mother is Mother.

I think for perhaps the first time, I saw her on that visit as an old lady. Lovely still, accomplished, the consummate perfectionist in all she does, but grown old and perhaps a bit dotty. "Lavina has been such a help," she told us at dinner, "I don't know what I'd do without her." I had the sense that Lavina was now looking after Mother as well as Dad, not to mention her assembled dependents back in Jamaica. "We had the most astonishing conversation just the other day," Mother continued. "It seems poor Lavina had several miscarriages herself before she had her children." I could feel Deirdre instantly stiffen. Oh, God, here we go again, I thought. I was just about to interrupt Mother before she rose into full flight, when she herself said something that stopped me cold: "So of course I told Lavina about my own troubles before I was able to have you, Dexter darling."

This I'd never heard before. "What troubles, Mother?"

"You know, darling; how I lost two babies before you. Lord knows I was terrified I'd lose you too. I don't know what I'd have done if that had happened, I really don't." Mother was suddenly close to tears. Deirdre was staring at her, wide-eyed.

"I never knew," I said to Mother. "You never told me this before."

"Oh, I'm sure I've mentioned it," Mother's tears retreated as quickly as they'd risen. "It's just you've been so preoccupied you haven't heard me." This too I let go, though I know for a fact that Mother's never before mentioned having miscarried. I wonder if she's confusing her own experience with Deirdre's, her losing grandchildren rather than children? I'd never before imagined my parents going through the same hell Deirdre and I have gone through, the devastating swoop of exhilaration suddenly crashing into bitter loss. Had Mother really lain in a hospital bed, as Deirdre had done, weeping for her lost child? What would my father be doing—weeping beside her? Maybe this is real, another piece of family history that's never been revealed. Surely she would have mentioned it at the time of our troubles. I was just about to ask her more, when Mother continued. "In any event, Lavina was very good. What she does, she says, is give thanks to her God for the children she has and the ones she's lost she kisses goodbye. I suppose it's what we all must do, isn't it?"

Deirdre and I looked across at one another, amazed, and none of us said anything else for the moment.

Another portrait of Mother, then. As a young woman who'd set aside whatever ambitions she may have had for herself in favour of marriage and children, losing her first babies. No wonder she clung to me so fiercely, told me repeatedly how precious I was, how gifted. I would have done the same if our third child had lived. Or if I'd been able to nurture and parent my phantom daughter. And my father's determination that I follow prudently in his footsteps, his subsequent disappointment with my choices—were these simply outgrowths of his own parental love, or was it his Spartan self protecting the woman he loved from her sorrow over losing my affection? Was his bitterness toward me a twisted form of his love for her, honed sharp through their previous losses? Was our perfect little family far from perfect after all, long before my fall from grace that I'd believed had introduced us all to imperfectability?

My love for Mother folded back over upon itself, soft and comforting, and I caught her by surprise giving her a long loving hug, right there in front of Deirdre, something I'd normally never do. Normal seemed at that moment to have taken a permanent leave of absence.

After dinner, while Deirdre and Mother cleaned up, I slipped into my father's room. He was propped up in bed but sleeping peacefully. The volume was turned low on the television, which was tuned to a nature program, about how and why elephants weep. The scene showed a herd of African elephants coming upon the scattered bones of the former matriarch of the herd. These ancient throwbacks gathered reverently around the bones and touched them tenderly with their trunks. The current matriarch, daughter of the dead giant, fondled her mother's skull, explored the brain cavity, and extended the tip of her trunk through the hollow eye sockets. A baby elephant picked up one of the ribs and held it in its mouth. The herd was making sounds that seemed to be of lamentation and praise. There was no doubt, said the deep male voice-over, that the animals recognized the bones as belonging to the dead matriarch and were responding to them with grief and affection.

I looked down at my father, unchanged from the last time I'd seen him. But entirely changed in my eyes. I thought of fly fishing with him, on those near-mystical mornings long ago, camping together in wild places, his reading Wordsworth to me by flashlight in the tent and decoding the stories etched across ice-sculpted stone. Discussing the origins of the universe with me, as though I were his friend and confidant. Affection and grief danced together in my memory. Regret at his sad condition, for one thing, but also a crush of shame that I'd discarded him so callously, written him off as an envious second-best to Gabriel. He'd done nothing to deserve being treated that way. I'd read him wrongly long ago and never been man enough, son enough, to tell him so and ask for his forgiveness. For a long time now I've hated the thought of my father drifting away, eventually to death, before we'd been able to reconcile. I wanted to tell him how much he'd meant to me, how much I appreciated all he'd taught me. Yes, how much I loved him. Looking closely at his gaunt face in the blue-white glare of the television amid the elephant's cries, I saw a small tic quivering on his temple, just above his left eye. In that tiny nervous pulsing I detected all the pathos of his debility, and the despair of our smashed relationship. I remembered that tic from our conversation in the Hotel Vancouver, when I finally broke away from him. I was starting a new life with Angela. The woman who was at that moment, unbeknownst to me, carrying my child. A child I'd lose as surely as my dad lost me. For the first time I reflected on what it must have meant for him that I completely withheld my respect and affection for him. Despite all his manly surety and strength of character, some part of him must have longed for his only son's love as I now long for my daughter's. To have cut him off as I did, turned my back on him, rejected his values and ambitions for me, must have bruised his spirit terribly. If only he could have said it. If only I could have understood. I know I can't go back to do it over again, the way I wish I'd done it the first time through. I can revisit it in memory, mourn the mistakes and squandered opportunities, but I've got to get over it and move forward, at least fortified with a keen awareness of the ultimate folly of ever withholding love.

I bent over and kissed my father tenderly on the forehead, my lips against his twitching skin. "I love you, Dad," I whispered to him. He stirred then unexpectedly and looked at me. It took him a few moments to focus.

"Dexter?" he said at last, his tongue attempting to moisten dry lips. "No need to worry, son. Why don't we go home and have some of Mom's hot chocolate?"

"I'd like that, Dad," I smiled to keep from sobbing, "I'd like that a lot."

"Good man," he smiled weakly and patted my hand. "We'll be alright, never you mind."

Then he slipped away into sleep again, back into the dream world.

I left the room feeling cleansed in his blessing.

That night, as we lay in bed together, I told Deirdre about the dream children.

"You think they're our lost babies?" she asked me after a long silence.

"I think so, yes. In fact, I'm sure of it. Do they come to you too?"

"No. Never that I can remember. I wish they did."

"I thought you wouldn't want to remember them."

"I didn't for the longest time; I just wanted to forget about all of that. Otherwise I may have gone mad. But somehow I don't feel the same any longer. Maybe I've forgotten as much as I needed to…" She paused for a moment and I could hear her heart pulsing in her chest. "Do you ever think we should try again?"

I'm startled she'd even ask. "I haven't dared to think it."

"Me neither. But sometimes now I do. Some days now I want a baby as strongly as I ever did back then."

I realized straight off that this was a watershed moment for us.

"Deirdre," I said, "I have something very difficult to tell you." I knew I must be absolutely honest with her if there was to be any hope for us. For me.

"Oh?"

"About Angela and me."

She said nothing and I could feel tension running through her like an alternating current.

"When I saw her in Toronto she told me something I'd never known and never even suspected."

Silence still.

"She told me that she had had my baby."

"Oh!" A small gasping sound, thick with surprise and hurt. I held onto Deirdre and caressed her, though her body was taut with resistance.

"Did you see the child?" she asked at last in a small voice.

"No. Angela placed her for adoption at birth. She has no idea where she is."

"A girl then?"

"Yes."

After a bit, "And how did you feel hearing this?"

"Angry at first. That she'd never told me; and then given the baby up without my even knowing about it."

"And are you still angry?"

"No. Strangely. No. Now I just feel immensely sad. But it was so obviously painful for Angela, her having to give her daughter up. It still is. I hadn't been through any of that myself, so layering my anger on top of her loss seemed unfair. I know she did what she thought at the time was the best thing for the child and I really can't begrudge her that." It was at that moment, in speaking with Deirdre, that I'd at last formatted my feelings. Though the loss was still there, the negative charge was gone. Without realizing it until then, I'd come to terms with the daughter I'll likely never know.

"No, I don't think you can." Deirdre took my hand in hers and squeezed it tight. I was amazed at how smoothly she was receiving this news. I'd been frightened of saying it to her, aware of her fierce disapproval of Angela, alarmed at the envy and hurt she must feel at my having had a child by another woman. But something else was taking effect at this moment, something stronger than envy or hurt. I realized that Deirdre was responding on a deeper level, a primal maternal level, to the common bond of lost children.

We talked long into the night after that, laughing at times, crying at others, holding one another tenderly, then eventually drifted off into a dreamless sleep. Next morning we made love, as sweet as in our courting days, as though all of what happened between us since then had not happened at all. Afterward we lay together in bed and I swear I could feel our souls rubbing against one another, a tender, languid commingling of spirits I hadn't experienced for years.

"Oh, look!" Deirdre points across the river. A dark band of boiling cloud—ink blue, black and grey—stretches across the horizon. As we watch, hand in hand, it seems to move like a great writhing creature across the sky. Thunder rumbles like the boom of cannons over the fields and into the valley. Bolts of forked lightning, uprooted trees of light, blink for a flash against the blue-blackness. All around us, leaves on the poplar trees quiver in the wind like imprisoned birds, flashing black and green, twirling on their short stems as though wanting to fly from the danger. In the riverbank willows, birds twitter nervously and everywhere rise sounds of rustling expectation. An astonishing freshness and clarity is in the light. Grasses shimmer an iridescent green; the stems of bushes glow with reds and yellows; tufted weeds shine like flourescent flowering heathers. The wind smells alive with grass and electricity.

The storm advances with apocryphal speed across the sky, blackening out the cerulean blue. Suddenly it's breaking over us, thunder smacking hard against the sky's membrane, booming the air with percussion. A smattering of raindrops. Then, within moments, a pelting of heavy rain, a drumming of hailstones, bracing waves of fresh, cool wind. We stand there mesmerized, exhilarated. Then we run together, hand in hand, shrieking through the wind-driven rain and hail. Soaked within seconds, we find a limestone shelf protruding from the riverbank and squeeze together under it, curled tightly in like sheltering animals. Deirdre's fine hair is plastered against her head, rain-soaked clothes clinging against slender limbs, her teeth chattering with the thrill of the storm. Huddled in the tiny cave, we kiss tenderly and I hold her wet body trembling against me.

Within minutes the storm has passed, rumbling and flashing away to the east. Wind and rain chase after it and suddenly the sun breaks clear of retreating clouds. Like startled ancestors at the dawning of the world, we crawl out from our cave, giddy. All the earth is dripping silver drops; a brilliant clarity shines through everything. Everywhere you look, things seem more alive and vibrant than ever, more real than real. And for a moment, just a moment, I swear I see the sun dancing in the sky.

Acknowledgements

For her wise advice and support during the early days of this story, I would like to thank Bernice Eisenstein in Toronto. Similarly, thanks to Alma Lee in Vancouver. I also appreciate Robert McCullough and Linda Palmer for guiding the story to Insomniac Press. Thanks to all the good folks at Insomniac: Publisher Mike O'Connor, designer Marijke Friesen and copy editor Emily Schultz. Thanks to Richard Almonte who was there in the early stages.

Special thanks to Adrienne Weiss for her incisive and sensitive editing of the story. My thanks as well to Tourism Vancouver and the marvellous Wedgewood Hotel in Vancouver for accommodation assistance. Lastly, and most especially, thanks to my companion Sandy for her loving encouragement throughout.